L.

MW01680813

Our Great Captains: Grant, Sherman, Thomas Sheridan, and Farragut

SALZWASSER
VERLAG

L. P. Brockett

Our Great Captains: Grant, Sherman, Thomas Sheridan, and Farragut

1st Edition | ISBN: 978-3-75255-444-1

Place of Publication: Frankfurt am Main, Germany

Year of Publication: 2022

Salzwasser Verlag GmbH, Germany.

Reprint of the original, first published in 1866.

OUR GREAT CAPTAINS:

GRANT, SHERMAN,

THOMAS SHERIDAN,

AND

FARRAGUT.

BY

L. P. BROCKETT, A. M.,

Author of a "History of the Great Rebellion," &c.

NEW YORK

1866.

PREFACE.

The biographies of living men who have achieved distinction, are always so attractive to the public, that we deem no apology necessary for presenting in a single portable volume, sketches of the lives of those who are pre-eminently our Great Captains. There have been, we are aware, four or five previous attempts to give publicity to the life and services of Lieutenant-General Grant; but while the greater part have dealt largely in fiction, none have attempted, as we have done, to give the later incidents of a military career now rounding into completeness, by the suppression, through his skilful and persistent strategy, of the Great Rebellion. The incidents of General Sherman's life have also been once or twice related, but with a want of appreciation of his peculiar and transcendent genius, which leaves much to be desired, and which we have endeavored to supply. No carefully prepared biographical sketch of Thomas, Sheridan, or Farragut has, we believe, been hitherto attempted.

In essaying thus to bring before our own countrymen, and the people of other lands, authentic narratives of the military career of these men, who have displayed abilities fully equal to those of the great captains of other lands in the past hundred years, we have been prompted by no vain-glorious desire to extol unduly our own military chieftains, or to bestow upon mediocrity the laurels due to extraordinary merit, but have made it our sole object to present the men as they were, and put on record, for our own and other times, the deeds for which they deserve the honor, admiration, and esteem of the loyal citizens of the Republic.

The bearing, influence, and effect of some of the great battles we have described, upon the struggle in which we are engaged, are not generally understood. We have tried to make these plain; and to show that through all the movements of our armies, the shock of battles, and the desperate conflicts for particular points, there has been a plan and purpose which has made them, not, as some of our unfriendly critics across the ocean have so often charged, mere collisions of brute force, without special aim or object, but portions of comprehensive strategy, having for its objects the overthrow of the Rebellion, and the re-establishment, at no distant date, of the authority of the Republic in every portion of our territory.

CONTENTS.

OUR GREAT CAPTAINS.

I.

Lieutenant-General Ulysses Simpson Grant.

ALTHOUGH war has been, during the whole historic period, so large a part of the business of the world, yet the number of great captains, commanders possessing the highest military genius, has been comparatively small. The "art of war" is not a science to be acquired simply by study; its conditions are ever changing, and tactics which are successful in one age may be ill adapted for another; a strategy which may be admirable in one country, may be utterly inadmissible in another; and movements which, in a country of wide plains, good roads, and few rivers, may be performed with celerity and certainty, may prove entirely impossible in a mountainous, heavily-wooded country, with swamps, thickets, miry streams, and wretched roads.

We must, then, in judging of the military abilities of a commander, take into account the age in which he lives, the people whom he commands, the enemy with which he has to contend, and the country he must traverse. We must look also to the quality of his mental action. If he possesses clear perceptions, foreseeing readily the measures of his antagonist; if he is fertile in resource, remedying difficulties, overcoming seeming impossibilities, and accomplishing his purposes in the face of the greatest obstacles; if he has the power, not only to plan combined operations, but to so control their details as that they shall not fail; if, above all, he possesses tact, and a control over his troops which enables him to wield them at his will to execute his purposes,—then he is entitled to a place among the world's great commanders. It was in these qualities that Alexander, Hannibal, Cæsar, and, in more modern times, Turenne, Marlborough, Frederick the Great, Wellington, and Napoleon surpassed the other generals of their time. But few as have been these illustrious names in the past, we hope to demonstrate that we have not simply *one*, but *several great captains*. Among these, none is more deserving of that title of honor than the general-in-chief of our armies.

It is now somewhere near one hundred years ago that two young Scotchmen of the name of Grant left their own land of the heather for the New World across the Atlantic. Though brothers, they did not choose the same location, one making his home in Canada, the other in Pennsylvania. The latter took up arms in defence of his adopted country, and after the peace settled upon a farm in Westmoreland county, Penn. Here in 1794, his son, Jesse R. Grant, father of the lieutenant-general, was born. In 1799, the attraction of new lands in the northwestern territory drew the sturdy Scotch farmer across the Ohio. For four or five years we lose sight of him and his family, the forests of Eastern Ohio being the favorite haunts of the Indian tribes, who reluctantly, and often only by compulsion, relinquished them to the inrolling tide of emigrants. In 1804, however, he had become one of the early settlers of the town of Deerfield, on the Western Reserve, and now in Portage county. In 1805 Mr. Grant died, leaving his son Jesse an orphan at the age of eleven years. Not long after, the boy was apprenticed to the tanning business, and when the barbarous alliance between the British and the Indians, in the war of 1812, had made the northern counties of Ohio an unsafe region for women and children, he removed with his mother and family to Maysville, Kentucky. In 1815 he returned to Portage county, and established himself at Ravenna as a tanner. The prevalence of ague and fever in Ravenna drove young Grant thence in 1820, and when after a few months he returned to Ohio, it was to establish himself in the southern part, near the banks of the beautiful river. Here, in June, 1821, he married Hannah Simpson, the daughter of an emigrant from Pennsylvania, and, like himself, a native of that State. The home of the young couple was at Point Pleasant, on the Ohio river, in Clermont county, but a few miles from the city of Cincinnati. Here, on the 27th of April, 1822, was born their eldest son, the hero of our story. The humble cottage which was his birthplace still stands, a frame building one story in height; and from its windows there is a pleasant view of the Ohio, and of the gently sloping Kentuckian farms on its further bank.

The name of the boy, bestowed at the instance of his maternal grandparents, was Hiram Ulysses, and so it remained until the time of his admission to the Military Academy at West Point, when, by the oversight of the member of Congress who appointed him a cadet, he was entered as Ulysses S. Grant; and after attempting in vain to have his baptismal name substituted, he submitted, and made his signature conform to that which had thus been imposed upon him. As his mother's maiden name was Simpson, the middle initial came to be regarded as standing for Simpson.

The tanner's son proved to be a sturdy little urchin, entirely devoid of fear; not precocious, but persevering, and with a Scotch pertinacity ot will in the achievement of any object on which he had set his heart, while at the same time he possessed an imperturbable good-humor which rendered him a general favorite.

There have been in Lieutenant-General Grant's case, as in that of most men who have attained high position, numerous stories of his boyhood and youth, which had their origin only in the imagination of the writers who have given them to the public. To repeat these would be an insult to the illustrious name we commemorate, but there are a few incidents which have been preserved by his father, which, as illustrating the traits of character which he has since developed, are worthy of record.

Mr. Grant relates that when Ulysses was but two years old, he took him in his arms and carried him through the village on some public occasion, and a young man wished to try the effect of the report of a pistol on him. Mr. Grant consented, though, as he said, "the child had never seen a gun or pistol in his life." The hand of the baby was accordingly put on the lock and pressed there quietly, until the pistol was discharged with a loud report. The little fellow exhibited no alarm, neither winking nor dodging, but presently pushed the pistol away, saying, "*Fick it again! Fick it again!*"

The story of his being unable to understand the meaning of the word *can't* has been too often told to need repetition. It need hardly be said that he has never yet succeeded in ascertaining its meaning in any thing which he has undertaken to do.

A still more characteristic incident is related of him by his father. When Ulysses was twelve years of age, his father wanted several sticks of hewn timber from the forest, and sent him with the team to draw them to the village, telling him that men would be there with handspikes to help load them on to the wagon. The boy went with the team, but on arriving at his destination the men were not there, and after some little delay they still did not appear. He had been sent for the timber, however, and he had no intention of going home without it. Looking about, he observed at a little distance a tree which had fallen over, and was leaning against another, its trunk forming an inclined plane. This, he reasoned, would enable him to get the timber into his wagon; accordingly he took out his horses, and hitching them to the logs, drew them up to the foot of the fallen tree, and, backing his wagon to the side of the inclined plane, he pushed and drew the timber, piece after piece, up the inclined plane, and shoved it into the wagon, and with his load secured, drove home triumphantly. The incident exhibits very forcibly the energy, pertinacity, and fertility of resource which have characterized the man in all his subsequent career.

In school the boy was faithful, diligent, and painstaking; not a genius, who acquired knowledge without study, but a boy who appreciated the value of an education, and who was not to be disheartened in his efforts to obtain one. However difficult his lessons might be, and however severe the study required to master them, he never gave up to discouragement, but if one method or resource failed, was always ready to try another. But the advantages of school training were limited by the want of good schools in the village, the small portion of the year (only three months) in which he could attend, and the straitened circumstances of his father, which did not permit him to send his son abroad for an education. The education, however, young Grant determined to have, and his father was also very desirous that he should obtain it. He had reached the age of seventeen, when it was decided that the effort should be made to secure an appointment as cadet at West Point. Application was first made to Hon. Thomas Morris, then U. S. Senator from Ohio, but Mr. Morris had already pledged himself to another applicant, and so informed Mr. Grant, but at the same time notified him of a vacancy in the gift of Hon. Thomas L. Hamer, the member of Congress from Grant's own district, the young man whom he had appointed having, for some cause, failed to enter. Mr. Grant immediately corresponded with Mr. Hamer, who promptly appointed Ulysses to the vacant cadetship. Having successfully passed his preliminary examination, the young cadet entered the Academy, July 1, 1839.

In the Military Academy, Grant was studious, attentive to all his duties, and though he had not enjoyed the advantages of many of his classmates in early education, he soon took a good position in scholarship, while his amiable disposition won him the friendship of all his classmates. The examinations at this period were very severe, and of Grant's class, which numbered one hundred in 1839, only thirty graduated in 1843. He stood No. 21, his standing being very high in artillery and infantry tactics, mathematics, engineering, and horsemanship, and fair in the other studies. During his last year he was commanding officer of cadets. Major-General Franklin, and Generals Ingalls, Steele, and Judah, were among his classmates. As there was no existing vacancy, he was on his graduation breveted Second-lieutenant of the Fourth Infantry regiment, and for a time after joining his regiment, then at Jefferson Barracks, near St. Louis, was required to perform the duties of a private soldier. In 1844 he removed with his regiment up the Red river, in Louisiana. There began now to be rumors of war between Mexico and the United States, in consequence of the annexation of Texas, and in 1845 General Taylor was sent to the border in command of an "army of occupation," and of this army young Grant's regiment, the Fourth Infantry, was a part. Grant had meantime been promoted to the rank of first-lieutenant of the Seventh Infantry; but preferring to remain with his old regiment, where there seemed more chance of seeing service, he accepted instead the second-lieutenancy, then vacant in that regiment.

In May, 1846, Lieutenant Grant, with his regiment, moved forward to Palo Alto and Resaca de la Palma, and in both those battles he distinguished himself for gallantry and courage. In the subsequent storming of Monterey, he received honorable mention from his commander for his good conduct. In April, 1847, after the capture of Vera Cruz, in which he had participated, the young lieutenant was appointed quartermaster of his regiment, and served in this capacity through the remainder of the campaign; but he showed no disposition to avail himself of his privilege of remaining in his own department in time of battle. In the autumn of 1847, at the desperate assault of Molino del Rey, and at the storming of Chapultepec five days later, Lieutenant Grant exhibited such daring, and acted so promptly and fearlessly, as to receive the high commendations of his superior officers, and to be promoted to a first-lieutenancy on the spot. Among those who spoke in the highest terms of his gallantry and daring on these occasions was Major Francis Lee, then commanding the Fourth Infantry. The following is the language of his report of the storming of Chapultepec:

"At the first barrier the enemy was in strong force,

which rendered it necessary to advance with caution. This was done; and when the head of the battalion was within short musket-range of the barrier, Lieutenant Grant, Fourth Infantry, and Captain Brooks, Second Artillery, with a few men of their respective regiments, by a handsome movement to the left turned the right flank of the enemy, and the barrier was carried. Lieutenant Grant behaved with distinguished gallantry on the 13th and 14th of September."

This, we presume, was the first of General Grant's *flanking* movements, a kind of strategy which has since proved so effective on more extensive fields. Colonel Garland, then in command of the First Brigade, added still stronger testimony to the military skill and admirable conduct of the young lieutenant on the same occasion. For this achievement he was brevetted captain, his rank to date from September 13, 1847. During the Mexican war Lieutenant Grant participated in fourteen battles.

After the close of the war the volunteers were mustered out of service, and the officers and soldiers of the regular army distributed among the forts and posts on the frontiers. In August, 1848, Lieutenant Grant married Miss Dent, a young lady residing near St. Louis, and soon after was ordered to Detroit, Michigan, and after a time to the post of Sackett's Harbor, N. Y., where in the quiet of peace he improved his leisure by the study of military science. In the autumn of 1851 the Fourth Infantry was ordered to the Pacific coast to preserve order, which was greatly endangered by the reckless and vicious immigrants who flocked thither after the discovery of gold. The battalion which Lieutenant Grant commanded was sent into Oregon, and had its headquarters for some time at Fort Dallas, in that territory. While on duty here, in August, 1853, Grant received his commission as captain. The times were, however, unfavorable to military advancement, and the young officer, who had now served eleven years in the army, desirous of getting on, and seeing but little prospect of promotion till he would become too old to value it, resigned his commission on the 31st of July, 1854, and returned to civil life.

His first essay seems to have been as a farmer, on a small farm belonging to his father-in-law, near St. Louis. But though industrious and pains-taking, he was not remarkably successful as a farmer. He was, after a time, appointed collector of taxes for the county; but his straightforward honesty and truthfulness were no match for the craft and deception of the delinquent tax-payers, and he could not make as full collections as men of a sterner and more unscrupulous character would have done. The duties of an auctioneer, an avocation tried for a brief period, were no better suited to his tastes. He felt that none of these pursuits were such as he could fill, either with credit or satisfaction to himself. In 1859, his father, who had for many years conducted the tanning business with success, proposed to him to go into the leather and saddlery business, in partnership with him, at Galena, Illinois. He accepted the offer, and the house of Grant & Son entered upon a prosperous business from the start. The quality of their goods was of the best, and their dealings were so honorable and fair that customers flowed in from all quarters, and the house soon became famous, and was rapidly attaining wealth. Meantime there were dark clouds lowering in the national sky, and hoarse mutterings of a storm which was soon to burst upon the land. The retired captain was not so absorbed in his business as not to be a careful watcher of the coming event. When at last the echo of the guns which were bombarding Fort Sumter, on the 12th and 13th of April, 1861, resounded over the land and gave token that the Rebel leaders had commenced war upon the nation, the quiet business man, without ado or delay, abandoned his business and gave himself to the cause of his country. The nation had educated him, and though he had served more than the prescribed time to which he was pledged in the army, he still felt that in the hour of his country's peril she had a strong claim upon him for further service. To raise a company, and march with it to Springfield and tender it to the governor, was his first act, and was soon accomplished. One of the members of Congress from Illinois wrote to Governor Yates, recommending Mr. Grant for a military command; but at that time, inexperienced in the work of selecting officers to command his troops, and naturally enough supposing that an officer should be a man of imposing figure and lofty stature, Governor Yates looked with some curiosity upon the small man clad in homespun, who seemed so diminutive in comparison with some of the stalwart gigantic applicants, and gave him no appointment.

It was not long, however, before the governor found himself embarrassed by his want of knowledge of the detail necessary in the organization of troops, and, calling upon his congressional friend, he inquired if that little man whom he had recommended to him understood these matters. The Representative answered by bringing Grant to the governor, and finding on inquiry that he was perfectly conversant with these details, the governor at once made him his adjutant-general. In this position he worked indefatigably, and soon succeeded in bringing order out of confusion. The governor was now called upon by the President to name two officers for promotion to the rank of brigadier-general, and proposed the name of his adjutant-general for one; but Grant declined, as he had not earned the promotion. In June, the three months' troops being organized, Adjutant-General Grant made a flying visi to his father at Covington, Ky., and while there a com mission was sent him from Governor Yates as colonel of the Twenty-first Illinois Volunteers. The colonel originally appointed to the command of this regiment, one of Governor Yates's fine commanding-looking men, had proved utterly wanting in military capacity, and his regiment had fallen into disorder. The governor had refused to commission him, and inquired of Grant by telegraph if he would take the command of the turbulent regiment. He consented, and hastened to join his regiment at Mattoon, where it was organized, and removed it to Caseyville for encampment. The new colonel made no display of authority, and was not in the least boisterous, but by the quiet influence of example, and the exercise of his remarkable tact, he soon had the regiment under the strictest discipline, and in a month, from being the most turbulent and disorderly regiment in the State, it became the model organization. At this time Quincy, Illinois, was thought to be in danger, and an application was made to the governor for a force for its protection. It was difficult to find transportation, for Quincy was a hundred and twenty miles distant, and the railroads were unable to furnish a sufficient number of cars. Colonel Grant heard of the governor's difficulty, and sent him word, "Send my regiment, and I will find the transportation." The governor at once gave orders to send the Twenty-first regiment, and before night it commenced its march on foot, and arrived in due season in excellent order.

The first service to which the Twenty-first Illinois was assigned was to guard the Hannibal and St. Joseph's railroad. Several regiments having been ordered to this service, it was necessary that one of the regimental commanders should become acting brigadier-general, and control the whole, as no brigadier-general had been assigned to the command. For this office Grant, though the youngest colonel on the ground, was selected, and took command at Mexico, Missouri, July 31, 1861. On the 9th of August, Colonel Grant was commissioned brigadier-general, and sent with an adequate force to Southern Missouri, where the rebel General Jeff. Thompson was threatening an advance. He visited Ironton, superintended the erection of fortifications there and at Marble creek, and, leaving a garrison in each place to defend it, hastened to Jefferson City, which was also threatened, and protected it from rebel attacks for ten days, when Thompson, having abandoned his purpose, General Grant left the Missouri capital to enter upon the command of the important district of Cairo.

It was while he was in Southern Missouri, his biographers say, that he issued his famous special order concerning Mrs. Selvidge's pie. The incident, which illustrates somewhat forcibly the quiet humor which is a marked characteristic of the general, was something like this:

In the rapid marches of his force in Southern Missouri, their rations were often scanty, and not very palatable, but the region was poor and sparsely settled, and, for the most part, there was no chance of procuring food from the inhabitants of the country through which they were passing. At length, however, they emerged into a better and more cultivated section, and Lieutenant Wickham, of an Indiana cavalry regiment, who was in command of the advance guard of eight men, halted at a farm-house of somewhat more comfortable appearance than any which they had passed, and entered the dwelling with two second-lieutenants. Pretending to be Brigadier-General Grant, he demanded food for himself and his staff. The family, whose loyalty was somewhat doubtful, alarmed at the idea of the Union general being on their premises, hastily brought forward the best their house afforded, at the same time loudly protesting their attachment to the Union cause. The lieutenants ate their fill, and, offering to compensate their hosts, were told that there was nothing to pay; whereupon they went on their way, chuckling at their adroitness in getting so good a dinner for nothing. Soon after, General Grant, who had halted his army for a short rest a few miles further back, came up, and being rather favorably impressed with the appearance of the farm-house, rode up to the door and asked if they would cook him a meal. The woman, who grudged the food already furnished to the self-styled general and his staff, replied gruffly, "No! General Grant and his staff have just been here, and eaten every thing in the house, except one pumpkin-pie."

"Ah!" said Grant; "what is your name?"

"Selvidge," answered the woman.

Tossing her a half-dollar, the general asked, "Will you keep that pie till I send an officer for it?"

"I will," said the woman.

The general and staff rode on, and soon a camping ground was selected, and the regiments were notified that there would be a grand parade at half-past six for orders. This was unusual, and neither officers nor men could imagine what was coming. The parade was formed, however, ten columns deep and a quarter of a mile in length. After the usual review, the assistant adjutant-general read the following:

"HEADQUARTERS, ARMY IN THE FIELD.

"*Special Order, No.* ——.

"Lieutenant Wickham, of the —— Indiana Cavalry, having on this day eaten every thing in Mrs. Selvidge's house, at the crossing of the Ironton and Pocahontas and Black river and Cape Girardeau roads, except one pumpkin pie, Lieutenant Wickfield is hereby ordered to return with an escort of one hundred cavalry and eat that pie also.

"U. S. GRANT,
"Brigadier-general commanding."

To attempt to evade this order was useless, and at seven o'clock the lieutenant filed out of camp with his hundred men, amid the cheers of the whole army. The escort witnessed the eating of the pie, the whole of which the lieutenant succeeded in devouring, and returned to camp.

The post of Cairo, the headquarters of the district to the command of which General Grant was now ordered, was one, from its position, of great importance to the Union cause. It commanded both the Ohio and the Upper Mississippi, and was the depot of supplies for an extensive region above, and subsequently below. Grant's command extended along the shores of the Mississippi as far as Cape Girardeau, and on the Ohio to the mouth of Green river, and included Western Kentucky. That State at this time was trying to maintain a neutral position, favoring neither the Union nor the rebels, a position which was as absurd as it was soon found to be impossible. The rebels were the first to cross the lines and take possession of the important towns of Columbus and Hickman, on the Mississippi, and Bowling Green on the Green river, all of which they fortified. General Grant was apprized of these violations of Kentucky's professed neutrality, and as they afforded him ample justification for occupying positions within the State, he quietly sent a body of troops on the 6th of September up the Ohio to Paducah, a town at the mouth of the Tennessee, and took possession of it at the time when the secessionists there were looking for the entry of the rebel troops who were marching to occupy it. The rage of these enemies of the country can be better imagined than described. Rebel flags were flaunted in the faces of our troops, and they were told that they should not long retain possession of the town.

This did not, however, in the least disturb the equanimity of General Grant. He issued a proclamation to the inhabitants, informing them of his reasons for taking possession of the town, and that he was prepared to defend the citizens against the enemy ; and added, significantly, that he had nothing to do with opinions, but should deal only with armed rebellion, and its aiders and abettors.

On the 25th of September he dispatched a force to Smithland, at the mouth of the Cumberland river, and took possession of that town also. The principal avenues through which the rebels had obtained supplies of food, clothing, arms, and ammunition, from the North, were thus effectually closed.

When General Grant was assigned to the command at Cairo, General McClernand's brigade and some other troops were added to his own brigade. Having taken possession of Paducah and Smithland, he now began to turn his attention to Columbus, Ky., an important position, held by the rebel Major-General Polk (a former bishop of the Protestant Episcopal Church) with a force of twenty thousand men. He had nearly completed his arrangements for attacking this post, when the Government ordered him to send five of his regiments to St. Louis; this left him too weak to make the attack with any hope of success. Meantime, there had been some correspondence between General Polk and General Grant, concerning an exchange of prisoners, of which each side had taken a considerable number. General Polk commenced the correspondence, proposing the exchange, and referred repeatedly in his communication to the Confederate army and the Confederate States. General Grant replied that he had no authority to make exchanges; that he recognized no southern confederacy himself, but would communicate with higher authorities for their views, and, should he not be sustained, would find means of communicating with him.

On the 16th of October, General Grant having learned that the rebel General Jeff. Thompson was approaching Pilot Knob, Mo., and evidently purposing an extensive raid through Southeastern Missouri, ordered fifteen hundred men, under Colonel Plummer, then stationed at Cape Girardeau, to move towards Fredericktown, Mo., by way of Jackson and Dallas, forming a junction at the latter place with Colonel Carlin, who had been ordered to move with three thousand men from another point, and, pursuing Thompson, to defeat and rout his force. The expeditions were successful. Thompson was found, on the 21st of October, not far from Dallas, on the Greenville road, and, after an action of two and a half hours, defeated and routed with very heavy loss. Colonel Plummer captured in this engagement forty-two prisoners and one twelve-pounder.

By this expedition, General Grant ascertained the position and strength of Jeff. Thompson's forces, and learned also that the rebels were concentrating a considerable force at Belmont, Missouri, nearly opposite Columbus, Ky., with a view to blockade the Mississippi river, and to move speedily upon his position at Cairo. Having received orders to that effect from his superior officers, General Grant resolved to break up this camp, although aware that the rebels could be reinforced to almost any extent from Columbus, Ky.

On the evening of the 6th of November, General Grant embarked two brigades, in all about two thousand eight hundred and fifty men, under his own and General McClernand's command, on board river steamers, and moved down the Mississippi. He had previously detached small bodies of troops to threaten Columbus from different directions, and to deceive the rebels as to his intentions. The ruse was successful, and the force which he commanded in person reached the vicinity of Belmont, and landed before the enemy had comprehended their intention. The Union troops, disembarking with great promptness, marched rapidly towards the rebel camp, a distance of about two and a half miles, and, forcing their way through a dense abatis and other obstructions, charged through the camp, capturing their camp equipage, artillery, and small-arms, and burned the tents, blankets, &c. They also took a large number of prisoners. The rebel force at the camp was not far from 4,000, but General Polk, learning of the attack, sent over as reinforcements eight regiments, or somewhat more than 4,000 more troops, under the command of Generals Pillow and Cheatham, and finally crossed the river himself and took command. General Grant having accomplished all, and more than he expected, and being aware that Belmont was covered by the batteries at Columbus, and that heavy reinforcements could readily be sent from thence, made no attempt to hold the position, but withdrew in good order. On their way to their transports, the Union troops were confronted by the fresh rebel force under Polk's command, and a severe battle ensued, during which a considerable number of the rebel prisoners made their escape; and there were heavy losses in killed and wounded on both sides, the Union loss amounting to nearly one hundred killed, and four hundred or five hundred wounded and missing, the larger part of whom were prisoners. What was the exact rebel loss has never transpired, but it is known to have been larger than this, the number of prisoners alone exceeding the total Union loss. The Union troops at length succeeded in reaching their transports and re-embarking, under the protection of the gunboats Tyler and Lexington, which had conveyed them, bringing with them two cannon which they had captured, and spiking two others, which they were obliged to abandon. This action, which was represented in some quarters as a Union defeat, proved to have been rather a Union victory, the advantages being decidedly on the part of General Grant, and his men having, by the action, gained confidence in themselves and in their commander.

On the 20th of December, General Halleck, who was then in command of the western department, reorganized the districts of his command, and enlarged the district of Cairo, including in it all the southern portion of Illinois, all of Kentucky west of the Cumberland river, and the southern counties of Missouri, and appointed General Grant commander of the new district. Large numbers of troops newly mustered into the service, and as yet untrained to military duties, poured into this district, some for service within its limits, others intended to reinforce the armies in other districts. General Grant maintained a vigilant supervision over these, and, whereever it was possible, subjected them to a thorough discipline, organization, and training, to qualify them for service, and then distributed them as rapidly as possible to the various posts within his district, or, when so directed, to other points. On the 10th of January, 1862, the troops under the command of General McClernand were sent in transports, convoyed by two gunboats, to Fort Jefferson, Ky., and landed there, the gunboats being ordered to lie off the fort. The rebels attacked these gunboats with three vessels the next day, but were beaten off after a brisk engagement, and pursued till they took refuge under the batteries of Columbus.

On the 14th of January, 1862, General Grant made an extended reconnoissance in force, moving in three columns, by different routes, to explore the country east of Columbus, and ascertain the rebel strength and position, with a view to an important enterprise soon to be undertaken. The reconnoissance was a severe and laborious one for raw troops, on account of the weather and the condition of the roads, but it was in every respect successful. On this march, General Grant issued general orders, the first, it is believed, issued during the war, prohibiting, under the severest penalties, all private plundering and straggling, and directing the order of march. The gunboats which had been constructed during the autumn and winter on the Mississippi, above Cairo, were now completed, and General Grant called for volunteers from the troops to man them, as there was a lack of sailors to make up the complement for their efficient management. The number of volunteers proved sufficient, and the gunboat flotilla, under the command of Flag-officer (afterwards Rear-Admiral) A. H. Foote, was soon ready for action.

Grant kept up his feint of attacking Columbus, and by his movements and general orders, issued for effect, led the rebels to concentrate at that point most of their available forces, while he was preparing for a flank movement in a different direction, which would compel them to evacuate that post without his striking a blow. Two large divisions were secretly concentrated at Paducah and Smithland, at the mouths of the Tennessee and Cumberland rivers, under the command of Generals C. F. Smith and Lewis Wallace; and the other two divisions under his command, which were apparently ready to pounce upon Columbus, were quietly withdrawn, and one being left to hold his base at Cairo, the other was transferred by night to Paducah, on the night of Feb. 2d, and, with the troops already there, moved directly upon Fort Henry on the Tennessee river. The gunboats were also moving for the same point, and arrived on the morning of February 6th, in advance of the troops, who were delayed by the condition of the roads. Grant was hastening forward as rapidly as possible, and was prepared to cut off the retreat of the garrison. Flag-officer Foote, having ascertained that the rebels were expecting reinforcements, resolved to attack the fort without waiting for the land forces to come up. He did so; and, after an engagement of an hour and a quarter, the garrison surrendered the fort, the rebel forces outside having made their escape to Fort Donelson.

General Grant came up within an hour, and the fort and its contents was handed over to him. The dispositions he had made would have insured its capture the same day, had Flag-officer Foote not anticipated the time of attack.

The capture of Fort Henry, however, was but one item in the programme which General Grant had marked out for accomplishment. Fort Donelson, a much larger and stronger work, and defended by a garrison of more than twenty thousand men, and lying nearly east of Fort Henry, still obstructed the passage of the Cumberland, and forbade the advance of the Union forces southward. To possess himself of this important fortress was the design of General Grant, and ordering up all the available forces of his district to join him on the strip of land lying between the Tennessee and Cumberland rivers, near the Kentucky line, on the 11th of February the three divisions constituting his force, under the command of Generals McClernand, C. F. Smith, and Lewis Wallace, moved by different routes towards Fort Donelson, and by the evening of the 12th were in front of the fort. General Grant proceeded at once to put them in position to invest the fort, though, owing to the non-arrival of the gunboats, which had been obliged to descend the Tennessee and ascend the Cumberland, the river front of the fort was still open. On the morning of the 13th the Carondelet, the only gunboat which had arrived, by General Grant's direction engaged the fort for two hours, and then withdrew. The object of this diversion was to give time for the remainder of his troops and the gunboats to arrive by way of the river. On the 14th, the gunboats and troops having arrived, a combined attack by the land and marine forces was ordered. The principal attack was made by the gunboats, which silenced the water-batteries; but, after a protracted contest, two of the iron-clads were disabled by plunging shots from the higher batteries, and two others so much injured that a single shot might disable them entirely. Under these circumstances, Flag-officer Foote, who had already been wounded, decided to withdraw from the action. General Grant now proposed to reduce the fort by siege, but on the morning of the 15th the enemy made a sudden and desperate sortie from their works upon the extreme right of the Union line, and at first broke it and captured two batteries of artillery. Very soon the troops were rallied, reinforcements brought up, and all but three of the captured guns retaken. The rebels in turn were reinforced, and again broke through the Union lines and drove back the supporting regiments, holding the position they had gained with great tenacity. At this time the Union centre had advanced and gained some successes in the rebel line, but so successful had the rebels been on the right that the day seemed lost. General Pillow, the second officer in command in the rebel fort, telegraphed to Nashville, "Upon the honor of a soldier, the day is ours." But while some of the Union officers gave way to despondency, no such feeling found a place in the heart of General Grant. At the darkest moment, he exclaimed to one of his staff, after comparing the reports of the officers sent into headquarters, "Good! we have them now exactly where we want them." General C. F. Smith, one of the ablest officers in the army, was ordered to make a vigorous assault with his fresh troops on the left of the line, and carry it at whatever cost; and, meantime, Lewis Wallace was to hurl his force against the enemy in their advanced position on the right, and drive them back at the point of the bayonet. General Smith's advance was one of the finest of the war. With his cap lifted, and his gray hair streaming in the wind, he galloped along the front of his men, unheeding the missiles which flew thick around him like the pattering of a heavy rain. "Steady! men; steady!" rang out in his clear tones; and steadily they advanced, though at every step their lines were thinned by the deadly minié balls. They reached the line of the rebel troops, and drove them back, back, till they had gained a position from which they could render the strongest portion of the fort untenable. Then rang out their hurrahs, and the whole army resounded with shouts of triumph. Wallace had done his work well; and at sunset the Union army occupied a position along the whole line which it was evident would give them the fort in another day. That night the rebel generals held a council to deliberate on their action for the morrow. General Buckner, who had held the position on the left, from which he had been driven by General Smith, declared that he could not hold his post a half-hour if the Union troops should attack, as they were certain to do, at daybreak; that his men were too much wearied and discouraged to fight, and proposed to treat with Grant for an armistice, and to capitulate on the best terms that could be obtained. Floyd and Pillow objected to this; they were unwilling to be taken prisoners,—Floyd, in particular, being conscious of a record as secretary of war which would put his life in peril. There was some talk of attempting to fight their way out, but Buckner declared that three-fourths of the troops would be sacrificed in the attempt; and it was finally arranged that Floyd and Pillow should relinquish their commands to Buckner, and escape with what troops they could take away, and Buckner should surrender with the remainder. Accordingly, Floyd and Pillow stole away during the night with one brigade of rebel troops, and embarking on some small steamboats in the river, made their escape to Nashville.

At dawn of the 16th, a messenger, bearing a flag of truce, approached the Union lines with a message for General Grant. It was as follows:

"HEADQUARTERS, FORT DONELSON,
FEBRUARY 16, 1862.

"SIR,—In consideration of all the circumstances governing the present situation of affairs at this station, I propose to the commanding officer of the Federal forces the appointment of commissioners to agree upon terms of capitulation of the forces and fort under my command, and in that view suggest an armistice till twelve o'clock to-day.

I am, sir, respectfully,

Your obedient servant,

S. B. BUCKNER, BRIG.-GEN., C. S. A.

TO BRIGADIER-GENERAL GRANT, commanding
United States forces near Fort Donelson."

The writer of this note knew what Grant did not, that he was powerless to continue the contest another hour, and that his two senior generals and a part of his troops had already fled; but Grant was fully assured that before sunset of that day he could carry the fort by force of arms, though perhaps with considerable loss; but he had no disposition to hold parley long with a traitor, nor to yield other and better conditions to him than such as he had the power to enforce within a few hours, and he accordingly sent back by Buckner's messenger the following brief but decisive reply:

"HEADQUARTERS, ARMY IN THE FIELD,
CAMP NEAR DONELSON, FEB. 16, 1862.

TO GENERAL S. B. BUCKNER, Confederate Army.

Yours of this date proposing an armistice, and appointment of commissioners to settle terms of capitulation, is just received. *No terms other than unconditional and immediate surrender can be accepted. I propose to move immediately upon your works."*

I am, respectfully,
Your obedient servant,
U. S. GRANT,
Brig.-Gen., U. S. A., commanding."

The rebel general was greatly chagrined at this reply, but, knowing his inability to sustain another assault, he was compelled to submit, which he did most ungraciously in the following letter:

"HEADQUARTERS, DOVER, TENN.,
FEB. 16, 1862.

TO BRIGADIER-GENERAL U. S. GRANT, U. S. A.

SIR,—The distribution of the forces under my command, incident to an unexpected change of commanders, and the overwhelming force under your command, compel me, notwithstanding the brilliant success of the Confederate arms yesterday, to accept the ungenerous and unchivalrous terms which you propose.

I am, sir, your very obedient servant,
S. B. BUCKNER,
Brig.-Gen., C. S. A.

By this surrender the Union troops received, and the rebels lost, over thirteen thousand prisoners, including one brigadier-general and numerous inferior officers, three thousand horses, forty-eight field-pieces, seventeen heavy guns, twenty thousand stand of arms, and a large quantity of commissary stores. The rebel loss, aside from this, was 230 killed, and 1,007 wounded, some of whom were prisoners. The Union loss was, killed 446, wounded 1,735, prisoners 150. The day after the capitulation two regiments of rebel Tennesseans, numbering 1,745 officers and men, who had been ordered to reinforce Fort Donelson, but were unaware of the surrender, marched into the fort with colors flying, and were at once made prisoners.

The capture of these forts having effectually flanked the rebel posts of Columbus and Bowling Green, Ky., the rebel commanders made all haste to evacuate them, Polk descending the river to island No. Ten, and Johnston making a hurried retreat to Nashville, Tenn.

The victory thus won caused the promotion of General Grant to the major-generalship, his commission dating Feb. 16, 1862. It may be as well in this place to meet the charge which was about this time industriously propagated, that General Grant was addicted to habits of intemperance. The masterly manner in which he had conducted the brief campaign just closed was in itself an indication that he could not have been, as was freely charged, an habitual drunkard; but we have other and conclusive evidence that the charge, however it originated, was wholly false. His father, and the officers of his staff, who have been with him throughout the war, testify that he is, and has been from his youth, one of the most abstemious of men, rarely or never tasting intoxicating liquors, even as a medicine.

On the 14th of February, General Halleck, foreseeing the result which soon followed, announced the formation of the new military district of West Tennessee, bounded on the south by Tennessee river and the State line of

Mississippi, and west by the Mississippi river as far north as Cairo. To the command of this new district he assigned General Grant, with permission to select his own headquarters.

In taking command of this new district, on the 17th of February, General Grant first issued the following congratulatory order to the troops which had aided in the reduction of Fort Donelson:

"HEADQUARTERS, DISTRICT OF WEST TENNESSEE,
FORT DONELSON, FEB. 17, 1862.

General Order, No. 2.

The General commanding takes great pleasure in congratulating the troops of this command for the triumph over rebellion gained by their valor on the thirteenth, fourteenth, and fifteenth instant. For four successive nights, without shelter, during the most inclement weather known in this latitude, they faced an enemy in large force, in a position chosen by himself. Though strongly fortified by nature, all the additional safeguards suggested by science were added. Without a murmur this was borne, prepared at all times to receive an attack, and with continuous skirmishing by day, resulting ultimately in forcing the enemy to surrender without conditions. The victory achieved is not only great in the effect it will have in breaking down rebellion, but has secured the greatest number of prisoners of war ever taken in any battle on this continent.

Fort Donelson will hereafter be marked in capitals on the map of our united country, and the men who fought the battle will live in the memory of a grateful people.

By order of
U. S. GRANT,
Brig.-Gen. commanding."

It was no part of General Grant's policy to rest satisfied with this victory. The enemy whom he had thus driven from one stronghold must be followed promptly, and driven successively from each one where they might seek shelter. The district of West Tennessee, now nominally, must be very soon really in his possession, and the rebel army captured or driven far towards the Gulf. Immediate preparation was therefore made for an advance. The gunboats were ordered to ascend the Cumberland, and a land force, consisting of a division of Grant's army, under command of General C. F. Smith, marched along the west bank of that river to keep them company.

On the 20th of February, Clarksville, the most important depot of supplies on the river, was captured without a fight, and supplies sufficient to sustain Grant's whole Army for twenty days were found there. This place was at once garrisoned and held, while the gunboats continued to ascend the river to open the way for the Army of the Ohio, under command of General Buell, which was marching from Bowling Green to occupy Nashville. On the 22d of February, General Grant, who remained for a time at Fort Donelson to organize the troops constantly arriving, and to send forward men and supplies, issued an order declaring his district under martial law; and on the 25th, published a general order received from General Halleck, prohibiting, under severe penalties, all pillaging, marauding, the destruction of private property, and the stealing and concealment of slaves, and defining the status of non-combatants, and the rules to be observed in obtaining forced contributions for supplies and subsistence.

After the fall of Nashville, the gunboats returned to

the Ohio river, and ascended the Tennessee river as far as Florence, Alabama. Their reconnoissance demonstrated the fact that there were no considerable bodies of rebel troops along the river, and that a base of operations could be established near the southern line of his district. In the interval which must necessarily elapse before this change could be effected, he removed his headquarters to Fort Henry, and continued the organization of the troops now constantly ascending the Tennessee river, sending small bodies in every direction to scour the country, who occasionally encountered the enemy, and, in one instance (at Paris, Tenn.) met and defeated a considerable rebel force, causing them to lose in killed, wounded, and prisoners, over one hundred men.

While engaged in this work of organizing troops, on the 11th of March, General Grant was presented with an elegant sword by four of the colonels of regiments constituting the garrison of Fort Henry.

The rebel commander-in-chief, Albert Sydney Johnston, after he had been compelled to abandon Nashville, concentrated his troops at Corinth, Mississippi, the point of junction of the Mobile and Ohio and Memphis and Charleston railroads, a position which, from its connections with the great network of railroads traversing the Southern States, was admirably adapted to the collection of troops from all quarters, and, from its great natural strength and capacity for fortification, could readily be made a most formidable position. To this point were brought, with the greatest possible rapidity, all the rebel troops which could be collected from the Southwest, and organized under the supervision of Generals Johnston, Beauregard, Bragg, Hardee, and Polk. Corinth was but little more than twenty-five miles from Savannah, Tennessee, the point first selected by General Grant as his base of operations, and was still nearer to Pittsburg Landing or Shiloh, on the west bank of the Tennessee, the point finally selected from strategic considerations by Major-General C. F. Smith, who was in command in the absence of General Grant at Fort Henry. General Buell with the army of the Ohio, which had been in the service longer than most of Grant's troops, was ordered by General Halleck to march across the country from Nashville and join Grant at Pittsburg Landing, and, the roads being heavy, made but slow progress.

Meantime the rebel commander, who had assembled at Corinth an army of full forty-five thousand men, under his ablest generals, with thirty thousand more under Van Dorn and Price, coming from Arkansas, well disciplined, and provided with all that was necessary to its efficiency, had conceived the plan of hurling his forces upon Grant before Buell could come up, and while Lewis Wallace's division was at Crump's Landing, some distance from the field of battle, and thus conquering the Union army in detail. The plan was well devised, and came very near being successful. Johnston at first fixed upon April 5th as the time for making the attack, and had he adhered to this determination he would very possibly have succeeded; but, desirous of obtaining Van Dorn's and Price's reinforcements before moving, he delayed one day, in the hope that they would come up, and that day's delay lost him the battle. The roads in that region were so heavy that though Pittsburg Landing was but twenty miles away, it took the rebel army two days to reach it. General Grant's suspicions had been aroused by the movements of some of the rebel reconnoitering parties on the night of the second of April, and he returned to the camp that night from Savannah, ten miles away, where his headquarters were, and reconnoitred in person.

As no sign of battle appeared, he returned to Savannah, leaving orders to fire a signal-gun if there were any appearances of an approaching battle. The Union army was surrounded by spies; rebel citizens who, while professing to be non-combatants, discovered and carried to the rebel headquarters every position and movement of the Union forces.

The forces under General Grant's command, constituting the army of West Tennessee, were organized in five divisions, commanded as follows: First division, Major-General John A. McClernand; second division, Brigadier-General W. H. L. Wallace; third division, Major-General Lewis Wallace; fourth division, Brigadier-General S. A. Hurlbut; fifth division, Brigadier-General W. T. Sherman. Of these generals, McClernand, W. H. S. Wallace, Hurlbut, and Sherman were at Pittsburg Landing, and Lewis Wallace at Crump's Landing, six miles distant. General Buell's forces, the Army of the Ohio, were twenty miles distant.

The troops were arranged in the following order: Prentiss's command, a subdivision of McClernand's, occupied the extreme Union left, resting on Lick creek, a distance of nearly three miles from the Tennessee river; next came McClernand; then W. H. L. Wallace, forming the right, with Sherman partly in reserve as a support on the right wing, extending along Snake creek. General Hurlbut's division acted as the supports of Prentiss on the left wing, and were also partly in reserve. The Union force that day in the battle did not exceed thirty-eight thousand. The rebel commander had thrown a detachment between Pittsburg and Crump's landings, and thus obstructed Lew. Wallace's division, and compelled them to make so extended a *detour* that they were unable to take any part in the first day's battle.

The battle commenced at daybreak of the 6th of April (Sunday), by a sudden and desperate attack on the extreme left, Prentiss's division, which was taken somewhat by surprise, but fought bravely. The rebel force was, however, massed so heavily upon them, that they at last gave way, and the greater part of them were captured. Hurrying these to the rear, the rebels next hurled their forces upon W. H. L. Wallace and Sherman. Wallace was mortally wounded, and his troops driven back some distance, but Sherman, making a stubborn resistance, held his position and repulsed the enemy, who however rallied and returned to the attack, flinging, meantime, a large force of fresh troops upon McClernand's division, and that general, though doing his utmost to keep his troops in line, was crowded back. The rebels next having tried in vain to break Sherman's lines, about two P. M. slackened their fire on him, and threw their principal force on General Hurlbut's division, gradually but surely pressing them back, till the greater part of the line was two and a half miles in rear of their first position, though still a half-mile from the river. Sherman meanwhile had taken a new line in a strong position, and repulsed all attacks, while Webster, General Grant's chief of artillery, gathering the batteries which had been scattered, and some of them deserted, opened a steady and destructive fire upon the enemy, who were making desperate efforts to turn the Union left, rout General Hurlbut, and gain possession of the landing. The fire of the artillery, aided by that of the gunboats Tyler and Lexington, which, coming within range, opened heavily upon the rebel ranks, caused them to give way a little, and General T. J. Wood's division, the advance of Buell's corps, coming up just at this time, aided in driving them back. At nightfall the rebels rested on their arms in what had been the Union camp; but the Union forces, though sadly shattered, looked forward with confidence to the morrow, when they felt certain they would be able to drive back and defeat the enemy. The rebel commander-in-chief, General Albert S. Johnston, had been mortally wounded early in the action, and died before evening, and General Beauregard was now in command.

Where, in this day of desperate fighting, was General Grant? That he was in the battle during the day was admitted, and was, indeed, evident from his own report, though, with characteristic modesty, he does not state when he reached the field. But his enemies, and among them some who should have had more manhood than to have brought false accusations against him, charged that he was surprised, and was, indeed, defeated, until General Buell's coming and taking command reversed the tables, and from the misfortunes of the first day's battle evoked the triumph of the second. It was also charged that he was unjustifiably absent on the morning of the first day's battle; that his place was with his troops; that he did not arrive till noon, and that he did nothing to prevent the demoralization which was taking place among his raw troops. To these charges, though knowing their falsity, General Grant has never deigned reply, but within the past few weeks we have had a refutation of them from the man of all others best qualified to testify to the truth in the case, Major-General Sherman. He states, in a letter to the editor of the "United States Service Magazine," that the battle-field was chosen by the late lamented Major-General Charles F. Smith, and that it was well chosen; that on any other the Union army would have been overwhelmed. He further says that General Grant was early on the field; that he visited his division in person about ten A. M., when the battle was raging fiercest; approved of his stubborn resistance to the enemy, and, in answer to his inquiry concerning cartridges, told him that he had anticipated their want, and given orders accordingly; and, remarking that his presence was more needed over at the left, rode off to encourage the hardly pressed ranks of McClernand's and Hurlbut's divisions.

"About five P. M.," continues General Sherman, "before the sun set, General Grant came again to me, and, after hearing my report of matters, explained to me the situation of affairs on the left, which were not as favorable; still, the enemy had failed to reach the landing of the boats. We agreed that the enemy had expended the *furore* of his attack, and we estimated our loss and approximated our then strength, including Lew. Wallace's fresh division, expected each minute. He then ordered me to get all things ready, and at daylight the next day to assume the offensive. That was before General Buell had arrived, but he was known to be near at hand. General Buell's troops took no essential part in the first day's fight, and Grant's army, though collected together hastily, green as militia, some regiments arriving without cartridges even, and nearly all hearing the dread sound of battle for the first time, had successfully withstood and repelled the first day's terrific onset of a superior enemy, well commanded and well handled. I know I had orders from General Grant to assume the offensive before I knew General Buell was on the west side of the Tennessee. . . . . I understood Grant's forces were to advance on the right of the Corinth road, and Buell's on the left (this was on the 7th), and accordingly at daylight I advanced my division by the flank, the resistance being trivial, up to the very spot where the day before the battle had been most severe, and then waited till near noon for Buell's troops to get up abreast, when the entire line advanced and recovered all the ground we had ever held. I know that, with the exception of one or two severe struggles, the fighting of April 7th was easy as compared with that of April 6th. I never was disposed, nor am I now, to question any thing done by General Buell and his army, and know that, approaching our field of battle from the rear, he encountered that sickening crowd of laggards and fugitives that excited his contempt and that of his army, who never gave full credit to those in the front line who did fight hard, and who had, at four P. M., checked the enemy, and were preparing the next day to assume the offensive."

Thus far General Sherman. Let us now resume the history of the battle. General Lew. Wallace's division had reached the battle-field on the evening of the 6th, too late to participate in the fighting of that day, but fresh and ready for the severe work of the morrow. General Nelson's division of Buell's army crossed the river during the night, and were also ready to commence fighting at dawn; but the remainder of Buell's army, owing to a deficiency of transportation and the want of pontoons, did not cross till the morning of the 7th. General Grant assigned Wallace's division to the right and Nelson's to the left of his line, and the divisions which formed the centre were those which had so bravely withstood the onset of the previous day. The attack on the 7th was made by the Union troops, General Nelson, on the left, opening with a destructive and galling fire, and advancing rapidly as the rebels fell back. In a short time the fighting was general along the whole line, and though the rebels maintained their position with great tenacity at some points, and were urged forward by their leaders, they at length began to break, and, when the remainder of Buell's troops came up towards noon, they gave evidence of thorough defeat, and, after an ineffective struggle, fled, abandoning their artillery and small-arms, about five o'clock, P. M. The battle had been the most sanguinary of the war up to that time. Of the Union troops, one thousand six hundred and fourteen were slain, seven thousand seven hundred and twenty-one were wounded, and three thousand nine hundred and sixty-three were missing, the greater part of them prisoners, making a total of thirteen thousand two hundred and ninety-eight *hors de combat*. The rebel losses, as stated by Pollard, were, killed, one thousand seven hundred and twenty-eight; wounded, eight thousand and twelve; missing, nine hundred and fifty-nine; making an aggregate of ten thousand six hundred and ninety-nine.

There is abundant evidence that the amount of missing, which includes the prisoners not wounded, is greatly understated, and from this statement it appears that the number of their killed and wounded was considerably in excess of that of the Union troops. The loss of cannon by the Union troops on the sixth was nearly or quite balanced by the loss of the rebels on the seventh. General Grant was slightly wounded in the ankle in this battle. The rebel loss of officers in high command had been very severe. Besides their commander-in-chief, General A. S. Johnston, General Gladden of South Carolina, General G. M. Johnston, *pseudo* governor of Kentucky, and Colonels Adams, Kitt Williams, and Blythe were killed; and Generals Breckinridge, Hardee, Cheatham, Johnson, and Bowen were wounded. General Grant's troops were too completely exhausted to make pursuit that night, and General Buell did not order any of his force, which was less wearied, to that duty. On the morning of the 8th, General Grant ordered Sherman to follow the retreating rebel force. He did so, and proceeding along the Corinth road, came upon the rebel cavalry, whom he drove from the field after a short skirmish, and, pressing forward, entered and destroyed the rebel camp and considerable quantities of ammunition. Proceeding onward, he found abundant evidences of a hasty and disorderly retreat, in the abandoned wagons, ambulances, and limber-boxes which strewed the road.

On the evening of the 8th, General Beauregard sent by flag of truce a note to General Grant, asking permission to send a mounted party to the battlefield to bury the dead, and that gentlemen wishing to remove the remains of their sons and friends might accompany the party. The next morning General Grant replied that, owing to the warmth of the weather, he had made heavy details of forces to bury the dead of both parties, and that it had been accomplished. He therefore declined to permit the approach of any party of the enemy to the battle-field.

General Halleck, the commander of the Mississippi department, on hearing of the battle of Pittsburg Landing, hastened at once to the field to take command in person, and on the 13th of April issued a general order expressive of his thanks to General Grant and General Buell, and the officers and men under their charge, for the results of the great battle. He also collected at the camp at Pittsburg Landing all the troops which could be spared from the other posts of the department, and reorganized the army in sixteen divisions, eight of which formed the Army of the Tennessee, under General Grant, four the Army of the Ohio, under General Buell, and four the Army of the Mississippi, under General John Pope. On the 30th of April this grand army moved forward to drive the rebels from their strongly fortified position at Corinth. As they approached the stronghold several sharp actions occurred between them and the rebels, which however resulted, in each instance, in the repulse of the latter. On the 17th of May the Union army commenced a series of regular approaches for the reduction of the city. On the 19th, General Grant urged General Halleck to allow him with his army to assault the enemy's works, as he was satisfied that the rebel army could be captured by a vigorous and concerted attack. General Halleck refused, preferring the method of slow approaches. General Grant still urged with great importunity, and a quarrel threatened between the two generals, the only one in Grant's military career. Halleck, however, adhered to his plan, and, in spite of frequent sallies on the part of the enemy, the parallels were drawn closer and closer, and on the night of the 28th of May, Generals Beauregard and Bragg, with their troops, evacuated Corinth, blowing up their caissons and magazines, and, moving southward along the Mobile and Ohio railroad, sought a safer position. They were pursued by General Pope, but without any considerable result, though their flight was somewhat accelerated, and by the end of June there was no rebel force within fifty miles of Corinth. Meantime, New Orleans and the forts below it had been surrendered to the Union forces under

Farragut and Butler, and Memphis had been captured by the Mississippi flotilla under Commodore Davis. On the 17th of July, General Halleck was summoned to Washington to take the position of general-in-chief of the armies of the United States, and the new department of West Tennessee created, embracing Northern Mississippi, West Tennessee, Western Kentucky, and Southern Illinois, and General Grant placed in command of it. General Curtis had succeeded General Pope in command of the Army of the Mississippi, now named the department of Arkansas, and General Buell still commanded the Army of the Ohio, which had for its department the region inclosed by the Tennessee river. General Grant made his headquarters for a time at Memphis, which, with its swarms of crafty secessionists, speculators, gamblers, and Jewish traders, desperate for gain, bid fair to be of more value to the rebels, when in possession of the Unionists, than when held by the rebels themselves, inasmuch as every thing in the way of supplies, which the enemy needed, was smuggled through the lines to them on one pretence or another. This illicit traffic General Grant broke up with a strong hand, and crushed the disloyal operators so effectually that the unscrupulous traitors and spies were almost beside themselves with rage.

Meantime, General Bragg was moving with all speed through Tennessee to Kentucky, and General Buell following, but not overtaking him; and when he doubled upon his track and again faced southward, Buell still pursued, and, after fighting an indecisive battle at Perryville, suffered him to make good his escape, with his plunder, into Tennessee again. This expedition of General Bragg was only one portion of a combined movement of the rebels, having for its object the expulsion of the Union armies from Northern Mississippi, West Tennessee, and West Kentucky, and the regaining of the territory they had lost within the previous seven or eight months. That portion of the programme having for its object the expulsion of Grant from his department was intrusted to Generals Van Dorn, Price, and Lovell. The first movement made by the rebels to this end was the capture of Iuka, a Union post about twenty miles from Corinth, and the subsequent battle of Iuka, in which Price attacked General Rosecrans, then one of Grant's lieutenants. The battle was a very severe one, but Price was severely beaten and compelled to evacuate the town. He retreated eastward instead of northward, as Grant had expected, and managed to join Van Dorn and Lovell in Tippah county, Mississippi, when the three, with a formidable force, determined to repossess themselves of Corinth, and thus compel Grant to loosen his hold on West Tennessee. General Grant comprehended their plans, and was ready to thwart them. It was at first somewhat uncertain whether they would attempt to seize Corinth, where Rosecrans was now stationed, or Bolivar, which was held by General Ord, another of Grant's lieutenants, with a considerable force, or Jackson, where General Grant had his own headquarters; their position near Pocahontas, on the Memphis and Charleston railroad, threatening all these about equally. This will be evident from a glance at the map, Jackson being the apex of an equilateral triangle formed by the junction of the Mobile and Ohio and Mississippi and Jackson railroads at Jackson, and their several crossings of the Memphis and Charleston railroad at Lagrange and Corinth. Corinth formed another angle of the triangle, and Pocahontas was nearly midway between that and Lagrange, and Bolivar about half-way between Lagrange and Jackson. But Grant had so arranged his forces and timed his movements, that whichever point might be attacked, a supporting force should be ready to strike the enemy in the rear, or to cut off his escape. General Hurlbut had been stationed between Pocahontas and Lagrange, and when it became evident that Corinth was the point aimed at by the enemy, he put himself in position to intercept his retreat along the Hatchie river, and General Ord was directed to move to his support. We need not describe in detail the battle of Corinth; suffice it to say that General Rosecrans defeated the combined rebel force after a severe battle on the 3d and 4th of October, and that the flying rebels were pursued and terribly punished by Hurlbut and Ord, and by General McPherson, whom he had detached from his immediate command for the purpose. A more thorough defeat and rout had not, up to that time, occurred during the war, nor a more decided and zealous pursuit. On the 25th of October, another change was made in the boundaries of the department of Tennessee. General Rosecrans was assigned to the command of the old department of the Ohio—now somewhat changed in boundary, and renamed the department of the Cumberland—in place of General Buell, relieved; and the department of Tennessee was extended down the Mississippi to Vicksburg. This new department General Grant divided into four districts, and assigned commanders to each, viz.: 1st. The district of Memphis, General W. T. Sherman, commander; 2d. The district of Jackson, General S. A. Hurlbut, commander; 3d. The district of Corinth, Brigadier-General C. S. Hamilton, commander; 4th. The district of Columbus, Brigadier-General T. A. Davies, commander.

There was still much trouble in regard to trade at

Memphis, and other points in his department. While some of those engaged in trade were men of high and honorable character, too many were unscrupulous speculators, who were ready, for the sake of gain, to smuggle through the lines weapons, ammunition, food, medicines, and other articles contraband of war, to the rebels. General Grant tried the most stringent rules and the most critical examination, but the evil still continued, and he was compelled to expel the Jews, who had been the principal offenders, from the department. Amid the almost universal corruption which prevailed at this period—very many officers in the army secretly engaging in cotton speculations, and neglecting their duty to acquire wealth in this way—General Grant's reputation for strict integrity, and avoidance of even the appearance of evil, was never questioned. He was remarkably sensitive to any thing which might seem to implicate his integrity in these matters. A friend, himself a man of unimpeachable honor, proposed to him, at this time, that he should designate Union men of high character to conduct the necessary trade. "No!" was his prompt reply, "I will do no such thing; for, if I did, it would be stated within a week, on the highest authority, that I was a partner with every man I appointed; and if any of them were guilty of misconduct, the blame and guilt would fall on my shoulders."

Vicksburg was now the goal of Grant's hopes; to capture that stronghold, the great object of his ambition. It was, indeed, a prize worth contending for. It was the key to the navigation of the Mississippi; strong by nature, in its terraced bluffs rising high over the Mississippi, it had been made tenfold stronger by the engineer's art, and was believed by the rebels to be utterly impregnable. From the very commencement of the war no pains had been spared in fortifying it, and when the loss of the forts below New Orleans and of Island No. Ten, and Memphis, had convinced the rebels that this fortress must be their main dependence in closing the river navigation, they redoubled their efforts to make it a perfect Gibraltar. Not simply the city itself was surrounded with earthworks—fort, bastion, redan, and rifle-pits—but Haines', Chickasaw, and Walnut bluffs, to the northwest, north, and northeast of the city, and Warrenton, commanding the lower approaches to it, were also strongly fortified, and iron-clad vessels of formidable character were built on the Yazoo river above, out of harm's way, to descend at the proper time and carry destruction among the gunboats of the Union squadron. It had been assailed before its defences were quite perfected, in the summer of 1862, by Admiral Farragut's squadron, but a long bombardment had proved ineffectual, so lofty were its bluffs, and so formidable at that time its batteries. An attempt during the same summer, by General Williams (who was killed in August of that year at Baton Rouge), to turn the current of the Mississippi through a canal across the peninsula formed by the bend of the Mississippi in front of Vicksburg, had proved a failure. General Grant was well aware how formidable was the enterprise he was about to undertake, and he made all possible preparation for it. The troops of the levy of July and August, 1862, were rapidly joining the army and rendering its numbers large, far beyond any former precedent. The supplies of food, ammunition, arms, clothing, &c., were also collected in vast quantities at suitable depots, for distribution to the forces of each district. Early in December, General Grant began to move his troops down the Mississippi Central railroad, for the purpose of a flank movement upon Vicksburg, to be executed in concert with an attack upon the north and northwest front of the city, by a force under General Sherman descending the river from Memphis. About the 15th of December, General Grant's headquarters were at Oxford, Mississippi, while his principal depot of supplies was at Holly Springs, thirty miles above, guarded by a sufficient garrison under a Colonel Murphy. A small rebel force, by a detour to the east, managed to make a dash upon Holly Springs on the 20th of December, but might easily have been driven off by the garrison, whose commander had been apprized of the attack by General Grant as soon as possible, and ordered to hold his ground and reinforcements should be sent to him. Colonel Murphy, however, was either a coward or traitor, and made but slight resistance, suffering the vast accumulation of supplies to fall into the hands of the rebels, who plundered and destroyed them, and then made all haste to escape. This mishap deranged General Grant's plans, compelling him to fall back to Holly Springs and order forward other supplies, and thus preventing him from making a simultaneous attack with General Sherman upon Vicksburg. Nor was he able to apprize General Sherman of the cause of his failure. Sherman went forward, made the attack upon Vicksburg, but, after a three days' struggle, was compelled to withdraw his troops, defeated but not dispirited at their want of success. Having renewed his stock of supplies, and the time for success in a movement southward, by way of the Mississippi Central railroad, having passed, General Grant next descended the Mississippi to Young's Point, Louisiana, a short distance above Vicksburg, where he devoted his whole attention to solving the problem of capturing the stronghold which frowned so loftily upon the Mississippi. The problem proved a knotty one. An assault on the water-front was impossible, and the heavy and repeated bombardments of the squadron, though seemingly sufficient to reduce any known fortress, made little impression upon this. The approaches by way of Chickasaw bluffs, strong enough in December to repulse Sherman's army, had been fortified since that time, until they left no hope of success in that direction. No siege was possible, because, the rear being open, supplies and men could be thrown in till the besieged could become the offensive party. There remained three alternatives, all attended with difficulty, and none giving very certain promise of success. These were the renewal of the canal project under more favorable auspices, with a view to rendering the position of Vicksburg worthless in a military point of view, and opening a new route for the navigation of the Mississippi through the canal; the approach to the city from the north and northeast by way of the Yazoo river, which at several points above communicated more or less directly with the Mississippi, and the passing of a land and naval force below Vicksburg, and attacking the fortress from the south.

That dogged pertinacity which, when a school-boy, led Grant never to give up till he had mastered a difficult problem, an heir-loom, perhaps, of his Scotch ancestry, now caused him to adhere to his purpose, hopeless as it seemed to the rebels, and indeed to our own Government, which at first seemed hardly willing to brook the delay. The canal was first tried, but owing to a sudden flood in the Mississippi, which broke the dam and overflowed the adjacent country, it was abandoned. Attempts were next made to enter the Yazoo by the old Yazoo pass, and subsequently by a more circuitous route, through

Steel's bayou, Black bayou, Duck creek, Deer creek, Rolling fork, and Sunflower river; but neither of these, though accomplishing much as raids into the enemy's country, proved successful in opening the way for an attack upon the city of Vicksburg. There remained, then, the last alternative of bringing his troops, with their supplies, to some point below Vicksburg, and thence attacking the fortress from below. How to do this was a serious question. From Vicksburg to Port Hudson, a distance of two hundred and thirty-two miles, every commanding bluff was fortified, and the batteries and earthworks at Port Hudson, Natchez, Grand Gulf, etc., were very formidable. Admiral Farragut had, indeed, run past the Port Hudson batteries, but had lost a ship-of-war in doing so; and there was no possibility of bringing troops for the purpose of attacking Vicksburg from New Orleans. To run the batteries in front of Vicksburg, with transports loaded with troops, was impossible; and to lead them through the swamps on the west side of the Mississippi, with their trains, at this time of the year (February and March), equally so. By opening an old channel of the Mississippi, into Lake Providence, and thence passing down the Tensas, and through a bayou discharging into the Mississippi some distance below Grand Gulf, it might be possible to send down some troops and supplies; but the work would necessarily be slow, as the route was tortuous, and only practicable for small vessels of light draft. Little as it promised, this route was tried, and a moderate amount of supplies forwarded. But it was necessary that a part of the gunboat squadron should be below Vicksburg, as well as transports to bring the troops and stores across the river, and to engage the batteries at Grand Gulf. Accordingly, after conference with Admirals Farragut and Porter, it was determined to send a part of the gunboats, and sixteen or eighteen transports, laden with forage and sup plies, past the batteries, in two divisions, on different nights. This was accomplished with only the loss of two transports, though under a most terrific fire continued for hours, and was one of the most heroic acts of the war.

Meantime the roads having improved, and the worst portions of them being corduroyed, General Grant commenced marching his troops by land, through the country west of the Mississippi, the Thirteenth Army Corps, General McClernand's, taking the lead, and the Seventeenth, General McPherson's, following; while the Fifteenth, General Shemran's, and a part of the Sixteenth, were left to take care of the communications and supplies, and to deceive the rebels as to the intentions of the commanding general. This march, which it was expected would terminate at New Carthage, thirty-five miles below Milliken's bend, the point of departure, was, from the condition of the roads, the breaking of the levee, etc., extended to Hard Times, Louisiana, a distance of seventy miles, and over roads which almost any other general would have pronounced impassable. The movement commenced March 29th, and occupied thirty days.

At first the attempt was made to land the troops near Grand Gulf, and the squadron engaged the batteries there with the intention of carrying the position, and thus affording a base of operations. But the resistance was too stubborn to be overcome by the gunboats, and, after a fight of five hours and a half, the admiral (Porter) ordered their withdrawal. During the night following the squadron and transports ran past the batteries, and the next morning commenced ferrying over the troops and landing them at Bruinsburg, ten miles below. Marching rapidly from this point northeastward towards Port

Gibson, the thirteenth and seventeenth corps encountered a considerable force of the enemy, whom they defeated after a sharp battle, and moved on to and across Bayou Pierre. The next day it was ascertained that Grand Gulf, which had been flanked by this movement, had been evacuated, and General Grant repaired thither with a small escort, and made arrangements to make it his base of supplies for a time. These arrangements occupied nearly a week. By his orders, as nearly as possible simultaneously with the landing of the two corps at Bruinsburg, General Sherman had made a strong demonstration towards Haines' Bluff and the Yazoo, and had thus attracted the attention of the rebels towards that quarter, where they believed the entire Union army were concentrated, and prevented them from opposing their landing below.

This being accomplished, Sherman's troops made all speed in marching to the rendezvous on the river, where the transports were in waiting to take them over to Grand Gulf.

Before leaving Young's Point, General Grant had also ordered an expedition by a competent cavalry force, under the command of Colonel, now General Benj. H. Grierson, to start from Lagrange, at the junction of the Mississippi Central and Memphis and Charleston railroads, to follow the lines of the Mobile and Ohio and Mississippi Central railroads, and destroy as much of these, and the Meridian and Jackson railroad, as possible,—capturing and destroying also all stores, ammunition, locomotives, and railroad cars possible, in their route. This expedition was thoroughly successful, and reached Baton Rouge on the 1st of May, at the time Grant was fighting the battle of Port Gibson. Other raids were ordered about the same time from Middle

Tennessee, which aided in breaking up the railroad communications and frustrating the plans of the rebels.

Our space does not allow us to go into details of the subsequent masterly movements by which, while apparently threatening an immediate attack on Vicksburg from the south, the garrison there, under the command of General Pemberton, were prevented from forming a junction with General J. E. Johnston's troops, then in the vicinity of Jackson, nor of the battle of Raymond, the capture of Jackson, and the destruction of the property and manufactories of the rebel Government there; the rapid march westward, the severe battles of Champion's hill and of Black River bridge, and the eminently skilful management of the corps of Generals Sherman and McPherson. Suffice it to say that General Grant interposed his army between the forces of Johnston and Pemberton, drove the former broken and routed northward, and compelled the latter to put himself and his defeated army as soon as possible within the defences of Vicksburg; and on the 18th the Union army sat down before Vicksburg, having completely invested it on the land side and opened communication with their squadron and transports by way of Walnut bluffs, above the river. On the 19th of May, and again on the 22d, General Grant ordered assaults upon the beleaguered city, neither of which were successful, except in gaining some ground and expediting the subsequent regular approaches. The army now became satisfied that the stronghold could only be captured by a systematic siege, and General Grant accordingly took all precautions to make that siege effective, and to prevent the rebel General Johnston from approaching with sufficient force to raise the siege. Day by day the parallels were brought nearer and nearer, and finally came so near that the rebels could not use their cannon, while the Union artillery from the adjacent hills, and from the squadron, constantly showered their iron hail upon the devoted city. The inhabitants and the rebel army dug caves in the bluffs, and endeavored to shelter themselves from the fiery storm, but these were often penetrated by the shells from the batteries, or blown up in the explosion of the forts. At length, on the third of July, General Grant was prepared to order an assault, which could not have failed of success, when overtures were made for a surrender, and the city was delivered into the hands of the Union army on the 4th of July, 1863,

It is stated that at the interview between General Grant and General Pemberton, after shaking hands, and a short silence, General Pemberton said:

"General Grant, I meet you in order to arrange terms for the capitulation of the city of Vicksburg and its garrison. What terms do you demand?"

"*Unconditional surrender*," replied General Grant.

"Unconditional surrender!" said Pemberton. "Never, so long as I have a man left me! I will fight rather."

"*Then, sir, you can continue the defence*," replied Grant. "*My army has never been in a better condition for the prosecution of the siege.*"

During this conversation, General Pemberton was greatly agitated, trembling with emotion from head to foot, while Grant was as calm and imperturbable as a May morning. After a somewhat protracted interview, during which General Grant, in consideration of the courage and tenacity of the garrison, explained the terms he was disposed to allow to them on their unconditional surrender, the two generals separated, an armistice having been declared till morning, when the question of surrender was to be finally determined. The same evening General Grant transmitted to General Pemberton, in writing, the propositions he had made during the afternoon for the disposal of the garrison, should they surrender. These terms were very liberal, far more so than those usually acceded to a conquered garrison.

The rebel loss in this campaign had been very great, larger than has often been experienced in the campaigns of modern times, and utterly without precedent in the previous history of this continent. The number of prisoners captured by the Union troops, from the landing at Bruinsburg to, and including the surrender of Vicksburg, was 34,620, including one lieutenant-general and nineteen major and brigadier-generals; and 11,800 men were killed, wounded, or deserters. There were also among the spoils of the campaign two hundred and eleven field-pieces, ninety siege-guns, and 45,000 small-arms. The Union losses had been 943 killed, 7,095 wounded, and 537 missing, making a total of casualties of 8,575, and of the wounded nearly one-half returned to duty within a month.

Having disposed of his prisoners at Vicksburg, General Grant dispatched General Sherman with an adequate force to Jackson to defeat and break up Johnston's army, and destroy the rebel stores collected there, in both which enterprises he was successful.

During the long period of two and a quarter years since he had entered the army, General Grant had never sought or received a day's furlough. But after this great victory, and while the thanks of the President, the Cabinet, Congress, and the people, were lavished upon him without stint, he sought for a few days' rest with his family, and received it. His stay with them was brief, and he returned to his duties, descending the

Mississippi—now, thanks to his skilful generalship, open to the navigation of all nations from its mouth to the falls of St. Anthony—to New Orleans, to confer with General Banks relative to the operations of the autumn. While here, on the 4th of September, he was seriously injured by being thrown from his horse while reviewing the troops of General Banks' department.

It had been the intention of the Government to place him in command of all the troops west of the Alleghanies and east of the Mississippi, on the resumption of active warfare early in September, but this accident unfortunately postponed that appointment. These troops were at this time comprised in three distinct armies—the Army of the Cumberland, under the command of General Rosecrans, the Army of the Tennessee, under General Sherman, and the Army of the Ohio, under General Burnside. The interest of the whole country was now concentrating on the movements of the first of these, the Army of the Cumberland. General Rosecrans, an able officer, had fought a great battle at Stone river, near Murfreesboro, Tenn., at the beginning of the year, with the rebel General Bragg, and had compelled that general to retreat to Tullahoma; but both armies had maintained a position of observation from that period until the last of June, when Rosecrans made a movement forward, and, threatening to flank Bragg, caused him to evacuate Tullahoma and retreat upon Chattanooga, a strong position, and one which it was very important to the United States Government to have in its possession, as it was the key to East Tennessee, which, though loyal, had long been in the possession of the rebels. General Rosecrans pursued slowly but steadily, and by an admirable flank movement compelled Bragg to march out of Chattanooga to give him battle, and occupied that important post meanwhile with a small garrison. At this critical juncture, Bragg was largely reinforced from the Army of Virginia, and the battle of Chickamauga was fought on the 19th and 20th of September, and the result was indecisive, since the Union army, though driven back and losing heavily, still occupied Chattanooga, the goal for which they fought, and had inflicted a loss equal to or greater than their own upon the enemy. The condition of the Army of the Cumberland was, nevertheless, precarious for the next two months, and that of the Army of the Ohio, which occupied Knoxville, Tenn., hardly less so. The rebels held possession of Lookout Mountain and Mission Ridge, and thus were able to lay an embargo upon both railroad and river communication with Nashville and Louisville, the real bases of the Army of the Cumberland, and had moreover captured a large train of supplies. Rations and forage could only be brought for the supply of the Army of the Cumberland by sixty miles' cartage over the worst roads in the Republic, and the force, augmented in October and November by two army corps from the Army of the Potomac, and by a part of Sherman's Army of the Tennessee, was for some months on half rations. It was at this time that General Rosecrans was relieved of the command of the Army of the Cumberland, and General Thomas made his successor, while General Grant was put in command of the grand military division of the Mississippi, comprising the three armies already named. He had not long assumed command when affairs put on a brighter aspect. By an adroit movement, the sixty miles of wagon road was reduced to ten, over a good road, and presently, by another equally adroit manœuvre, the navigation of the Tennessee below Chattanooga was secured, and arrangements made for the speedy repair of the Nashville and

Chattanooga railroad. Still, so sanguine was Bragg that he should soon obtain possession of Chattanooga, that on the 21st of November he sent this message by flag of truce to General Grant: "Humanity would dictate the removal of all non-combatants from Chattanooga, as I am about to shell the city!"

The reply to this threat came promptly, but it was not fully delivered until the evening of the 25th of that month.

General Grant had been devising means and ways for the expulsion of the rebel forces from the valley of Chattanooga and its vicinity, and his plans were just ripe for execution when this summons came from Bragg. That general had been betrayed into the indiscretion of sending Longstreet with about twenty thousand troops to besiege Knoxville, and had thus fatally weakened his force. Giving instructions to General Burnside to lure him on, and while delaying his progress by occasional, and, apparently, strenuous resistance to fall back after each battle, till Longstreet was securely entrapped, he made rapid dispositions to punish Bragg most severely for his audacity. Pontoons were secretly transported to the Tennessee, near the mouth of North Chickamauga creek, and a sufficient body of troops crossed in boats to drive off any rebel troops in the immediate vicinity; and then, at a preconcerted signal, the pontoons were laid, a cavalry force crossed, and sent to cut the railroads leading to Knoxville effectually, and, a large body of troops following them, took possession of an isolated hill between the Atlanta railroad and the river. This movement was made under General Sherman's direction. General Hooker, meantime, was dispatched with a sufficient and resolute force to take possession of Lookout Mountain and drive the rebels from it. He marches down Lookout Valley, and seems to be intending to reach and ascend a pass ten miles below, but, when out of sight of the rebel camps on the brow of the mountain, suddenly turns, ascends, and attacks them in the rear, and after a series of gallant engagements succeeds in driving them, with heavy loss, from the mountain, which, the next morning, was crowned with the Union flag.

On the previous day, simultaneously with Sherman's movements, General Thomas had moved out of Chattanooga with a heavy force, and, after a sharp action and a brilliant charge, obtained possession of Orchard Knob and another eminence in front of Chattanooga, on which the rebels had a strong redoubt, and which commanded a part of Mission Ridge and the principal forts of the rebels on that ridge.

On the 25th of November, General Grant directed General Sherman to make persistent and repeated demonstrations against Fort Buckner, situated on Tunnel Hill, the northern extremity of the continuous Mission Ridge, not in the expectation that he would be able to carry the fort by his assaults, but to draw the attention of the rebels in that direction, while he was preparing to attack them from Fort Wood. Sherman's first assault was made about 10 A. M.; it was repulsed, as were other successive assaults delivered on one and the other slope of the ridge on which Fort Buckner stood defiant, and, as the rebels believed, impregnable. The assaulting columns were reinforced again and again, and, though not successful in carrying the fort, they had accomplished all that Grant desired; they had drawn thither a large portion of the rebel force, thus weakening the garrisons of Forts Breckinridge and Bragg, further south on the same ridge, and had been able to gain and hold a position far up the slope, from which, when the time came, they could deliver a crushing blow upon the rebel fort. It had been announced to the corps in a general order, that the firing of six guns was to be the signal for the movement of the fourth army corps (General Gordon Granger's) to the assault of Fort Breckinridge, the largest and most formidable of the enemy's works on Mission Ridge, situated nearly a mile below Fort Buckner. This fort was about two miles distant, and nearly northeast of Fort Wood, the earthwork on the summit of Orchard Knob, where Thomas's army were assembled. A little past 3 P. M., General Sherman sent word to General Grant that he could hold his position, and at twenty minutes to four the signal-guns boomed from Fort Wood, and the divisions of Wood, Sheridan, and Baird, forming the fourth army corps, sprang to their positions, and in five minutes were marching steadily towards the ridge. The rebel batteries on the summit, and the rifle-pits which girded the slope and the base of the ridge, commenced at once a sweeping fire over the plain which the assaulting party must cross, and the Union batteries—Forts Wood and Negley, Forts Palmer and King, from a point nearer Chattanooga, Bridge's battery from the base of Orchard Knob, and Moccasin Point battery, from the other side of the Tennessee—hurled in reply their heavy shot and shell, at long range, on the rebel forts and rifle-pits. Undismayed by the tempest of shot, and shell, and bullets that rained so fiercely upon them, the veteran troops pressed steadily and swiftly forward, cleared with a hurrah the rifle-pits at the base of the ridge, sending the rebel troops which had occupied it back as prisoners, and instantly ascending the precipitous slope, a slope so steep that it would task severely the powers of a skilful climber to reach the top unopposed; yet, with an ardor that nothing could restrain, upward, still upward they went, though every step was attended with loss from the fire of the thirteen batteries on the summit, and the volleys of musketry which belch forth from the rebel rifle-pits and barricades half way up the slope. These last are soon carried with a shout, and their occupants sent reeling down the slope under the fire of their own batteries, and, without stopping for breath, the Union soldiers push on up a steep so precipitous that the cannon in the forts cannot be depressed sufficiently to reach them, and it is only the musketry fire from the rebels on the summit which opposes them. The rebels did not, would not, believe that they could reach the top. Bragg himself declared it utterly impossible. Five minutes before the Union troops captured Fort Breckinridge, an old lady, at whose house on the summit Bragg made his headquarters, said to him, "General, what shall we do if the Yankees do get up here?" "Oh! never fear," was Bragg's reply, "they cannot reach the top; every man of them will be killed before they get near it." "But," said the old lady to a Union officer, "he had hardly said so, when they came swarming up, and General Bragg and General Breckinridge had to ride for their lives." The top of the ridge was gained; Fort Breckinridge, after a brief but sharp struggle, was captured; and Bragg's army, routed, and abandoning all their artillery and most of their small-arms, fled, tumbled, and rolled down the eastern slope of the ridge. Instantly Sherman advanced and drove the rebels from Fort Buckner, while Hooker, who had been moving from the eastern slope of Lookout mountain since early morning, and had ascended Mission Ridge some distance below, came upon Fort Bragg two miles below, and drove its garrison into the valley of the Chickamauga.

General Bragg was answered. The non-combatants were not removed from Chattanooga, and that redoubtable general, partly from the loss of most of his cannon, and partly from the entire rout of his forces and their rapid retreat eastward, was unable to fulfil his threat of shelling the city.

But General Grant had not yet done with General Bragg or his troops. On the morning of the 26th, long before dawn, Davis's division of the fourteenth corps were in rapid pursuit of the retreating foe, and very soon after sunrise three corps, Hooker's, Palmer's, and Sherman's, were on their way, and, overtaking the rear of the enemy, drove them in confusion from Chickamauga depot, capturing and destroying large quantities of supplies and some cannon; and thence pushing forward to Pigeon Ridge and Graysville, still skirmishing wherever the rebels would make a stand, drove them eastward to Ringgold Gap, where they fought for a time desperately, having every advantage of position, but were eventually driven from the Gap and beyond Red Clay station on the Dalton and Cleveland railroad; and that railroad being destroyed, thus eventually cutting off all communication between Bragg and Longstreet, the pursuit was given over, and the shattered columns of Bragg's army were gathered at Dalton, where Bragg was at once displaced from command, and Hardee, and eventually J. E. Johnston, put at the head of the rebel army.

Meantime, General Grant had directed General Sherman, after pursuing the enemy a few miles, to turn northward, and, marching with all practicable speed, put himself in communication with General Burnside and compel

Longstreet to raise the siege of Knoxville. This was accomplished, and Longstreet, who, enraged at having been outwitted, had dashed himself in vain against the defences of Knoxville, found himself compelled, on the 4th of December, by the near approach of Sherman's army, to abandon the siege and retreat towards Virginia, while both Foster's and Sherman's cavalry pursued.

With this movement the campaign of Chattanooga closed, a campaign hardly less brilliant than that of Vicksburg, and one which paralyzed for months the rebel army in the Southwest.

On the 7th of December it was announced that from the commencement of the war, up to that date, the armies under General Grant's particular command had captured four hundred and seventy-two cannon, ninety thousand prisoners, and more than a hundred thousand stand of small-arms.

On the 8th of December the President of the United States sent the following dispatch to General Grant:

WASHINGTON, DEC. 8, 1863.

MAJOR-GENERAL GRANT:

Understanding that your lodgment at Chattanooga and Knoxville is now secure, I wish to tender you, and all under your command, my more than thanks—my profoundest gratitude, for the skill, courage, and perseverance with which you and they, over so great difficulties, have effected that important object. God bless you all!

A. LINCOLN.

On the 10th of December, General Grant issued the following congratulatory order to the army under his command. Its quiet, self-possessed, and appreciative tone, while they contrast favorably with the boastful character of some of the general orders of officers whose achievements were far less conspicuous than his, remind us forcibly of the orders of that other great commander, whom in so many traits of character he strikingly resembles, the Duke of Wellington.

HEADQUARTERS, MILITARY DIVISION OF THE MISSISSIPPI,
IN THE FIELD, CHATTANOOGA, TENNESSEE,
Dec. 10, 1863.

General Orders, No. 9.

The general-commanding takes this opportunity of returning his sincere thanks and congratulations to the brave armies of the Cumberland, the Ohio, the Tennessee, and their comrades from the Potomac, for the recent splendid and decisive successes achieved over the enemy. In a short time you have recovered from him the control of the Tennessee river, from Bridgeport to Knoxville. You dislodged him from his great stronghold upon Lookout mountain, drove him from Chattanooga valley, wrested from his determined grasp the possession of Missionary Ridge, repelled with heavy loss to him his repeated assaults upon Knoxville, forcing him to raise the siege there, driving him at all points, utterly routed and discomfited, beyond the limits of the State. By your noble heroism and determined courage you have most effectually defeated the plans of the enemy for regaining possession of the States of Kentucky and Tennessee. You have secured positions from which no rebellious power can drive or dislodge you. For all this, the general-commanding thanks you, collectively and individually. The loyal people of the United States thank and bless you. Their hopes and prayers for your success against this unholy rebellion are with you daily. Their faith in you will not be in vain. Their hopes will not be blasted. Their prayers to Almighty God will be answered. You will yet go to other fields of strife; and with the invincible bravery and unflinching loyalty to justice and right which have characterized you in the past, you will prove that no enemy can withstand you, and that no defences, however formidable, can check your onward march.

By order of

Maj.-Gen. U. S. GRANT.

T. S. BOWERS, A. A. G.

The honors lavished upon General Grant for this and his previous successes, were not confined to the thanks sent him by the President. On the 17th of Dec., 1863, a joint resolution passed both houses of Congress, and received the Executive approval, which, in addition to the thanks of the national Legislature, provided for a gold medal, with suitable emblems, devices, and inscriptions, to be prepared and presented to General Grant. This token of a nation's grateful regard was designed by the artist Leutze. On one face of the medal was a profile likeness of the hero, surrounded by a wreath of laurels—his name and the year of his victories inscribed upon it; and the whole surrounded by a galaxy of stars. The design for the obverse was the figure of Fame seated in a graceful attitude on the American Eagle, which with wings outspread seems about to take flight. In her right hand she holds her trumpet, and in her left a scroll on which are inscribed Corinth, Vicksburg, Mississippi river, and Chattanooga. On her head is an Indian helmet with radiating feathers. In front of the eagle is the emblematic shield of the United States. Below the group, sprigs of the pine and palm, denoting the North and South, cross each other. Above the figure of Fame in a curved line is the motto, "Proclaim Liberty throughout the Land." The edge is surrounded by a circle of Byzantine stars, exceeding the number of the present States of the Union. Resolutions of thanks were also passed by the Legislatures of most of the loyal States; and numerous costly presents (swords, pistols, &c.) were made by admiring friends. None of these honors, however, produced on the part of the recipient of them any elation, or changed in the least the simplicity and modesty of his manners, or his earnest devotion to the work of putting down the rebellion. His health was not fully re-established, after the severe injuries he had received at New Orleans, but he toiled more continuously and patiently than any officer in the service. The communications of his army with its bases at Nashville and Louisville, which had long been broken or in indifferent condition, must be put in the best order, and abundant stores accumulated at Chattanooga, Nashville, and Knoxville, for the coming campaign into the heart of Georgia. His men, worn down by short rations and severe labors, must be recruited by the best of care to the highest degree of efficiency, and withal there must be during the winter months a severe and crushing blow struck upon some vital point of the Confederacy in the Southwest. He had hoped to join in a co-operative movement with the Department of the Gulf on Mobile, but his plans in that direction were thwarted by some adverse influences. He then determined upon an expedition from Vicksburg eastward to reach Meridian, Miss., and, if possible, Selma and Montgomery, Ala.; this expedition to be joined at or near Meridian by a cavalry force dispatched simultaneously from Lagrange southward, and the two to traverse at will the central portions of Mississippi and Alabama. The enterprise was a bold and daring one; the army which should undertake it must cut loose from their base, and obtain their subsistence mainly from the enemy's country—and this with a force of twenty or twenty-five thousand men was not an easy matter. The management and leadership of the principal column, which was to move eastward from Vicksburg, he assigned to his tried and able lieutenant, General William T. Sherman, and the command of the cavalry co-operating force to his chief of cavalry, General W. Sooy Smith. The expedition started early in February, and penetrated as far as Meridian; but the cavalry failing to join them, they advanced no further eastward, but returned to Vicksburg after an absence of a month. In consequence of this failure on the part of the cavalry to connect, which was not wholly their fault, the expedition did not produce all the results expected from it by General Grant; but it greatly crippled the resources of the rebels, made their railroads worthless as communications, and by the alarm it awakened prevented the forces in the vicinity of the Gulf from joining Johnston, who had now succeeded Hardee in the command of the rebel army at Dalton.

While this expedition was in progress General Grant was summoned to new and higher responsibilities. Congress resolved to revive the grade of Lieutenant-General, which had been conferred by brevet only, on General Scott, but as an actual rank in time of war had only been bestowed on General Washington; and a law to that effect having been passed, the President at once conferred the commission on General Grant, and the Senate confirmed it. The commission bore date March 2d, 1864, and on the 9th of that month the President presented to him in person this commission, assuring him of his own hearty personal concurrence in the measure. General Grant replied very briefly, but evidently with deep feeling. On the 12th of March, the President, by official order, assigned to the lieutenant-general the command of the armies of the United States; at the same time appointing General W. T. Sherman commander of the grand military division of the Mississippi, which General Grant had previously commanded; and General McPherson, an able and accomplished officer, to succeed General Sherman in command of the Army of the Tennessee; while General Halleck, hitherto general-in-chief, was relieved from duty, and made chief of staff to the army, at Washington.

General Grant had, in January, 1864, visited all parts of his command, the military division of the Mississippi, and carefully observed its condition, but his position as lieutenant-general required that he should spend some time in ascertaining the condition of the other Western departments, and that he should arrange with General Sherman the future movements of the spring and summer campaign. This done, he returned as speedily as possible, and made every preparation for the coming campaign in Virginia. He purposed taking command in person of the forces destined to assail Richmond, though keeping a vigilant oversight of the movements in other parts of the country. General Sherman, with his magnificent force, composed of the three armies, of the Cumberland, the Tennessee, and the Ohio, had been ordered to move, as nearly as possible, simultaneously with the armies in Virginia, so that there should be no reinforcements sent from one rebel army to the other, as there had been during the previous autumn.

The force with which Grant took the field against

Lee, was such a one as has seldom been under a single commander, or concentrated upon a single object. It consisted, in fact, of three armies; the Army of the Potomac, under the command of Major-General Meade, consisting of three corps of infantry recruited up to their full strength, and numbering each nearly fifty thousand men, with such corps-commanders as Hancock, Warren, and Sedgwick; a cavalry corps of extraordinary ability, commanded by the gallant and fiery Sheridan, and a reserve corps of about 40,000 men, one-third of them colored troops, under the command of the brave and trusty Burnside; the Army of the James, under the command of Major-General Butler, composed of two corps, one that was hitherto known as the Army of Eastern Virginia and North Carolina, the other a fine corps, partly composed of colored troops, under the command of General Gilmore, hitherto forming a part of the Army of the Department of the South; and the Army of the Shenandoah, commanded by Major-General Franz Sigel, and composed of the Army of Western Virginia, under General Crooks, and to which was subsequently added the Nineteenth army corps, formerly from the Department of the Gulf, commanded by General Emory, and with these a considerable cavalry force. But, though seeking the accomplishment of a common object—the reduction of Richmond—these armies were moving from different points, and over different fields, to effect it. Lee's forces lay south of the Rapidan, stretching eastward from Orange Court-house, and his cavalry guarding his left flank towards Gordonsville, and his right near Chancellorsville. The Army of the Potomac, which for months had been confronting him, lay north of the Rapidan, its headquarters being at Culpepper Court-house, and its camps extending from Brandy Station to Robertson's river. To this army was assigned the opening of the conflict, and the mighty task of driving back Lee's vast force, which possessed the advantage of interior lines. The Army of the James had for its first duty the seizing, by an adroitly executed feint, the position at Bermuda Hundred, lying on the south or right bank of the James, nearly midway between Richmond and Petersburg; and, if it should prove practicable, the interposition of a sufficient force permanently between Richmond and Petersburg, and the capture of the latter city. The Army of the Shenandoah, though not at first existing under that title, had for its first mission a movement upon Staunton, Waynesboro, and Lynchburg, with the intent of crippling the resources and effectually cutting off the supplies of Lee's army from the West, and at the same time guarding against any sudden movement of a rebel force down the Valley of the Shenandoah, and into Maryland and Pennsylvania.

Every thing being thus prepared, the order was given on the night of May 3d, for the army of the Potomac to break up camp, and on the morning of the 4th, the three corps crossed the Rapidan, the Second corps (Hancock's) in front, crossing at Ely's ford, the Fifth (Warren's) and the Sixth (Sedgwick's) immediately following, crossing at Germanna ford. This movement, which aimed at flanking Lee's right, as his army were strongly intrenched at Mine run, was at once observed by General Lee, who, with his usual promptness, made a counter movement to match it. From a short distance south of Germanna ford, eastward to and beyond Chancellorsville, stretches a tract of dense, tangled forest and undergrowth, fifteen or twenty miles in length and about five miles wide, traversed by few and indifferent roads, known as the "Wilderness." It was in the eastern part of this that the battle of Chancellorsville was fought, in May, 1863. Into this desolate and difficult region the army of the Potomac plunged, almost immediately on crossing the Rapidan; and against their line, at right angles, between the Fifth and Sixth corps, Lee flung Longstreet's corps, on Thursday, May 5th, before they had had the opportunity of getting into position, and while they were yet embarrassed by the dense and tangled undergrowth of the forest. The weight of the first attack fell on Sedgwick's corps, which, though losing heavily, succeeded in holding its own. Drawing back momentarily, Longstreet returned to the attack with still greater desperation, and at first seemed to be carrying all before him, but Sedgwick's veterans would not yield, and the enemy, sorely disappointed, withdrew; then a fresh force was hurled against the centre (Warren's corps), but, though gaining a temporary advantage, was finally foiled, and beaten back. The battle lasted far into the night, but with indecisive results. At 4 o'clock, A. M., on Friday, 6th of May, Lee renewed the attack, again massing his force, and attempting to break through the right and centre: the attack was repulsed, and by 6 A. M., Hancock commenced driving the rebels, who fell back to a high ridge, with a marsh in front,—a position they had previously fortified. Through the day the fighting was terribly severe, each party in turn gaining some slight success, though at the expense of terrible slaughter. Towards dark an attack was made on the extreme right of the Union lines, and they were turned, and the right completely flanked. General Grant showed his military skill and fertility of resources by extending his left and centre, which were still firm, southward, and bringing his right into a new position, changing his base meanwhile to Fredericksburg and the Rappahannock. He thus flanked Lee in turn, and out of threatened defeat evoked success. He had also gained another advantage, in getting out of the Wilderness into a more open country, where he could use his artillery with greater effect. Moreover, Burnside, with a part of the reserves, had come up in season to take part in the fight of Friday afternoon. An advance at daybreak on Saturday (May 7th) showed that Lee had fallen back. Grant pursued vigorously, and came upon him near Spottsylvania Court-house, where he had taken a new and very strong position. On Sunday, Monday, and Tuesday there was some sharp fighting, but without any decisive result. On Wednesday the fighting was more severe, but still without marked result. On Wednesday night (11th), General Grant directed Hancock's (Second) corps to be transferred to the left, taking up a position between Sedgwick's (Sixth) and Burnside's (Ninth) corps. This movement was made for the purpose of turning the enemy's right, and at the same time forcing them further from their connections with Richmond. At half-past 4 A. M., on the 12th, the Second corps (Hancock's) moved on the enemy in a most terrible bayonet-charge, which proved a perfect surprise to the rebels, winning the day, capturing thirty heavy guns, and over four thousand prisoners, including two generals. The Fifth and Ninth corps also made successful charges. This was the first great success of the campaign, and it rendered the rebels desperate; they made repeated and obstinate charges in the attempt to retake the positions captured by Hancock, continuing their struggles, though at terrible cost, till 3 o'clock on Friday morning. On Friday, Lee re-formed his lines, moving further to the right, and Grant kept pace with him. On Friday night the rebels attacked the Fifth corps (Warren's), but were repulsed with severe loss. From the 12th to the 18th of May there was a lull in the fighting, both armies resting, and receiving large reinforcements. On the 18th, General Hancock attacked the right flank of the rebels, and gained two lines of his intrenchments. Burnside was also engaged the same day, but without decisive result. General Grant had already planned another flanking movement, by way of Guiney's station, to Milford bridge, which occupied the next three days, and which was successfully executed, except some loss of wagons and ambulances, from an attack of Ewell. Lee meantime had moved and occupied a strong position between the North and South Anna. After some hard fighting, in which the Union troops reaped partial success, General Grant found their position too strong for direct attack, and again prepared to make a flank movement. Ordering the army to recross the North Anna, and making an attack with his right wing, to cover the movement, he burnt the bridge of the Virginia Central railroad, rapidly crossed the Pamunkey, and on the 31st of May had his entire army across the Pamunkey, and within fifteen miles of Richmond. Here again he found Lee ready to receive him, and, with reinforcements received from the Shenandoah valley, presented a full front. For two or three days there was cavalry fighting and skirmishing, but no general engagement. On the first of June the Sixth corps took up a strong position near Cold Harbor, where they were joined by a force under General W. F. Smith, detached from the army of the James. Here, on the third of June, a stubborn and desperate battle was fought, which resulted in the possession of Cold Harbor by the Union forces. The same day the Union troops attacked the rebel position, and a bloody and protracted engagement followed, but they failed to carry the rebel works. Finding that to dislodge the enemy from his position by direct attack would require too great a sacrifice of life, General Grant now determined on the bold measure of crossing the James river, and making his attack on Richmond from that side. This movement was made in the face of the enemy, though without his knowledge, in three days, viz., from the 12th to the 15th of June.

General Butler had meantime been executing his part of the programme with great skill. He had occupied Bermuda Hundred, and fortified his position there; had cut the railroad below Petersburg, and made a dash upon that city, but had not succeeded in capturing it; had laid siege to Fort Darling, but had been unable to hold his position against the rebel force; had repelled the rebel attacks upon his lines, and was in position to welcome the approach of the army of the Potomac, and render it valuable assistance. The army of West Virginia, under General Sigel, had been less successful. On the 15th of May he encountered a considerable rebel force at Reed's hill, near Mount Jackson, in the valley of the Shenandoah, and was severely handled. He was then relieved of command, and succeeded by General Hunter, who at first met with better fortune. He defeated General Sam Jones, near Staunton, and killed him; took 1,500 prisoners and several guns, driving the rebels to Waynesboro. On the 8th he formd a junction with Crook and Averill; and, while General Sheridan moved towards Gordonsville, and defeated the rebels at Trevilian station, Hunter pressed on towards Lynchburg destroying railroads and bridges on his way, but finding it strongly defended did not venture to attack, and Early marching against him, in turn, with a large force, retreated into the mountains, and made a forced march into Western Virginia. On this march his army suffered terribly, and he lost heavily in guns and wagons.

Sheridan, meantime, had made his famous raid around Lee's lines, destroying railroads, trains, depots of supplies, releasing our prisoners, and capturing many of the enemy. He penetrated within the first line of works around Richmond, and having cut all Lee's communications, reached Butler's headquarters in safety, five days after starting.

The rebel General Early, finding himself unopposed, extended his expedition down the Shenandoah, crossed into Maryland, occupied Hagerstown and Frederick, and plundered extensively, fought two or three battles with the militia, which had been called out to oppose him, threatened Baltimore and Washington, approaching within two miles of the latter city, but finding that the Nineteenth corps, from New Orleans, and the Sixth, from the Army of the Potomac, were ready to attack him, and that General Couch, from Pennsylvania, was threatening his rear, he hastened back into Virginia, taking with him most of his plunder.

General Grant, having reached the south side of the James, ordered an immediate attack on Petersburg. This would probably have proved successful but for the lack of co-operation on the part of the cavalry force, through some misunderstanding. A series of attacks were made upon the rebel works, and by the 22d of June the city was invested, except on the north and west. There was sharp fighting that day for the posses sion of the Petersburg and Danville or South side railroad, which was finally held by the Union troops. Meantime, an extensive raid was made by Wilson and Kautz's cavalry upon the Weldon railroad, several miles of which they destroyed, together with stores, &c. Before they could reach our lines, however, they were surrounded by a large rebel force, and lost seven or eight hundred men. After an interval of comparative quiet, during which General Grant had succeeded in running a mine nearly under the confederate fortifications, he ordered a feint to be made on the north side of the James, to divert General Lee's attention from an assault which he purposed making on Petersburg at the time of exploding the mine. The feint, better known as the action of Strawberry Plains, was successful in turning the enemy's left, and capturing four heavy guns. On the 30th of July the mine, which was charged with eight tons of powder, was exploded, and the assault commenced. There was a disagreement between the commanders, and fatal delays occurred, which permitted the rebels to recover from their first panic, and make effectual resistance, and the movement failed of success, and entailed heavy losses upon the troops engaged in it. Not disheartened by this failure, General Grant continued his operations with renewed energy. The battle of Deep Bottom, on the north side of the James, occurred on the 12th of August. The Second corps alone was engaged, and dislodged the enemy from his position, taking 500 prisoners, six cannon, and two mortars. On the 18th of August, the Fifth corps (Warren's) moved on Reams station, on the Weldon railroad, surprised the rebel force guarding it, and took possession of the road. On the 19th a large rebel force attacked Warren with great impetuosity, and breaking the right centre. The Union troops rallied, however, and being reinfored by two divisions of the Ninth corps, retrieved measurably the fortunes of the day, holding a part of the road, though with a loss of nearly 4,000 men.

During the next five weeks there were no movements

of great importance in the vicinity of Richmond or Petersburg, though a little advance had been made by occasional attacks upon the enemy's lines. On the night of the 28th September, General Ord crossed the James to the north side, and early on the morning of the 29th advanced on the intrenchments at Chaffin's farm, and carried them without serious loss, capturing nearly 300 prisoners and fifteen pieces of artillery. General Birney, at the same time, moved up the Newmarket road, and carried the intrenchments there with perfect ease. The Union forces then took possession of Fort Harrison, and advanced as far as Laurel Hill. On the 30th, the rebels made a desperate effort to capture Fort Harrison, but failed, and the Union cavalry, on the 1st of October, made a reconnoissance within less than two miles of Richmond. On the 7th of October, the rebels attempted to turn the right flank of the army of the James, but after some temporary success and some sharp fighting they were severely repulsed. On the 29th of October, General Grant ordered a reconnoissance in force against the rebel position at Hatcher's run. A severe battle ensued, with considerable loss on the part of the Union troops, but the position was held until General Grant ordered their withdrawal.

Dissatisfied with the inefficiency which had existed in the Shenandoah valley, and Northern Virginia and Maryland, General Grant advised, in August, the organization of a new and larger department, to be called the Department of the Shenandoah, and the appointment of Major-General Philip H. Sheridan to its command. This was done, and after careful watching of the enemy for some time, General Sheridan decided that the time for action had come. He had at this time under his command the Army of Western Virginia, and the Sixth and

Nineteenth corps. On the 19th of September was fought the battle known as that of Oqequan creek, in which, after a sharp contest, General Sheridan, by a brilliant cavalry charge, drove Early's army from the field in confusion, capturing over 2,000 prisoners and a large number of guns. On the 22d he attacked them again at Fisher's Hill, routing them completely, capturing their artillery, horses, and ammunition, and pursued them as far as Staunton, causing them a loss in the two engagements of over 10,000 men. On the 9th, the rebel General Rosser attacked Sheridan again at Fisher's Hill, but was grievously defeated. On the 19th of October, General Early attacked the Union forces again, when General Sheridan was absent, and in the morning defeated it, driving the Union troops three miles, and taking twenty-four cannon; but Sheridan coming up, rallied his men, reformed them, and defeated the rebels in turn, utterly routing them, capturing fifty-four pieces of artillery, including all his own.

General Sherman had fulfilled, in the most brilliant manner, the work assigned to him. After a campaign of extraordinary vigor and many hard-fought battles, he took possession of Atlanta on the 2d of September. Hood, who was in command of the rebel force, rallying from his severe defeats, attempted to cut Sherman's lines of communication with his base; and Sherman giving him, for good reasons, every facility of doing so, sent General Thomas with two corps to the Tennessee river to look after Hood, who was by this time in Alabama, and then tearing up the railroad between Atlanta and Chattanooga, and cutting loose from his base, started with a large force across the country, nearly three hundred miles, to Savannah, which was surrendered to him on the 22d of December.

Meantime, Hood rashly pushed on after Thomas, whose instructions were to draw him on, and after fighting a severe battle at Franklin, on the 30th of November, in which he lost in killed, wounded, and prisoners, eighteen generals and about 7,000 of his troops, attempted to invest Nashville; but on the 15th of December General Thomas attacked and routed him completely, pursuing him to the Tennessee river. Hood's losses were about 17,000 men in these two engagements.

An expedition was planned late in the season by General Grant against Wilmington, and sailed on the 13th of December from Hampton roads, under the command of General Butler, accompanied by a naval squadron under Rear-Admiral Porter. This expedition was unsuccessful, and the troops returned to City Point; but soon after, a second expedition, under the command of General A. H. Terry, embarked for the same destination, and on the 15th of January captured Fort Fisher, and effectually sealed the harbor of Wilmington. On the 6th of February, General Grant ordered another movement with four corps of the army to Hatcher's Run, with the intention of establishing his lines in closer proximity to the Weldon railroad. The struggle was a desperate one, and on the second day the enemy was successful, as before, in finding a gap in the Union lines, through which he broke, causing a considerable loss; but the Union soldiers were able the next day to regain the ground they had lost and hold it, and established themselves permanently four miles in advance of their previous position. On the 25th of March the rebels, by a sudden attack in mass, seized Fort Steadman, near Petersburg, and captured the garrison; but the Union troops rallying promptly, retook the fort, and drove the rebels back into and beyond their lines, and the Sixth and Second corps advancing at the same time, gained and held a portion of their lines. The Union loss in this affair was about 2,000, that of the rebels over 6,000, of whom 2,800 were prisoners.

On the 29th of March, the Union army was, by General Grant's order, put in motion, with a view to occupying the Southside Railroad. For this purpose, he ordered General Sheridan, on the 29th of March, to move with his cavalry force, returned three days before from the great raid, by way of Reams' Station to Dinwiddie Courthouse, and, threatening the Southside Railroad in the direction of Burkesville Junction, compel Lee to send a force westward to protect it, and the Second and Fifth corps, as in the previous attacks upon the line of the Southside Railroad, to cross by the Vaughan and Halifax roads, Hatcher's Run, and endeavor to gain possession of the Boydton plank-road. The movement was on a larger scale than any previous one; and the weakness of the enemy, as developed in the Fort Stedman affair, gave promise of success. Portions of the Twenty-fourth and Twenty-fifth corps, under command of General Ord, were brought across the river, and stationed along the line of the Vaughan road to maintain the connection between the Sixth and Second corps, in full strength. The first day the movements were all successful. The cavalry reached Dinwiddie; the Fifth corps had a sharp fight for the possession of the Quaker road, but drove back the enemy; the Second corps had very little fighting. The 30th of March also passed without serious fighting, and the Fifth corps had taken position on the White Oak road and the Boydton plank-road, the Second corps being near and within supporting distance. On the 31st, the Fifth corps, attempting to advance on the White Oak road, towards Five Forks,

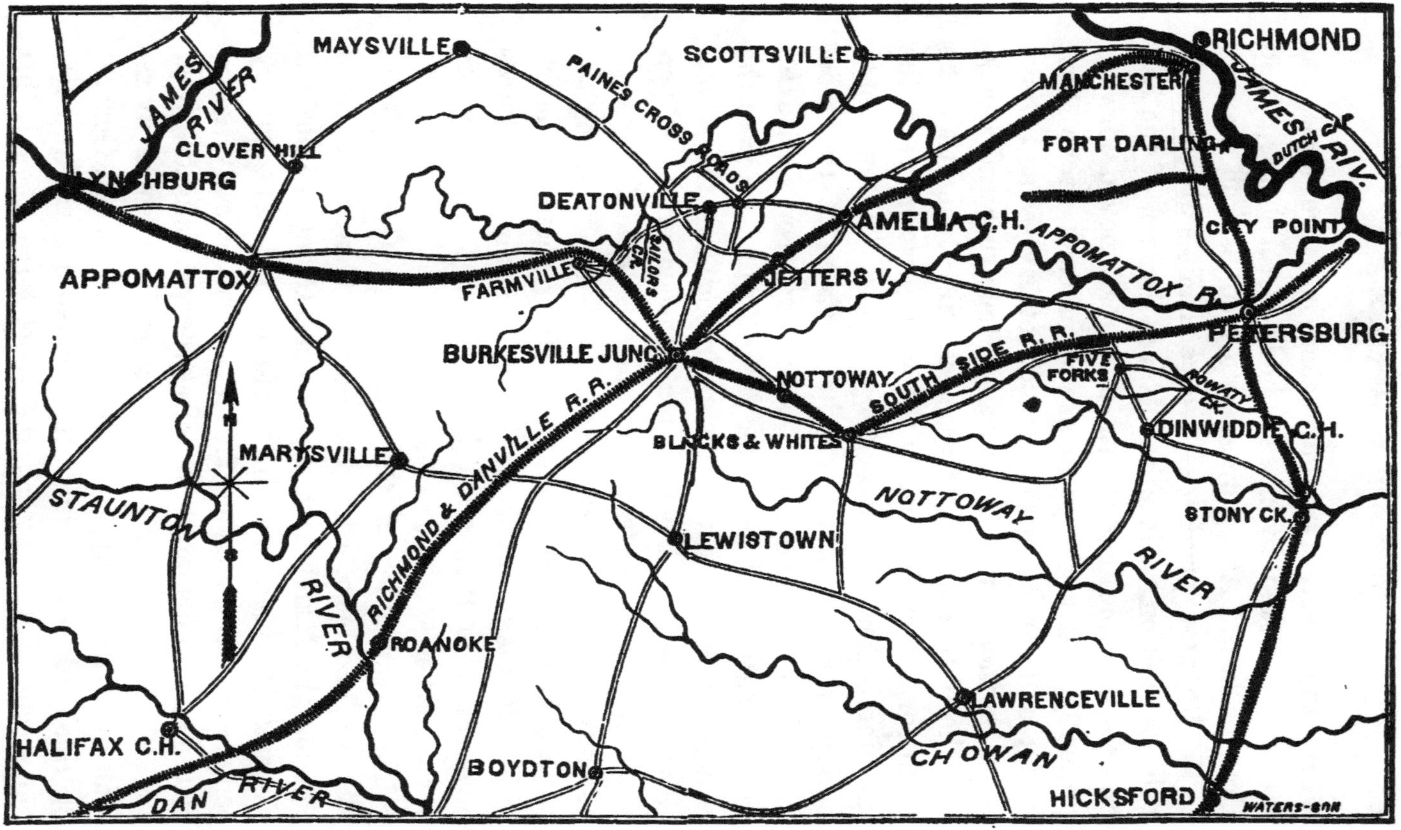
RICHMOND
MANCHESTER
JAMES RIV.
DUTCH G.
FORT DARLING
CITY POINT
SCOTTSVILLE
MAYSVILLE
PAINES CROSS ROADS
DEATONVILLE
AMELIA C.H.
APPOMATTOX R.
JETTERS V.
PETERSBURG
SAILORS CR.
FARMVILLE
APPOMATTOX
LYNCHBURG
JAMES RIVER
CLOVER HILL
BURKESVILLE JUNC.
NOTTOWAY
SOUTH SIDE R. R.
FIVE FORKS
ROWATY CK.
DINWIDDIE C.H.
BLACKS & WHITES
RICHMOND & DANVILLE R. R.
MARYSVILLE
STAUNTON
RIVER
NOTTOWAY
RIVER
STONY CK.
LEWISTOWN
ROANOKE
LAWRENCEVILLE
HALIFAX C.H.
BOYDTON
CHOWAN
HICKSFORD
DAN
RIVER
N
WATERS-SON

where the enemy were intrenched in large force, was met and attacked by a heavy body of rebel troops, and Crawford's and Ayres' divisions driven back in disorder to the Boydton plank-road, where Griffin's division still held its position. Meantime Miles's division of the Second corps, witnessing the rapid retreat, moved forward promptly, and striking the enemy in flank drove them back; and Griffin, with so much of Ayres' and Crawford's divisions as could be rallied, following and attacking the rebels, forced them back, till at nightfall the Fifth corps occupied nearly the same position as in the morning. But this temporary repulse had opened a passage through which another division of the rebel forces flung themselves with great fury upon Sheridan's cavalry, cutting off for a time Merritt's division from the remainder of the cavalry, and imperilling the whole. General Sheridan, however, took the command in person, and rallying his troops, and placing them dismounted behind temporary barricades, succeeded in repulsing the attacks of the rebels, and compelling them to desist. When it was too dark for longer fighting both forces bivouacked on their arms, within a few hundred yards of each other.

The commander of the Fifth corps, General G. K. Warren, had been ordered to report to General Sheridan at midnight, March 31st, and General Grant had notified General Sheridan that he would do so. The cavalry commander was anxious for his assistance early, as he had made up his mind to defeat the rebels before him, and driving them westward to carry Five Forks by assault, the next day. As he did not appear, General Sheridan addressed him a note, dated 3 A. M. April 1st, requesting him to attack the rebel force, then in his front, in the rear at daylight, and he would attack them in front at the same time. General Warren made no answer, but did not attack. Sheridan, however, assailed them at the time appointed, and drove them west of Chamberlain's Creek, and between 7 and 8 o'clock found Warren near J. Boisseau's house, four or five miles north of Dinwiddie. He now directed him to be ready to move on the enemy when he should receive orders, and himself proceeded to invest Five Forks on two sides with his cavalry, and a little after noon ordered up the Fifth corps to attack on the east side. General Warren moved with apparent reluctance, and infused no confidence into his men; and though the intrenchments were finally carried, and the enemy routed and driven westward, General Sheridan was so much dissatisfied with General Warren that he relieved him of his command, as General Grant had authorized him to do, and put General Griffin in his place. The next day the enemy were driven by Miles' division of the Second corps, and Crawford's and Ayres' of the Fifth, from a strong position which they held at the junction of the White Oak and Claiborne roads, and pursued to Sutherland's Station on the Southside Railroad, and thence by a front and rear attack to the river road along the banks of the Appomattox.

Meantime the troops which manned the lines around Petersburg had kept up a frequent and heavy bombardment along the lines, and on the 2d of April the Sixth and Ninth corps and the provisional corps assaulted the fortifications with great fury, and after a short but severe struggle broke through to the Southside Railroad, and commenced tearing it up. They captured many prisoners and guns in this bold assault, and of course rendered both Richmond and Petersburg untenable. During the night both were evacuated, and were occupied on the morning of the 3d of April by Union troops.

Not delaying to enter the captured cities, General Grant pressed on to capture the rebel general and his army. The pursuit was unremitting, and after actions of greater or less extent at Deep Creek, Paine's Cross-roads, Deatonsville, Farmville, and High Bridge over the Appomattox, and Appomattox Station, the rebels leaving at each point artillery, wagons, and supplies, on the 9th of April General Lee surrendered his army to General Grant. The terms granted by the conqueror were liberal in the extreme. They were as follows:

"Rolls of all the officers and men to be made in duplicate; one copy to be given to an officer designated by General Grant, the other to be retained by such officers as General Lee should designate. The officers to give their individual paroles not to take arms against the United States until properly exchanged, and each company or regimental commander to sign a like parole for the men of their commands. The arms, artillery, and public property to be packed and stacked, and turned over to the officer appointed by General Grant to receive them. This not to embrace the side-arms of the officers, nor their private horses or baggage. This done, each officer and man to be allowed to return to their homes, not to be disturbed by United States authority so long as they observe their parole and the laws in force where they may reside."

The surrender perfected, though its provisions were much abused, General Grant passed through Richmond, and thence to Washington, whence on the evening of April 14th he took the train for Philadelphia to visit his family, and while on his way was overtaken by the sad intelligence of the assassination of the President, and returned immediately to the capital.

Meanwhile, with that comprehensive grasp of mind which characterizes him, and that admirable perception of character which has always enabled him, when the choice was his, to select the men best adapted for carrying out his plans, General Grant had been directing, in other quarters of the vast territory of the Union, important movements, all tending to the one end of crushing the rebellion. Under his suggestion, General Sherman had made his famous campaign of sixty days in the Carolinas, flanking Charleston and compelling its surrender, capturing Columbia, Cheraw, Fayetteville, and, in concert with Schofield and Terry (who had joined him after capturing the city of Wilmington), Goldsborough; and having, after a fortnight's delay to recruit, moved forward, had added Smithfield and Raleigh to his captures, and held Johnston in a position where he must surrender. At the West, General Thomas had sent a magnificent cavalry force under General Wilson to capture Selma, Montgomery, Columbus, Ga., West Point, Macon, etc.; an infantry force to aid General Canby in the Department of the Gulf; Schofield and the Army of the Ohio to assist in the reduction of Wilmington; and finally, Stoneman, with a large body of cavalry, through Southwest Virginia and Western North Carolina, to attack Johnston and Lee in the rear; and this force, having thoroughly broken the Virginia and East Tennessee Railroad, had struck the North Carolina Railroad above Salisbury, captured that place with all its stores, released its prisoners, and effectually barred Johnston's further retreat. In the Southwest, General Canby, acting under his direction, in concert with the fleet under Admiral H. K. Thatcher, had, after a siege of about two weeks, captured Spanish Fort, Blakely, and Mobile, the surrender being made on the 12th of April.

The last sad funeral rites for the martyred President were hardly passed, when a special messenger from General Sherman brought to Washington a memorandum for a treaty between the rebel General Johnston and himself, for a complete cessation of hostilities and surrender by all the armies of the rebels. A Cabinet meeting was called, and although the consummation was greatly to be desired, the terms of the memorandum were found objectionable, and it was disapproved. Convinced that General Sherman's error was not the result of ambition or disloyalty, but only of his earnest desire to see the war ended, General Grant went immediately to Raleigh, *incog.*, and after consultation with General Sherman, finding Johnston desirous of surrendering on the terms which he had granted to Lee, directed General Sherman to make those terms to the rebel general, and accept the surrender without any reference to his presence. This matter settled, he returned to Washington, where a few days later he received the intelligence of the capture of the rebel President. After flying visits to New York, West Point, Chicago, etc., he has returned to the abundant and wearisome, though necessary labors attending the reduction of the army and the return of peace.

In person General Grant is rather below the middle size, but of firm, well-knit figure, with a pleasant countenance, a firmly-set mouth and chin, clear gray eyes, brown hair, and a full beard, inclined to auburn. He smokes almost incessantly; is quiet, reticent, thoughtful, yet quick and prompt in action. There is not a particle of jealousy in his composition. He accords most heartily to his lieutenants all the honors they can claim, and even turns honors meant for himself upon them. A man of less real greatness and magnanimity, placed in his position, would have winced under the encomiums showered upon Sherman and Sheridan, especially when comparisons not in his favor were drawn, as they have been ; but he only honors these brave generals the more. His resolute, unyielding determination and perseverance is a marked feature of his character. Even his wife says, "Mr. Grant is a very obstinate man," though she would not for the world have him one whit less obstinate. He has never yet, under any circumstances, been drawn or driven into making a speech, and seldom writes a long letter, though he can write, as his reports prove, with great force and clearness. The "wise man" assures us that "greater is he that ruleth his own spirit than he that taketh a city." While Lieutenant-General Grant has no mean reputation as a captor of cities, he is eminently entitled to Solomon's encomium for that extraordinary self-command which, under all the trying circumstances in which he has been placed, has enabled him to remain calm and imperturbed, never falling into a passion, never lifted into excitement or exultation. In this particular he surpasses Washington, and stands far above most of the great captains of the Old World. A man thus self-poised, brave, loyal, truthful and pure, may well command the armies of the mightiest of Republics, for he will make no evil use of his authority, and the heart of the nation doth safely trust in him.

II.

Major-General William Tecumseh Sherman.

If it be one of the attributes of genius to rise superior to the most adverse circumstances, and triumphing over detraction, depreciation, and abuse, to secure to itself a high place in the records of history, then it must be admitted that General Sherman has given no doubtful proof of the possession of a high order of genius. The sacrifices which his loyalty had prompted him to make were not appreciated; his warnings of the magnitude of the Rebellion fell on inattentive ears, and were regarded as the apprehensions of a distempered imagination; his estimate of the force necessary for the successful prosecution of the war at the West, though since proved to have been within the bounds of strict moderation, were then considered as the ravings of a melancholic madman; and the press—the great engine of power in this country—having been offended in the person of some of its baser members, by the strictness of General Sherman's discipline, undertook, with full confidence, the work of writing him down. Thenceforward, for many months, he was persistently represented as the "crazy general," "the madman," the "lunatic;" as incapable, by reason of his mad fantasies, of any successful military operation, or of commanding any considerable body of men. But, like "Banquo's ghost," Sherman would not stay down. His zeal, loyalty, and success constantly contradicted the misrepresentations of his enemies, and the fiercer their maledictions, the more he displayed the resources and abilities of a successful commander. Through all this period of bitter misrepresentation, one man defended him, believed in him, trusted him, and insisted on his advancement. That man was the present Lieutenant-General U. S. Grant. Never for a moment did he lose his confidence in his abilities and genius; and, with that fine discrimination of character which is a marked trait in his character, he insisted, at every step of promotion conferred upon himself, on advancing General Sherman also, let who might oppose. At length, after more than two years' endurance, the storm of detraction began to cease, and ere long those who had been most virulent, finding that they were powerless to injure him, became his most vehement admirers, until now, it would be hard to find any who would acknowledge that they had ever spoken disparagingly of one who has proved his claim to be reckoned among the ablest generals of modern times.

WILLIAM TECUMSEH SHERMAN, a son of the late Hon. Charles R. Sherman, for some years one of the judges of the Supreme Court of Ohio, and brother of Hon. John Sherman, U. S. Senator from Ohio, was born in Lancaster, Ohio, February 8th, 1820. His education, up to his ninth year, was obtained in the schools of his native town; but on his father's death, in 1829, he became a member of the family of Hon. Thomas Ewing, and after enjoying the advantages of good schools, at the age of sixteen entered the Military Academy at West Point, being a classmate of Generals George H. Thomas and W. Hays of the Union army, and of Generals Ewell, McCown, and Bushrod R. Johnson of the rebel army. He graduated June 30, 1840, ranking sixth in his class, and was immediately appointed second lieutenant in the Third Artillery, and ordered to duty in

Florida, where he served through the next year. In November, 1841, he was promoted to a first-lieutenancy. His service in Florida was enlivened by some encounters with Billy Bowlegs' band, in one of which he achieved some distinction in rescuing his little squad of men from the utter destruction with which that wily savage had threatened them. Late in the year, Lieutenant Sherman was ordered to Fort Moultrie, Charleston harbor, where he remained for several years.

In 1846 he was sent to California, where he was made acting assistant adjutant-general, and performed his duties with such marked ability, that, in 1851, Congress conferred upon him the brevet of captain, to date from May 30th, 1848, "for meritorious services in California, during the war with Mexico." In 1850 he was promoted to the rank of captain, and made commissary of subsistence, being assigned to the staff of the commander of the Department of the West, with headquarters at St. Louis. He married, the same year, the daughter of his friend, Hon. Thomas Ewing. Soon after, he was transferred to the military post of New Orleans, where he became acquainted with the leading men of Louisiana. In 1853, he resigned his commission in the army, and removed the same year to San Francisco, where he was for four years the manager of the banking house of Lucas, Turner & Co.

In 1857, some of his friends in Louisiana, secretly, as it afterwards appeared, making preparation for a secession movement, resolved to establish a State Military Academy, and sought to secure his services as president and superintendent. Their real object was carefully concealed, and the reasons given for its establishment were, that it would enable them more readily to suppress any insurrection among the slaves; that it would be of service in preparing them to repel Indian incursions, which were giving trouble in the adjacent States of Arkansas and Texas; that it would give them a nucleus for a military force in case of an attack by a foreign enemy, or should the acquisition of Mexico become desirable. By such plausible arguments, Mr. Sherman was induced to accept the presidency of the Louisiana Military Academy, without a suspicion of the treasonable purpose which had led to its establishment. He entered upon his duties early in 1858.

Soon after the commencement of the presidential campaign of 1860, he became convinced of the disloyal sentiments of a majority of the leading men of the State, and of the motives which had led them to establish the Military Academy, and they put forth their utmost powers of persuasion to induce him to unite with them in their revolutionary schemes. The thoroughness with which he had trained his pupils, and his cool, calm, soldierly bearing, had convinced them of his value to their cause if he could once be induced to join it. For this purpose they unfolded their plans, and sought by the offer of high military position to win him from his allegiance. It was all in vain. Manly, honest, straightforward, and thoroughly loyal, neither the love of gold or fame could cause him to swerve for an instant from his duty to his country. Convinced that war was inevitable, he dispatched the following letter to the chief magistrate of Louisiana on the day of its date:

JANUARY 18, 1861.

GOVERNOR THOMAS O. MOORE,
BATON ROUGE, LA.

SIR—As I occupy a *quasi*-military position under this State, I deem it proper to acquaint you that I accepted such position when Louisiana was a State in the Union, and when the motto of the seminary was inserted in marble over the main door, "*By the liberality of the General Government of the United States. The Union, Esto Perpetua.*" Recent events foreshadow a great change, and it becomes all men to choose. If Louisiana withdraws from the Federal Union, *I* prefer to maintain my allegiance to the old Constitution as long as a fragment of it survives, and my longer stay here would be wrong in every sense of the word. In that event, I beg you will send or appoint some authorized agent to take charge of the arms and munitions of war here belonging to the State, or direct me what disposition should be made of them. And furthermore, as President of the Board of Supervisors, I beg you to take immediate steps to relieve me as Superintendent, the moment the State determines to secede; for on no earthly account will I do any act, or think any thought, hostile to or in defiance of the old Government of the United States.

With great respect, &c.,

(Signed) W. T. SHERMAN.

There spoke the true hero and patriot, "On no earthly account will I do any act, or think any thought, hostile to or in defiance of the old Government of the United States." The same principle has actuated him in all his subsequent career. Other generals, both in the East and the West, have been suspected of disloyal leanings; but even the bitterest detractors of General Sherman have never dared to whisper the slightest hint of disloyalty in connection with his name.

His resignation was accepted, for what could the rebels do with a man who was so thoroughly and determinedly loyal? He removed in February with his family to St. Louis, and shortly before the attack on Fort Sumter visited Washington. Here he found, to use his own language, that "the men in authority were sleeping on a volcano, which would surely burst upon them unprepared." Thoroughly conversant as he was with the intentions and plans of the leaders of the rebellion, he was astonished at the apathy and incredulity of the Government on the subject. None of the Cabinet believed that there was to be any serious conflict. At most, they thought it would be an affair of sixty or ninety days. Sherman knew better, and in the hope of arousing the Government to action before it should be too late, he addressed a letter to General Cameron, then Secretary of War, in which he forewarned him in the most earnest language of the imminency of war and the entire want of preparation for it. He stated also that he was educated at the expense of the United States, and feeling that he owed every thing to his country, he had come to tender her his services as a soldier. He also waited upon the President, and, stating to him his views, tendered his services. The President replied, laughing, "We shall not need many men like you; the whole affair will soon blow over." He urged, when the fall of Sumter came, the importance of a gigantic army, not called out for three months, but for the war, to put down the rebellion at once, and denounced the calling out of three months men as being as absurd as the attempt to extinguish the flames of a burning building with a squirt-gun. Neither the Government nor the people were then prepared to comprehend the justice and clearness of his views, and he passed for an ultraist. At the organization of the new regiments of the regular army in June, 1861, he was appointed colonel of the new 13th infantry, his commission dating from May 14, 1861.

His first actual service in the war was at the battle of Bull Run, or Manassas, as the rebels named it. Colonel Sherman commanded the third brigade in the First (Tyler's) division. That brigade consisted of the 13th, 69th, and 79th New York, and the 2d Wisconsin infantry regiments, and Ayres' regular battery—all troops since renowned for their gallantry. There have been many conflicting statements and opinions in regard to this battle, but the best military authorities seem to have settled the point that the fighting of that day was not discreditable to either army, composed as both were of raw troops. It is evident from the reports of the rebel commanders that they themselves regarded the day as lost, till the unexpected arrival of Johnston's troops turned the scale, and communicating a sudden panic to the Union troops, who had previously fought well, led to that disgraceful rout which has made that day infamous. But whatever may be thought or said of the fighting of other portions of the army, there is abundant evidence that Sherman's brigade fought with desperate and determined valor. "A part of Hunter's and Heintzelman's divisions," says Major-General McDowell in his report, "forced the enemy back far enough to allow Sherman's and Keyes's brigades of Tyler's division to cross from their positions on the Warrenton road. These drove the right of the enemy, understood to have been commanded by Beauregard, from the front of the field, and out of the detached woods, and down the road, and across it, up the slopes on the other side." They did more than this: pressing forward, they came upon an elevated ridge or plateau, where occurred the severest fighting of the day. Sherman led his brigade directly up the Warrenton road, and held his ground till the general order came to retreat. Colonel Bowman, in a biographical sketch of General Sherman in the "U. S. Service Magazine," mentions an incident connected with this battle which we have not seen elsewhere. It was as follows. The order given to Tyler's division was to cross Bull Run when possible, and join Hunter on the right. In obeying this order, Sherman led off, with the 69th New York in advance. On their march they encountered a party of the enemy retreating along a cluster of pines; and Lieutenant-Colonel Haggerty, then in command of the 69th, rode over, without orders, to intercept their retreat, and was instantly killed by the enemy's fire. Haggerty was much beloved by his men, and they, furious at his loss, sprang forward and opened fire, which was returned. "But," says Colonel Sherman, "determined to effect our junction with Hunter's division, I ordered the fire to cease, and we proceeded with caution towards the field, where we then plainly saw our forces engaged." Burnside, then a colonel commanding one of the brigades in Hunter's division, was at this time sorely pressed and nearly overwhelmed by the enemy and was only relieved by the timely advent of Sherman's brigade, which under his orders turned not aside either to the right hand or the left, till the orders it had received were obeyed. "It was Sherman's brigade," says Burnside, "that arrived about twelve-and-a-half o'clock, and by a most deadly fire assisted in breaking the enemy's lines." The promptness and strict obedience to orders which characterized Sherman's conduct on that day have been marked traits in his subsequent career.

The vigor and determination with which Colonel Sherman fought his brigade on this occasion, made their share of the losses much heavier than those of any other brigade in the Union army; his total of killed, wounded, and missing, being six hundred and nine, while that of the whole division was but eight hundred and fifty-nine, and of the entire army, aside from prisoners and stragglers, but fifteen hundred and ninety. The flight of the panic-stricken fugitives towards Washington disgusted Colonel Sherman, and he was very severe in his denunciations of the militia officers, especially those in his own command, for their part in the panic. Conscious of their misconduct, some of these officers resented his rebukes, and sought to injure his reputation. The Ohio delegation in Congress having learned the good conduct and valor of Colonel Sherman, urged his promotion, and on the 3d of August he was confirmed a brigadier-general of volunteers, his commission dating from May 17th, 1861.

Early in August, General Anderson having been assigned to the command of the department of the Ohio, General Sherman was made second in command, and sent soon afterwards with a force of seven thousand men, composed of volunteers and Kentucky home-guards, to occupy Muldraugh's hill, a point of considerable strategic importance, south of the Rolling fork of Salt river. The home-guards which there, as elsewhere, proved entirely unreliable, soon abandoned his camp for their homes, and the reinforcements intended to strengthen his command were sent elsewhere. He now found himself with only five thousand troops, badly armed, and in an unfriendly region, confronted by the rebel General Buckner with a rebel force of twenty-five thousand men. While affairs were in this discouraging condition, General Anderson's health failed so completely, that he resigned, and, on the 8th of October, General Sherman was appointed his successor.

In no part of the country, and at no time during the war, were the prospects more gloomy than in the department of the Ohio at this period. The greater part of the population of Kentucky capable of bearing arms had joined the rebel army. Those who remained behind were divided in sentiment, but most of them, from one cause or another, unfriendly. The force at Sherman's command was wholly inadequate, and what he had were poorly armed. He was deficient also in munitions of war, and in the means of transportation, while in his front were rebel forces outnumbering his own at almost every point, well supplied and confident of success. If the rebel generals had known his actual condition, they could have captured or driven his forces across the Ohio in ten days. There were in his camps numerous newspaper letter-writers, who, if loyal, were far from being discreet, and whose communications made public the very facts which it was all-important to conceal from the enemy. These he excluded from his lines by a stringent general order, and thus brought down upon his head all the indignation of the press.

But a greater cause of alarm arose from the fact that the Secretary of War, General Cameron, utterly failed to comprehend the necessities of his position, or the importance of holding it. No one doubts the loyalty of General Cameron, but there can be no question that his failure to comprehend the magnitude of the contest, and the necessity of having a large and well-appointed army promptly on the ground, to meet and crush out the rebellion during its first year, was the means of protracting it through the years which followed. In the end, the result may be better for the nation, but it reflects, nevertheless, on the incapacity of the secretary.

General Sherman had an interview with Secretary Cameron, at Lexington, Kentucky, in October, in presence of Adjutant-General Thomas. In this interview, he explained to the Secretary the critical situation of his command, and the numbers and condition of the enemy's troops, and to the question what force was necessary for a forward movement in his department, which then included all east of the Mississippi and west of the Alleghanies, he replied promptly, "Two hundred thousand men." "The answer," says Colonel Bowman, "was the inspiration or the judgment of a military genius, but to the mind of Mr. Secretary Cameron, it was the prophecy of a false wizard," or, we may add, the raving of a maniac. The secretary and the adjutant-general at once pronounced Sherman crazy, and made themselves merry over his extravagant demands, which the adjutant-general was so indiscreet as to repeat and allow to find its way into print, together with the details of the strength of Sherman's position, thus informing the enemy of the weakness of his lines.

On the 3d of November, General Sherman telegraphed to General McClellan, then general-in-chief, detailing the position and number of his several forces, showing that everywhere, except at a single point, they were outnumbered, and concluded his dispatch with the remark, "Our forces are too small to do any good, and too large to be sacrificed." In reply, General McClellan inquired, "How long could McCook (one of Sherman's generals) keep Buckner out of Louisville, holding the railroad, with power to destroy it inch by inch?" Here was no hint of any intention of sending reinforcements, but a probable purpose of abandoning Kentucky. Sherman, with that sensitiveness which is peculiarly the attribute of a gallant soldier, felt that he had incurred the displeasure of the War Department by his frankness and his estimate of the power and capacity of the enemy, and that, under the circumstances, he could not conduct the campaign successfully; he therefore asked to be relieved, and was succeeded by General Buell, who was at once reinforced and enabled to hold his defensive position till Grant was ready to move in the spring.

Meantime, the press had revenged itself upon Sherman by pronouncing him crazy, and he was shelved by being put in command of Benton barracks, near St. Louis. Not long after, General Halleck succeeded General Fremont in command of the Western Department, and he was too good a judge of character to allow a man of General Sherman's abilities to be detained as the commandant of recruiting barracks. He was accordingly detailed to forward reinforcements and supplies from Paducah to General Grant, then engaged in the siege of Fort Donelson, and after the capture of that stronghold, he was put in command of the Fifth division of Grant's army, and with it went into camp at Pittsburg Landing. The Fifth division was composed almost wholly of raw troops, who had never been under fire. In the short period which elapsed before the battle of Shiloh, the men were drilled and trained as well as time would permit, but they were still but indifferently prepared for the fierce battle which was so soon to come.

When the battle of Shiloh commenced, April 6th, 1862, General Sherman had just taken his position at Shiloh church, three miles out from the landing, on the main road to Corinth. He was strongly and advantageously posted. His first line of battle was formed on the brow of a hill, or rather a ridge, on the west of Lick and Owl creeks, which served as a natural fortification. The men, by lying down or falling back a few steps, were well covered, and by rising and advancing a few paces could deliver their fire with terrible effect. The rebel commanders soon appreciated the fact that this position must be carried at all hazards if they would win the day. Hence their assaults upon it were well-directed, rapid, and persistent. A part of Sherman's regiments were panic-stricken, broke, and fled; but this he had expected and was not disconcerted by it, and rallying the remainder, he fought the enemy undismayed through the day, and at 4 P. M., deliberately made a new line behind McArthur's drill-field, placing batteries on chosen ground, where he could protect a bridge which it was necessary for General Lew. Wallace's division, then every moment expected, to cross, and here repelled the assaults of the enemy and drove them back. General Grant visited him twice that day, approved of his movements, and directed him to assume the offensive at daylight the next day. He did so, and after some severe fighting, the rebels were compelled to retreat. On the morning of the 8th of April, he made a reconnoissance with his division along the Corinth road, met and drove from their position a considerable force of rebel cavalry, and captured a number of prisoners, and large quantities of arms, ammunition, &c. But it was not merely by his admirable management of his division that he saved the day. Colonel Bowman well says of his conduct in that battle, "There was not a commanding general on the field who did not rely on Sherman, and look to him as our chief hope; and there is no question that but for him our army would have been destroyed. He rode from place to place, directing his men; he selected from time to time the positions for his artillery; he dismounted and managed the guns; he sent suggestions to commanders of divisions; he inspired everybody with confidence; and yet it never occurred to him that he had accomplished any thing worthy of remark."

General Nelson, himself a division commander in that

battle, said, "During eight hours, the fate of the army on the field of Shiloh depended upon the life of one man; if General Sherman had fallen, the army would have been captured or destroyed." General Halleck, who arrived on the field two or three days after the battle, said, in a letter to the Secretary of War, "It is the unanimous opinion here that Brigadier-General Sherman saved the fortunes of the day; he was in the thickest of the fight, had three horses killed under him, and was twice wounded."

General Grant, in his report of April 9th, 1862, speaks of his services as follows: "I feel it a duty, however, to a gallant and able officer, Brigadier-General W. T. Sherman, to make a special mention of his services. He not only was with his command during the entire two days of the action, but displayed great judgment and skill in the management of his men. Although severely wounded in the hand on the first day, his place was never vacant. He was again wounded, and had three horses killed under him." Again, after the capture of Vicksburg, under date of July 26, 1863, General Grant wrote to the War Department, of General Sherman: "At the battle of Shiloh, on the first day, he held, with raw troops, the key-point of the landing. It is no disparagement to any other officer to say, that I do not believe there was another division-commander on the field who had the skill and experience to have done it. *To his individual efforts I am indebted for the success of that battle.*"

A cavalry officer, who was in the battle of Shiloh, gives some interesting incidents of his bearing on that day, in a communication quoted by Colonel Bowman. "Having," he says, "occasion to report personally to General Sherman, about noon of the first day at Shiloh,

I found him dismounted, his arm in a sling, his hand bleeding, his horse dead, himself covered with dust, his face besmeared with powder and blood. He was giving directions at the moment to Major Taylor, his chief of artillery, who had just brought a battery into position. Mounted orderlies were coming and going in haste; staff officers were making anxious inquiries; everybody but himself seemed excited. The battle was raging terrifically in every direction. Just then there seemed to be unusual commotion on our right, where it was observed our men were giving back. 'I was looking for that,' said Sherman; 'but I am ready for them.' His quick, sharp eyes flashed, and his war-begrimed face beamed with satisfaction. The enemy's packed columns now made their appearance, and as quickly the guns which Sherman had so carefully placed in position began to speak. The deadly effect on the enemy was apparent. While Sherman was still managing the artillery, Major Sanger, a staff-officer, called his attention to the fact that the enemy's cavalry were charging towards the battery. 'Order up those two companies of infantry,' was the quick reply; and the general coolly went on with his guns. The cavalry made a gallant charge, but their horses carried back empty saddles. The enemy was evidently foiled. Our men, gaining fresh courage, rallied again, and for the first time that day, the enemy was held stubbornly in check. A moment more, and he fell back over the piles of his dead and wounded."

During the advance upon Corinth which followed the battle of Shiloh, Sherman's division was continually in the lead, and carried, occupied, and reintrenched seven distinct rebel camps. On the 30th of May, 1862, Beauregard retreated from Corinth, and it was occupied the same day by Sherman's division. "His services as division commander in the advance on Corinth," writes General Grant, "I will venture to say, were appreciated by the now general-in-chief (General Halleck) beyond those of any other division commander." At the earnest request of Generals Halleck and Grant, General Sherman was promoted to the rank of major-general of Volunteers, to date from May 1st, 1862.

On the 20th of June he advanced from Corinth and captured the important post of Holly Springs, Mississippi, thoroughly destroying trestle-bridges and track on the Mississippi Central railroad, so as to prevent any sudden approach of the enemy.

Memphis, which had surrendered to our naval forces in the spring of 1862, and was now in General Grant's department, was in a sad condition. Around it, in all directions, a guerilla warfare raged furiously, and the city itself had become so thoroughly interested in the contraband trade with rebels, that a prominent rebel officer avowed his belief that it was more valuable to them in the hands of the Federal Government than before its capture. General Grant had no intention of allowing this state of things to continue, and knowing General Sherman's hearty loyalty and decision of character, he appointed him to the command of the district of Memphis, with an injunction to suppress both the guerillas and the contraband trade. This was accomplished within the next six months so thoroughly, that for many months subsequent, the place bore a high character for loyalty, and the guerrillas confined their raids to regions where they were in less danger of losing their lives.

In December, 1862, General Grant made the first movements in his operations against Vicksburg. His first step was to appoint General Sherman to the command of the Fifteenth army corps, and to direct him to make some reconnoissances near Tallahatchie river. These completed, he unfolded to him his plan for the capture of Vicksburg. Sherman, at the head of four picked divisions, was to embark at Memphis, on the 20th of December, and rendezvous at Friar's point, and from thence move directly on Vicksburg, and attack it; while Grant himself, with a large force, was to proceed down the Mississippi Central railroad to Jackson, Mississippi, and hold and engage the enemy's forces there, and, these defeated, move to the rear of Vicksburg. Holly Springs, on the Mississippi Central, was to be his depot of supplies, and he had already accumulated there the stores necessary for the expedition. Sherman started promptly on the 20th,* but on the same day Holly Springs was attacked by the enemy under Van Dorn, and disgracefully surrendered, and its stores destroyed. General Grant, who was below Holly Springs at the time, was

* Sherman's general order on setting out with this expedition is a remarkable document. Then, as always, he was opposed to all military trading expeditions, and to permitting a motley and irresponsible herd of camp-followers to accompany and betray the purposes and numbers of the expedition. The order was as follows: "The expedition now fitting out is purely of a military character, and the interests involved are of too important a nature to be mixed up with personal and private business. No citizen, male or female, will be allowed to accompany it, unless employed as part of a crew, or as servants to the transports. No person whatever—citizen, officer, or sutler—will, on any consideration, buy or deal in cotton, or other produce of the country. The trade in cotton must wait a more peaceful state of affairs. Any person whatever, making reports for publication, which might reach and inform, aid, or comfort the enemy, should be treated as a spy. A citizen following the expedition in defiance of the above orders, should be conscripted, or made a deck-hand on the transports."

compelled to return towards Memphis, and accumulate new supplies before he could move forward, and at the same time was unable to communicate with Sherman.

Unaware of this failure, Sherman pressed on, and disembarking on the 26th and 27th of December near the mouth of the Yazoo, ordered a general advance at once upon the city, and before night drove the enemy from his outer lines. On the 28th and 29th the assault was renewed, and on the latter day a series of brilliant charges were made with the utmost fury. There have been few instances of as desperate fighting during the war. "Blair's brigade in the advance, emerging from the cover of a cypress forest, came upon an intricate abatis of young trees felled about three feet above the ground, with the tops left interlacing in confusion. Beyond the abatis was a deep ditch with a quicksand at the bottom, and several feet of water on the sand. Beyond the ditch was a more impenetrable abatis of heavy timber. All this was swept by a murderous fire from the enemy's artillery. Yet through and over it all the brigade gallantly charged, and drove the enemy from his rifle-pits, at the base of the centre hill, on which the city lay. Other brigades came up in support, and the second line was carried; and still up the hill pressed the heroic advance. But it was all in vain. The city was impregnable to so small a force, and reluctantly the storming party yielded up their hardly earned conquests, Blair's brigade losing one third of its men in the daring assault. Under a flag of truce, Sherman buried his dead and cared for his wounded, and then promptly re-embarked. At this juncture General McClernand arrived, and assumed command by virtue of his priority of commission. Sherman at once announced the fact to his "right wing of the Army of the Tennessee," praising their zeal, alacrity, and courage, and adding, "Ours was but part of a combined movement, in which others were to assist. We were in time; unforeseen contingencies must have delayed the others. We have destroyed the Shreveport road; we have attacked the defences of Vicksburg, and pushed the attack as far as prudence would justify; and having found it too strong for our single column, we have drawn off in good order and in good spirits, ready for any new move. A new commander is now here to lead you. I know that all good officers and soldiers will give him the same hearty support and cheerful obedience they have hitherto given me. There are honors enough in reserve for all, and work enough, too."

The patriotism and manliness of this order will be more evident if we bear in mind that General Sherman had just suffered the mortification of a repulse for which he was in no sense blameworthy, the reasons which had compelled General Grant to fail in his part of the attack being unknown to General Sherman; and that the subordinate officers not cognizant of all the facts, and the newspaper correspondents who had an old grudge to revenge, were heaping undeserved reproach upon him. There was, beside this, the mortification of being required to yield his command to a man like General McClernand, a civilian general, overbearing, ambitious, and conceited, who never scrupled in the endeavor to exalt his own reputation on the misfortune of others, or to avail himself of their plans without ascribing to them any portion of the credit. Yet Sherman acquiesced gracefully and with true patriotism in the change, and in handing over the command to McClernand, sought to transfer to him also the affection and good-will of his officers and men.

But time makes all things even. This attack on Chickasaw bluffs, for which Sherman was denounced in the most violent and unmeasured terms by the Western papers, was subsequently fully justified and approved by General Grant in his report to the War Department, in which he says: "General Sherman's arrangement as commander of troops, in the attack on Chickasaw bluffs, last December, was admirable; seeing the ground from the opposite side from the attack, afterwards, I saw the impossibility of making it successful."

The troops which embarked at the mouth of the Yazoo, under the command of General McClernand, consisted of part of two army corps, the Fifteenth, of which Sherman still retained the command, and the Thirteenth, which was properly McClernand's. They proceeded at once to Arkansas Post, and, following out a plan proposed by Sherman before the attack on Chickasaw bluffs, carried the position, capturing seven thousand prisoners, several cannon, and a large quantity of supplies.

In the subsequent operations of General Grant for the reduction of the rebel stronghold of Vicksburg, General Sherman bore a distinguished part. His first achievement was the relief of Admiral Porter's fleet of gunboats on the Sunflower river. It had been a favorite plan with General Grant to reach the Yazoo river with gunboats, from some point above Vicksburg, and descending it to Haines' bluff, make an assault from that point upon the city, which he believed would result in its capture. The attempt had been made through the Yazoo pass, but had failed. Admiral Porter, who was co-operating with General Grant, thought he had discovered another route which promised better success, through the interlacing streams which irrigate the tract between the Mississippi and the Yazoo. He asked the co-operation of a skilful and resolute land force; and General Grant detailed General Sherman, with one division of his Fifteenth army corps. The gunboats pushed on through Steele's and Black's bayous, into Deer creek and Rolling fork, an affluent of Sunflower river, which is itself a tributary of the Yazoo, while the troops, following a more circuitous route, were necessarily a day or two in the rear. On the 21st of March, the admiral having entered the Sunflower river, found it full of obstructions, with formidable batteries ahead, the enemy in heavy force, with artillery in front and on both flanks, and the stream too narrow to manœuvre successfully. Fearing that the enemy might blockade his rear by felling obstructions, he sent a pressing message to Sherman, then many miles distant, to come immediately to his relief, and awaited his coming with the deepest anxiety, the enemy meantime endeavoring to pass him on one or the other flank. Sherman received his message at seven o'clock on the morning of the 22d, and started instantly with rather more than a brigade, in a forced march over the most intolerable roads, to relieve him. He pushed on with the utmost speed; but while yet several miles distant, a part of the rebel force attempted to push across his flank, in order to reach the boats first, and as they came in sight, the gunboats opened fire on them. At the sound of the cannon, Sherman, with his little band, struck out in a straight line for the point whence the firing proceeded, and by the greatest urgency brought his men through in about an hour, and flung his force upon the rebels, who, astonished at his appearance, fled instantly. Another hour, and the gunboats would have been lost inevitably. As it was, it required the utmost skill and generalship on the part of both commanders to force their way back, with the goal unattained.

When General Grant determined to attack Vicksburg from below, by moving his force down the west side of the Mississippi, landing at Grand Gulf, or below, and marching first eastward to Jackson, he confided his plan to General Sherman, and required of him a movement, by way of feint, involving some danger and requiring a high degree of military tact. The Thirteenth and Seventeenth corps (McClernand's and McPherson's) were put at once upon the line of march, over that wearisome slough of mud between Milliken's bend and Hard Times, Louisiana; but Sherman's corps was ordered to remain at Milliken's bend, and keep up the semblance of siege of the city from that position; and when Grant was ready to land his troops at Bruinsburg, he sent a dispatch to Sherman, who thereupon embarked his troops on transports, and moving directly on Haines' bluff, landed, and, with the co-operation of the gunboats, prepared to assault. The gunboats maintained a terrible fire for four hours to cover their landing. These demonstrations were continued for two days with great success. The enemy regarding it as a *bona fide* attack, concentrated almost their entire force at Haines' bluff, and General Grant was thus enabled to land his troops without opposition, and to proceed towards Port Gibson without encountering any very large force. This accomplished, General Sherman made a forced march of over sixty miles of terrible roads in six days, and joined General Grant at Grand Gulf on the 6th of May. The next day the whole army advanced, and on the 12th Sherman's and McClernand's corps had some skirmishing at Fourteen Mile creek, while McPherson fought a sharp but successful battle at Raymond. Generals Sherman and McPherson then marched by different routes towards Jackson, and while Sherman approached and attacked on the south side, McPherson assailed it on the north. Johnston, the rebel general, planted artillery, and stationed a small infantry force under cover in front of Sherman, but massed his troops against McPherson. This ruse General Sherman promptly detected, and sending a reconnoitering party to the right, flanked the position, and held himself in readiness to support McPherson's attack; but after a sharp battle, that general had defeated the rebels, who had fled northward. Sherman was now left at Jackson to destroy the railroads, bridges, factories, arsenals, machine-shops, &c., belonging to the enemy. He did this effectually, and, early on the 16th of May, received orders from General Grant to move with all speed till he came up with the main forces near Bolton. In one hour from the time of receiving the dispatch, he was in motion with his troops. On reaching Bolton, he found that the army had gone on and fought that day the battle of Champion hills, and orders were left for him to go on to Bridgeport, and by noon of the 17th he had reached that point. From thence he assumed the advance, starting before dawn of the 18th, crossing the Black river on a pontoon bridge, and marching rapidly towards Vicksburg. Before night of that day, by a rapid detour to the right, he threw himself on Walnut hills, and compelled their evacuation by the enemy, passing between Snyder's and Walnut bluffs, and thus cutting the rebel force in two. This brilliant manœuvre accomplished two results, both of the greatest importance. It compelled the evacuation of Haines' bluff, Snyder's bluff, and Walnut and Chickasaw bluffs by the enemy, with all their strong works, and it enabled General Grant at once to open communication with the fleet and his new base on the Yazoo and Mississippi, above Vicksburg. Of General Sherman's conduct during this preliminary portion of the campaign,

General Grant wrote to the War Department: "His demonstration at Haines' bluff in April, to hold the enemy about Vicksburg, while the army was securing a foothold east of the Mississippi; his rapid marches to join the army afterwards; his management at Jackson, Mississippi, in the first attack; his *almost unequalled* march from Jackson to Bridgeport, and passage of Black river; and his securing Walnut hills on the 18th of May, attest his great merit as a soldier." It is worthy of notice, that the position thus gained by General Sherman, by a rear attack, was the one against the front of which his troops had been hurled in vain less than five months before.

On the morning of the 19th of May, at 2 A. M., General Grant ordered a general assault on the enemy's lines, and, of the three corps engaged, Sherman's alone succeeded in making a material advance. A second assault was ordered for the 22d. This, though conducted with great bravery and daring, proved unsuccessful, and resort was had to the slower but surer process of a siege. The city was surrendered on the 4th of July, and its reduction conferred lasting renown on General Grant and his brave Army of the Tennessee. To the remainder of that army the surrender brought rest and relaxation from their severe labor; but Sherman's troops, increased by the addition of the 13th army corps, were ordered immediately to look after Johnston. That rebel commander had made great efforts to collect a force sufficient to enable him to raise the siege of Vicksburg, but had found it impossible to do so. He had, however, hovered in the rear of Grant's army, prudently keeping the Big Black river between his force and theirs, but was on the alert to do them a mischief. On the very day of the surrender Sherman moved eastward, found and drove Johnston's force back to Jackson, and promptly invested it there, at the same time sending his cavalry to cut the railroads, and destroy railroad bridges, culverts, depots, cars, &c., above and below the city on the Mississippi Central railroad, and east on the Jackson and Meridian railroad. Johnston made one desperate sortie, but, finding General Sherman prepared for him, evacuated the city hastily on the night of the 16th, at the only point not yet completely invested, abandoning every thing, except the arms of the soldiers, to the Union troops. Of this last triumph General Grant said, "It entitles General Sherman to more credit than usually falls to the lot of one man to earn."

For two months General Sherman and his army corps rested, lying in camp along the Big Black river, a rest much needed after the hardships of the siege and subsequent pursuit of Johnston; but the opportunity was improved by the commander to refit and recruit his force, and to bring and keep them in the highest state of efficiency for service whenever they should be called upon. The time soon came. On the 22d of September, General Grant telegraphed him from Vicksburg to send a division at once to reinforce Rosecrans, who had just fought the severe and disastrous battle of Chickamauga. At 4 P. M., the same day, Osterhaus' division were on the road to Vicksburg, and the next day ascending the river to Memphis. On the 23d the order came for General Sherman to follow with the remainder of his corps. He started instantly, every thing being in order for immediate movement, and on the 27th was on his way to Memphis by water. Owing to the low state of the river and the scarcity of fuel, the voyage was very slow, and the general found it necessary frequently to land forces and gather fence-rails, and other fuel, to hasten their progress. They finally reached Memphis on the 2d, 3d, and 4th of October, Osterhaus' division having, meantime, advanced as far as Corinth. At Memphis he found orders from General Halleck to move his corps, and all other available troops in his vicinity, to Athens, Alabama, following and repairing the railroad, and depending on the country through which he passed for his supplies. Work was instantly commenced on the railroad, and prosecuted day and night, but, finding he could move his trains more rapidly by turnpike with an escort, he dispatched them by that route, and finally sent forward his fourth division in the same way.

The rebels having learned of this movement, and being alarmed by it, collected as rapidly as possible bodies of troops at Salem, Mississippi, and Tuscumbia, Alabama, to prevent the advance of Sherman, and his reinforcement of Rosecrans. At Salem, the rebel General Chalmers had collected three thousand cavalry and eight pieces of artillery, and moved forward with this force to the Memphis and Charleston railroad to obstruct Sherman's progress. Having been informed of this, General Sherman on the 11th of October put his whole force in motion towards Corinth, and himself started for that place in advance by special train, having a battalion of the 13th regular infantry (his own old regiment) with him as escort. As he approached Colliersville, twenty-four miles from Memphis, his train was fired upon, and it was discovered that Chalmers was investing the place, which was defended by a small garrison of Union troops in a stockade. Springing from the train, and forming his escort, he ordered them to charge the rebels, which they did with great effect, scattering them in all directions, and relieving the little garrison. Having driven the rebels from the vicinity, he proceeded the next day to Corinth, from whence he sent General Blair to Iuka with the first division, and, as fast as they came up, pushed the other divisions along, with orders to stop at Big Bear creek, five miles east of Iuka. Before leaving Memphis he had sent a request to Admiral Porter to send the gunboats up the Tennessee, and to General Allen, at St. Louis, to send a ferry-boat to Eastport. Both had complied with his wishes, and he resumed work on the railroad with all possible energy, sending General Blair, meanwhile, with two divisions to drive the enemy out of Tuscumbia, which he accomplished on the 27th of October, having previously encountered the rebels in a severe fight at Cane creek.

While General Sherman was thus making as rapid progress as he could in reopening communications between Memphis and Chattanooga, General Grant had been advanced to the command of the grand military division of the Mississippi, comprising the three armies of the Cumberland, the Ohio, and the Tennessee, and had asked and obtained for General Sherman the command of his own army of the Tennessee. He was informed of this while at Iuka, and immediately commenced reorganizing his new command; and on the day of the battle of Cane creek he sent General Ewing with a division to cross the Tennessee, and move with all speed to Eastport. On the 27th of October, a messenger arrived from General Grant, ordering him to drop all work on the railroad east of Bear creek, and push on to Bridgeport. With prompt obedience he immediately ordered all his columns towards Eastport, as the only practicable point where the Tennessee could be crossed. On the 1st of November, General Sherman himself crossed, and passed on to the head of the column, leaving the rear in charge of General Blair, and marched to Rogersville and the Elk river. Finding that river impassable, and there being no time for building a bridge or constructing pontoons, he marched on by the north side of the Elk river to Fayetteville, and crossing there, headed his column for Bridgeport; and having prescribed the route for each division, he hastened forward to Bridgeport, telegraphed to General Grant the position of his troops, and on the 15th of November, with his escort, entered Chattanooga. He was welcomed by General Grant, and at once received orders to move his troops, as soon as they came up, across the Tennessee, and effect a lodgment on the terminus of Missionary Ridge, and at the same time demonstrate with a part of his force against Lookout mountain. His men were much exhausted by their long and terrible march from Memphis, and most generals would have craved a brief period of rest for them, but General Sherman was too thorough a soldier to hesitate a moment in his obedience, and he accordingly directed Ewing's division on Trenton, to make the intended demonstration on Lookout mountain, and himself returned to Bridgeport, rowing a boat down the Tennessee from Kelly's ferry, and instantly put his other divisions in motion, in the order in which they had arrived. The roads were horrible, but by the most incessant exertion night and day, he succeeded in crossing three divisions over a pontoon bridge at Brown's ferry by the 23d of November, while the fourth division was left behind in Hooker's camp, in consequence of the breaking of the bridge. The three divisions were the same day concealed behind the hills opposite the mouth of Chickamauga river, and the same night, by a dexterous manœuvre, he moved a force silently along the river, and captured every guard but one of the enemy's picket of twenty men. By daylight, on the 24th of November, he had crossed eight thousand men on steamboats and pontoon boats to the east bank of the Tennessee, and they had thrown up a strong rifle trench, commanding both the Tennessee and the Chickamauga river, as a *tête du pont.* At dawn two pontoon bridges were begun—one thirteen hundred and fifty feet long, over the Tennessee; the other, across the Chickamauga, perhaps two hundred and fifty feet. At 1 P. M., both were done, and the remainder of the three divisions crossed, and marched from the river *en échelon*, so arranged as to be able to deploy promptly to the right on meeting the enemy. After these came a considerable cavalry force, which crossed the Chickamauga, and dashed eastward, to cut the railroad lines upon the Chattanooga and Knoxville and Cleveland and Dalton roads. The movements of the infantry were so completely concealed by a rain and fog, that they pushed on up the hill which forms the terminus of Missionary Ridge, unseen, surprised the enemy, and took the log and earthwork fort which crowned the hill by half-past three o'clock P. M. The enemy, enraged at finding himself so completely outmanœuvred and outflanked, opened upon Sherman's troops with artillery and musketry, but the Union artillery, which had been dragged up the steep ascent, opened in turn and soon silenced him. Looking at the ridge from the summit of this hill, however, it was evident that the grand objective was the next or second spur, which was higher, steeper, and on the broad plateau at the top had a very strong and extensive earthwork, known as Fort Buckner. To carry this must be Sherman's effort on the following day. The commander-in-chief held a consultation with his leading generals that night, and fully aware of Sherman's abilities and prompt obedience, assigned to him a difficult task, and one which, for the time, could not increase and might diminish his reputation, because the motives on which he acted might not be fully understood. As he expected, General Sherman promptly, and without objection, accepted his part of the duty of the morrow. He was to make a persistent demonstration against Fort Buckner, sending up column after column to assault it, and thus drawing the rebel troops from Forts Bragg and Breckinridge below to Tunnel hill, on which Fort Buckner was situated, leave those forts fatally weakened, when General Grant would send a storming column to capture them, and the enemy thus assailed in rear and flank would be compelled to relinquish his position on the ridge. It was not expected that Sherman's assaults would be successful, though, to be effective, they must cost heavy losses; but it is not saying any thing derogatory to the other able generals who participated in these battles, to say that to none other would General Grant have felt willing to have assigned a task requiring such firmness and self-sacrifice without any immediate hope of reputation or fame, but rather a certainty of reproach, utterly undeserved, attaching to it; and had he been disposed to propose it to any other, he could hardly have failed to have met with a protest. General Sherman accepted the duty, however, as he would have done any other, satisfied that it was his part to perform whatever duty was assigned to him, without complaint, so it would inure to the overthrow of the rebellion and the end of the war.

"Before dawn on the 25th of November," says Colonel Bowman, "Sherman was in the saddle, and had made the entire tour of his position in the dim light. It was seen that a deep valley lay between him and the precipitous sides of the next hill in the series, which was only partially cleared, and of which the crest was narrow and wooded. The further point of the hill was held by the enemy, with a strong breastwork of logs and fresh earth, crowded with men and carrying two guns. On a still higher hill beyond the tunnel he appeared in great force, and had a fair plunging fire on the intermediate hill in dispute. The gorge between these two latter hills, through which the railroad tunnel passes, could not be seen from Sherman's position, but formed the natural *place d'armes*, where the enemy covered his masses to resist Sherman's turning his right flank, and thus endangering his communications with the Chickamauga depot."

General Corse was to have the advance, "and," says General Sherman, "the sun had hardly risen when his bugle sounded the 'Forward.'" Down the valley and up the steep sides of the hill in front they moved briskly, and though at every step they encountered a murderous fire from the enemy's artillery, yet they managed in spite of all opposition to carry and hold a secondary crest or ledge of rocks on Tunnel hill, although their position was swept by the fire of the breastworks in front. For more than an hour a conflict of the most desperate character raged, the Union troops now surging up close to the breastwork, and apparently about to spring over, and anon dashed back far away to their original position. To draw the fire partially from these struggling heroes, General Sherman opened a fire with his artillery upon the breastwork, throwing shot and shell into it with great accuracy. He also sent two columns, one to the left of the ridge and one to the right, abreast of the tunnel, to distract the enemy's attention, and thus support Corse's attack. About ten o'clock A. M., the fight increased in intensity, and General Corse was severely wounded. Two brigades of reinforcements were sent up, but the crest was so crowded that they had to fall away to the west side of the hill, and at once the enemy's reserves, which had been lying in the gorge under cover of the undergrowth, sprang out upon their right and rear. Thus suddenly assailed, they fell back in some confusion to the lower edge of the field, where they re-formed in good order, and repelled the attempts of the enemy to pursue. As these brigades constituted no part of the real attack, this temporary rebuff was of no practical importance. General Corse's column and the two brigades on the right and left still held their position stubbornly on the crest. They might not be able to drive the enemy from the hill, but neither would they be driven from it themselves.

Regarding this as the main attack, and determined to repel it, the enemy now began to draw, from his line below, troops to mass against these stubborn assailants. "At three P. M.," writes General Sherman, "column after column of the enemy was streaming towards me, gun after gun poured its concentric shot on us from every hill and spur that gave a view of any part of the ground." From Orchard knob General Grant watched, with deep interest, the struggle; and when, after another charge of the most determined character had almost, but not quite, won the goal, opposed, at the very last, by the heavy reinforcements which the enemy had just brought up, the commander-in-chief sent a division over to support him, Sherman sent it back, with a message, that he had all the force necessary, and could hold his position on Tunnel hill. Then came the moment so long watched for, when the blow to which Bragg had unwisely exposed himself, was to be struck, and the patient and gallant heroes on Tunnel hill were to be avenged. Hooker had already placed himself in rear of the enemy, on Mission ridge, and was at that moment thundering against the walls of Fort Bragg, the southernmost of the rebel earthworks on the ridge, which he carried a little later—and at twenty minutes to four, the fourth army corps of Thomas' army charged in solid column up the ridge, and carried Fort Breckenridge; and the rebel general and all his garrisons and army were forced, after a very brief conflict, to fly in hot haste down the eastern slope of Missionary ridge, and take refuge in the valleys beyond. The battles of Chattanooga were won. Sherman's part in this conflict had been, as we have said, not the brilliant one of the victor, before whom the enemy fly in confusion; rather had he at the first to bear the odium of having sacrificed his men in a fruitless though persistent assault on a fortification which could not be carried by direct attack; but when the whole plan of the battles came out, and their mutual relations were seen, it became evident that the glorious successes of that day were due as much to the persistency and stubbornness with which General Sherman held the crest of Tunnel hill, as to the brilliant charge of the fourth corps against Fort Breckenridge. Without the former the latter could not, by any possibility, have proved successful. But with the victory came no rest for Sherman's war-worn veterans. The same night Sherman's skirmishers followed the enemy, and long before dawn the next morning Sherman was himself in the saddle, leading a division of Howard's corps in swift pursuit of the flying foe. The remainder of his army, and portions of Thomas's, as well as Hooker's grand division, followed closely and persistently, skirmished with the enemy at two or three points, and finally compelling him to stand at bay at Ringgold, had a sharp action, but defeated the rebels with considerable slaughter. General Grant now acceded to General Sherman's request, to be allowed to destroy thoroughly the railroad communications of the enemy with Knoxville, and thus effectually prevent the reunion of Longstreet and Bragg.

Meantime, General Burnside, now besieged at Knoxville, had sent an urgent appeal to General Grant for relief. Grant had already ordered General Granger to march thither with his corps, but he had not yet got off, and moved with reluctance and complaint. Nor had he the number of men which General Grant had directed him to take. "I therefore determined," says General Grant, "notwithstanding the fact that two divisions of Sherman's forces had marched from Memphis, and had gone into battle immediately on their arrival at Chattanooga, to send him with his command." Accordingly, Sherman received command of all the troops designed for relieving Knoxville, including Granger's. "Seven days before," wrote Sherman, "we had left our camps on the other side of the Tennessee, with two days' rations, without a change of clothing, stripped for the fight, with but a single blanket or coat per man, from myself to the private included. Of course, we then had no provisions, save what we gathered by the road, and were ill-supplied for such a march. But we learned that twelve thousand of our fellow-soldiers were beleaguered in the mountain-town of Knoxville, eighty-four miles distant, that they needed relief, and must have it in three days. This was enough; and it had to be done." The railroad bridge over the Hiawassee was repaired and planked, and at daylight of the 1st of December the army crossed upon it, and marched to Athens, fifteen miles, through deep mud. On the 2d of December they hurried forward to London, twenty-six miles distant, while the cavalry pushed on in advance to endeavor t save the bridge over the Tennessee, held by the rebel General Vaughan's brigade. They found him strongly posted in earthworks with heavy artillery, and were compelled to wait for Howard's infantry to come up. During the night, Vaughan retreated, destroying the pontoon bridge, and running several locomotives and a number of cars into the Tennessee, but leaving his guns and provisions. But one day remained, and less than half the distance was traversed, and the bridge gone. General Sherman, therefore, sent word to Colonel Long, the commander of the cavalry brigade, that General Burnside must know within twenty-four hours that he was on his way to relieve him, and directed him to select his best mounted men, start at once, ford the Little Tennessee, and push into Knoxville, at whatever cost of horseflesh. The road was long and almost impassable for mud, but Colonel Long was off before dawn, and reached there the same evening. The army turned aside at Philadelphia, and struck the Little Tennessee at Morgantown, but were obliged to extemporize a bridge, and crossed in the night of the 4th of December, and on the morning of the 5th received a message from General Burnside that Long's cavalry had arrived in season, and that all was well. The forced march was continued to Marysville, where a staff-officer of General Burnside arrived on the evening of the 5th, with the announcement that Longstreet had raised the siege the night before.

General Sherman now sent forward Granger's two divisions to Knoxville, and at once ordered the remainder of his gallant army to halt and rest, for their work was done. For himself, he went to Knoxville; and, having found every thing safe there, returned leisurely with his army, except Granger's divisions, to Chattanooga. The three months which had elapsed since they left Vicksburg had been passed in a campaign unparalleled in the history of war. Without a moment's rest, after a march of four hundred miles, without sleep for three successive nights, they crossed the Tennessee river, fought their part in the battles of Chattanooga, pursued the enemy out of Tenesssee, then turned north more than a hundred miles, and compelled Longstreet to raise the siege of Knoxville. These marches had been made much of the time without regular rations or supplies of any kind, through mud and over rocks, sometimes barefooted, and in a mountainous region, in the depth of winter, without a murmur.

It is related of one of these veteran heroes, that after his return to Chattanooga, he was, in passing through the camps, challenged by a sentinel belonging to the Eleventh corps, and made answer that he "belonged to the Fifteenth corps." "Where's your badge?" asked the sentry. "What badge?" inquired the veteran. "The badge of your corps. We wear a crescent to designate our corps." "Badge?" answered the hero. "Oh yes! Forty rounds of ammunition in our cartridge boxes; sixty rounds in our pockets; a march from Memphis to Chattanooga; a battle and pursuit; another march to Knoxville; and victory everywhere. That's all the badge we want."

General Sherman possesses a highly cultivated mind, well trained by study and observation in a wider range of topics than usually come within the scope of military men; and in his letters and reports the evidences of this thorough and thoughtful culture are often noticeable, a single expression sometimes embodying some great principle on which Vattel, Montesquieu, or Jomini would have expended a hundred pages. We shall see instances of this further on. In all matters of military law, principle, or custom he displays a profound knowledge, and a facility in applying them to existing cases which few military writers have possessed. His letters on the proper treatment of disloyal people in conquered territory are models of military learning and judicial ability, and will in all the future be quoted as authorities. One of these, addressed to Assistant Adjutant-General Sawyer at Huntsville, Alabama, and bearing date Jan. 24th, 1864, is so clear and satisfactory in its enunciation of the position of our government in relation to these disloyal residents, that we cannot forbear quoting a considerable portion of it.

After citing historical precedents, and the authority of Napoleon and William of Orange, for his views, he proceeds to say:

"The war which now prevails in our land is essentially a war of races. The Southern people entered into a clear compact of government, but still maintained a species of separate interests, history, and prejudices. These latter became stronger and stronger, till they have led to a war which has developed fruits of the bitterest kind.

"We of the North are, beyond all question, right in our lawful cause, but we are not bound to ignore the fact that the people of the South have prejudices, which form a part of their nature, and which they cannot throw off without an effort of reason, or the slower process of natural change. Now, the question arises, should we treat as absolute enemies all in the South who differ from us in opinion or prejudice,—kill or banish them? or should we give them time to think and gradually change their conduct, so as to conform to the new order of things, which is slowly and gradually creeping into their country?

"When men take arms to resist our rightful authority, we are compelled to use force, because all reason and argument cease when arms are resorted to. When the provisions, forage, horses, mules, wagons, &c., are used by our enemy, it is clearly our duty and right to take them, because otherwise they might be used against us.

"In like manner, all houses left vacant by an inimical people are clearly our right, or such as are needed as storehouses, hospitals, and quarters. But a question arises as to dwellings used by women, children, and non-combatants. So long as non-combatants remain in their houses, and keep to their accustomed business, their opinions and prejudices can in no wise influence the war, and, therefore, should not be noticed. But if any one comes out into the public streets and creates disorder, he or she should be punished, restrained, or banished, either to the rear or front, as the officer in command adjudges. If the people, or any of them, keep up a correspondence with parties in hostility, they are spies, and can be punished with death, or minor punishment.

"These are well-established principles of war, and the people of the South, having appealed to war, are barred from appealing to our Constitution, which they have practically and publicly defied. They have appealed to war, and must abide *its* rules and laws. The United States, as a belligerent party claiming right in the soil as the ultimate sovereign, have a right to change the population, and it may be, and is, both politic and just, we should do so in certain districts. When the inhabitants persist too long in hostility, it may be both politic and right that we should banish them and appropriate their lands to a more loyal and useful population. No man will deny that the United States would be benefited by dispossessing a single prejudiced, hard-headed, and disloyal planter, and substituting in his place a dozen or more patient, industrious, good families, even if they be of foreign birth. I think it does good to present this view of the case to many Southern gentlemen, who grew rich and wealthy, not by virtue alone of their industry and skill, but by reason of the protection and impetus to prosperity given by our hitherto moderate and magnanimous Government. It is all idle nonsense for these Southern planters to say that they made the South, that they own it, and that they can do as they please,—even to break up our Government, and to shut up the natural avenues of trade, intercourse, and commerce.

* * * * *

"Whilst I assert for our Government the highest military prerogatives, I am willing to bear in patience that political nonsense of slave-rights, State rights, freedom of conscience, freedom of press, and such other trash, as have deluded the Southern people into war, anarchy, and bloodshed, and the foulest crimes that have disgraced any time or any people.

"I would advise the commanding officers at Huntsville, and such other towns as are occupied by our troops, to assemble the inhabitants and explain to them these plain, self-evident propositions, and tell them that it is for them *now* to say whether they and their children shall inherit the beautiful land which by the accident of nature has fallen to their share. The Government of the United States has in North Alabama any and all rights which they choose to enforce in war,—to take their lives, their homes, their lands, their every thing; because they cannot deny that war does exist there;

and war is simply power, unrestrained by Constitution or compact. If they want eternal war, well and good; we will accept the issue and dispossess them and put our friends in possession. I know thousands and millions of good people who, at simple notice, would come to North Alabama and accept the elegant houses and plantations now there. If the people of Huntsville think differently, let them persist in war three years longer, and then they will not be consulted. Three years ago, by a little reflection and patience, they could have had a hundred years of peace and prosperity, but they preferred war. Very well. Last year they could have saved their slaves, but now it is too late; all the powers of earth cannot restore to them their slaves, any more than their dead grandfathers. Next year their lands will be taken, —for in war we can take them, and *rightfully* too,—and in another year they may beg in vain for their lives. A people who will persevere in war beyond a certain limit ought to know the consequences. Many, many people, with less pertinacity than the South, have been wiped out of national existence."

The expedition of General Sherman into Central Mississippi was projected by that general, but sanctioned and ordered by General Grant. It was a grand conception, the marching a movable column of twenty-two thousand men, cut loose from any base, for a hundred and thirty miles through the enemy's country, and in modern times has hardly been surpassed except by Sherman himself in his later movements. That it failed of accomplishing all that was intended, and was in its results only a gigantic raid, carrying terror into the very heart of the Confederacy, and crippling the resources of the enemy beyond effectual reparation, was not the fault of General Sherman, but of the co-operating cavalry force, which failed to make its movement at the proper time, and with the necessary resolution and energy to effect a junction which might have swept Mississippi and Alabama out of the grasp of the rebels.

Brigadier-General W. S. Smith was ordered to leave Memphis on the 1st of February, with a force of 8,000 cavalry, and move down the Mobile and Ohio railroad, from Corinth to Meridian, destroying the road as he went. At Meridian he was to form a junction with General Sherman, who left Vicksburg on the 3d of February, and marched eastward with a force of twenty thousand cavalry, twelve hundred infantry, and a train carrying twenty days' rations. General Smith failed to move at the proper time, and, indeed, did not leave Memphis till the 11th of February; and the rebels, meantime, had collected a sufficient force on his route to oppose his progress, and induce him to turn back, after one or two skirmishes. Meantime, Sherman had performed his part of the expedition well. Moving directly across the State of Mississippi from Vicksburg, through Clinton, Jackson, Quitman, Enterprise, and Meridian, he encountered no formidable opposition, and destroyed the rebel communications and stores beyond their power to replace them, and brought off large numbers of the able-bodied negroes and their families from that region, the centre of the cotton-growing country, and great numbers of horses, mules, and army wagons. Finding that General Smith would not probably effect a junction with him, he turned his face westward from Meridian, after a stay of three or four days, meeting with no serious annoyance from the rebels, who followed at a respectful distance.

The purpose of the expedition was to cut off Mobile

from Johnston, and so annoy, harass, and cut up Polk's force in Central Mississippi as to prevent its going to the relief of Mobile, at which Farragut was pounding away with his fleet. The failure of General Smith to co-operate deranged this plan in part, and the assault on Mobile was necessarily postponed for the time.

On the 12th of March, 1864, the general order of the War Department was issued, by virtue of which Lieutenant-General Grant was put in command of all the armies of the Union, and by the same order General Sherman was assigned to the command of the grand military division of the Mississippi, the position vacated by General Grant. This division included the departments of the Ohio, the Cumberland, the Tennessee, and, for the time, Arkansas. The forces under his command numbered more than one hundred and fifty thousand men, and were to be still further increased. His subordinate commanders were General Thomas, at the head of the Army of the Cumberland, General McPherson, an accomplished officer, who succeeded him in the command of the Army of the Tennessee, General Schofield, commanding the Army of the Ohio, General Hooker, commanding two corps from the Army of the Potomac, General Hurlbut, at the head of the large and efficient Sixteenth army corps, General Howard, previously of the Army of the Potomac, and General Logan, who commanded his own old corps, the Fifteenth; and, besides these, nearly a score of able corps and division commanders, conspicuous for their ability in previous fields,—men like Stoneman, Kilpatrick, Palmer, Wood, Johnson, Davis, Rousseau, Newton, Geary, Williams, Baird, and Brannan.

At an interview which General Sherman had with the lieutenant-general, within a week after his promotion, the plans for the coming campaign were fully discussed, and it was agreed that a simultaneous forward movement of the Eastern and Western armies should be made early in May, the one having Richmond, and the other Atlanta, for its objective. Less than two months remained before the time of making this movement, and in that time a vast amount of supplies must be sent forward to Chattanooga, sufficient for at least sixty days beyond the current expenditure of the army; arms, ammunition, and cannon must be collected in immense quantities; the scattered army corps concentrated at Chattanooga, and thoroughly reorganized and trained; the cavalry remounted, and increased in numbers and efficiency, and all the details for a gigantic campaign completed. With that promptness and celerity which has uniformly characterized his operations, General Sherman, while visiting all the posts and garrisons of his command, took measures to perfect all these arrangements, and accomplished them so thoroughly, that on the 7th of May he moved forward with his army from its several camps at Ringgold, Gordon's mill, and Red Clay. His grand army numbered ninety-eight thousand seven hundred and ninety-seven effective men, and two hundred and fifty-four pieces of artillery. It was divided as follows: The Army of the Cumberland, Major-General Thomas commanding, sixty thousand seven hundred and seventy-three men, and one hundred and thirty guns; the Army of the Tennessee, Major-General McPherson commanding, twenty-four thousand four hundred and sixty-five men, and ninety-six guns; the Army of the Ohio, Major-General Schofield commanding, thirteen thousand five hundred and fifty-nine men, and twenty-eight guns. Of these troops, six thousand one hundred and forty-nine were cavalry, four thousand four hundred and sixty artillery, and the remainder infantry. The force opposed to him consisted of Hardee's, Hood's, and Polk's corps, the whole under the command of General Joseph E. Johnston, and numbered, according to General Johnston's report, about forty-five thousand, of whom four thousand were cavalry. The rebels received during the campaign, according to the same report, reinforcements to the amount of about twenty-one thousand, of which nearly seven thousand were cavalry. Sherman's army received only a sufficient number of reinforcements, and men returning from furlough and hospital, to keep his army about up to the original standard; while Johnston represents the number of troops turned over to Hood as about six thousand greater than that with which he commenced the campaign, although he acknowledged a loss of about fifteen thousand previous to the battles near Atlanta.

The two armies were very differently situated in one respect. Johnston's, if compelled to fall back, would be only approaching nearer to his base of supplies; while Sherman, already fully three hundred and fifty miles from his primary base at Louisville, and one hundred and seventy-five from his secondary base at Nashville, was compelled at every step forward to increase the distance, while his lines of communication were one, or, for part of the way, two lines of railroad, and some slight assistance, at certain stages of river navigation, from the Tennessee river. To guard this long line of communications from the roving bands of rebel guerrillas, as well as the regular cavalry of the rebel army, was, in itself, no easy task, and by most generals would have been regarded as entirely impracticable, while every stage of progress towards his objective, one hundred and thirty miles distant from Chattanooga, only added to his difficulties. The rebel authorities constantly prophesied his utter discomfiture from this cause alone, and continually declared, till the phrase became a by-word, that they had "now got Sherman just where they wanted him." Yet it is one of the best evidences of his skilful generalship that, during a campaign of more than five months, General Sherman kept this line of nearly five hundred miles of communications wholly within his own control, and, with rare ability, turned every effort of the enemy to sever or destroy his lines to their own signal disadvantage.

The portion of Northern Georgia through which General Sherman must necessarily penetrate in order to reach Atlanta, the goal of his hopes, is characterized by peculiar topographical features. Parallel ridges of hills of considerable height, and with bold rugged faces and narrow and steep defiles, with valleys often gloomy and dark, threaded by rapid and generally deep streams, extend from north to south, broken through, in an east and west line only, by the Coosa river and its principal affluent, the Etowah. South of this latter river the country is somewhat more open, though broken by isolated peaks and narrow passes, and presenting a rough and difficult region for military movements. The route of the Chattanooga and Atlanta railroad was through several of these mountain passes or gaps; and these, in addition to their great natural strength, had been carefully fortified, and were impregnable to an attack in front. General Johnston, an officer inferior in ability to no one in the rebel army, had made the most herculean exertions to prepare against every possible contingency of attack from the Union forces, and throughout the campaign displayed extraordinary skill in falling back, when compelled to retreat from one stronghold to another, in such a way as to lose neither prisoners nor material.

The first point to be carried was Dalton, a position of great strength, occupied by a part of Johnston's force, which extended to Buzzard's Roost gap, a high and narrow defile in the Great Rocky-faced Ridge, a spur from the Chattoogata mountain. This defile, which was protected by a strong abatis, artificially flooded with the waters of Mill creek, and commanded by batteries which swept every foot of it, was the only gateway to Dalton from the northwest, and through it the railway passed. General Sherman sent McPherson's troops, by way of Snake Creek gap, towards Resaca, a town lying on the railroad, eighteen miles below Dalton, and subsequently (on the 10th of May) ordered Hooker's and Palmer's corps, and Schofield's Army of the Ohio (Twenty-third corps), to follow; while Thomas, at first with his whole army, and subsequently with Howard's corps, demonstrated vigorously against Buzzard Roost gap. Johnston, finding that he was outflanked, fell back over a good road to Resaca, which he reached before McPherson had been able to attack; and Howard, passing the gap, entered Dalton and pressed on Johnston's rear. Arrived at Resaca, and occupying a strong position, Johnston prepared to give battle; but while preparing to gratify him with a fight, General Sherman had pontooned the Oostanaula, which flows south of Resaca, and sent Sweeney's division forward to threaten Calhoun, the next point of importance on the railroad, while he dispatched also a cavalry division to break the railroad still further south, between Calhoun and Kingston, thus compelling a further retreat in any event. On the 14th, there was heavy fighting in front of Resaca, without any perceptible advantage being gained by the Union troops, but on the

15th the attack was renewed, and Hooker's corps gained one of Johnston's strongest positions, capturing four guns and many prisoners. That night, Johnston ascertaining the danger of being flanked, escaped with his army, burning the bridge over the Oostanaula behind him.

The losses of the Union army in these battles had been heavy, nearly 5,000, a large proportion of whom, however, were but slighty wounded, and soon returned to duty. Johnston's loss was not far from 3,500, a thousand of whom were prisoners, eight guns, and a considerable amount of stores. After the evacuation, Sherman pressed on in pursuit, detaching, on the 17th, Jefferson C. Davis's division of the Fourteenth corps to Rome, which was captured and garrisoned. The rebel army was overtaken at Adairsville, and a sharp artillery engagement ensued, when they continued their retreat; and on the 18th, after some heavy skirmishing, Johnston crossed the Etowah, and Kingston fell into Sherman's hands, and he gave his troops a few days of needed rest, while he superintended the repair of the railroads, the reopening communications to the Chattanooga, and the bringing forward of supplies for his army.

On the 23d of May, having supplied his men with twenty days' rations, General Sherman moved forward, this time leaving the route of the railroad, which, just after crossing the Etowah, entered a long and dangerous defile known as Allatoona Pass, and turning directly southward, advanced towards Dallas, which would enable him to flank the pass. Johnston, in order to protect his railroad communication, was compelled to leave his fortified lines and advance upon Sherman's army. His cavalry first came in collision with Hooker's corps at Burnt Hickory, on the 24th; and on the 25th again at Pumpkinvine creek, which ended in a general though compelled him to cross, which he did in good order, protecting his crossing by a strong *tête-du-pont.* On the 7th of July, General Schofield effected a strong and commanding lodgment on the east bank of the river, surprising the rebel guard, capturing a gun, and laying a good pontoon and trestle-work bridge, and two days later, General Sherman had secured three good points for passing the river; and Johnston, who till that time had held his position on the river-bank, now found himself compelled to fall back to Atlanta, and leave Sherman indisputable master of the Chattahoochie. Atlanta was but eight miles distant, and strong as it undoubtedly was, General Sherman was determined to capture it. But first he found it necessary to give his troops a little rest; and meanwhile he put in operation a plan for cutting off Johnston's supplies, which was characteristic as showing the mental grasp and far-reaching foresight of the man in all military movements. He knew that when Johnston had crossed the Chattahoochie his supplies must come mainly from the direction of the Montgomery, Atlanta, and West Point railroad, as Central and Southern Alabama, Georgia, and Mississippi were the source from which the beef, pork, and corn were derived. Foreseeing that he should drive him to Atlanta, he had collected a force of two thousand cavalry, well-appointed, at Decatur, Alabama, more than two hundred miles in his rear, and had sent them orders, on receiving notice by telegraph, to push immediately south, and break the railroad from Montgomery, at Opelika, and as far as possible east and west from that point, and then move on to join him at Marietta. This would also prevent Johnston from receiving reinforcements from Mobile or other points west. The order was given on the 9th, and the cavalry, under the command of the gallant Rousseau, a strongly intrenched line between Kenesaw and Lost mountains. Pressing him again, and assaulting his lines, General Sherman compelled him to give up Lost mountain, and the works connecting it with Kenesaw; and, as the Union army still crowded upon him, he partially changed his position, and making Kenesaw his salient, covered Marietta with his right wing, and intrenched his left behind Nose's creek, thus securing his railroad line. Still the relentless pressure continued, the crossing of the Chattahoochie, near Sandtown, being threatened. On the 22d, Hood's corps sallied and assaulted the Union lines, but were repulsed with heavy loss, some seven or eight hundred being killed, wounded, or captured. The time had come when Sherman must either assault Johnston's position, or again make the effort to outflank him; and believing that the effect of an assault, even if repulsed, would be better on the *morale* of his army than a flank movement at that time, he ordered an assault at two points on the 27th. It was repulsed by the rebels with great loss on the part of Sherman's army in killed and wounded, nearly three thousand being put *hors de combat*, while the enemy, being behind their intrenchments, received but little damage. The Union troops were not, however, in the least disheartened, and Sherman, by a skilful manœuvre (throwing McPherson's entire corps forward towards the Chattahoochie), compelled the evacuation of Marietta on the 2d of July, and the Union army entered it next morning. He at once moved upon the enemy, hoping to find him in confusion in the crossing of the Chattahoochie; but the rebel commander had provided well against any chances of danger, and remained strongly intrenched on the west bank of the river till the 5th of July, when another flank movement of Sherman, accompanied by active skirmishing, not severe engagement near Dallas. Then followed, the same day, the severe struggle near New Hope church, with heavy losses on both sides; and after three days' skirmishing and manœuvring, the bold and daring assault of Johnston on McPherson at Dallas on the 28th, which resulted in the repulse of the rebels with fearful slaughter, their loss being over three thousand, and McPherson's less than one thousand. During these four days of battle, Sherman had been extending his lines to the left to envelop the rebel right, and occupied all the roads leading eastward to Allatoona and Ackworth. After the bloody battle at Dallas, General Sherman sent his cavalry to seize and occupy Allatoona Pass, in the mean time making demonstrations looking to a further movement southward; but on the 1st of June he pushed McPherson rapidly to the left, and reached Ackworth. Johnston sullenly abandoned his position at New Hope church, and on the 4th of June fell back to Kenesaw mountain. General Sherman now examined Allatoona Pass in person, and finding it admirably adapted for a secondary base, which he needed in that vicinity, had it fortified and garrisoned, and the railroad communications repaired, and on the 9th of June full supplies were brought into his camp from Chattanooga by rail. Receiving reinforcements here, he moved forward, and began again to press Johnston in his strongly fortified position, extending in a triangle, and covering the northern slopes of Pine, Kenesaw, and Lost mountains. On the 11th of June he made his dispositions to break the rebel line between Kenesaw and Pine mountains. There was considerable artillery practice for several days, and on the 14th the rebel General Polk was killed.

On the morning of the 15th it was found that General Johnston had abandoned Pine mountain, and maintained marched at once, and within twelve days had broken up thirty miles of the railroad, defeated the rebel General Clanton, and reached Marietta on the 22d, with a loss of only thirty men. Roswell, and the extensive factories of army clothing for the rebels there, were burned on the 7th of July.

On the 17th of July, the grand army moved forward, and formed its lines on the Peach-tree road; and while Thomas was crossing Peach-tree creek in force by means of numerous bridges, thrown over in face of the enemy's intrenched lines, McPherson and Schofield had swung round upon the Augusta railroad, beyond Decatur, and broken it effectually. There was heavy fighting daily during these movements, and, on the 20th of July, General Hood (who had succeeded Johnston in the command of the rebel army on the 17th) made a sudden and desperate assault upon the Union lines, aiming to take advantage of a gap between Newton's division, of Howard's corps, and Johnson's, of Palmer's corps. These two divisions, and the remainder of Hooker's corps, sustained the full brunt of the attack of Hood's entire army, and after a terrible battle drove the enemy back to his intrenchments, with a loss of full five thousand men, while the Union loss was only seventeen hundred and thirty-three, which fell almost entirely on Hooker's corps, all of which, except Newton's corps, went into the fight without their usual intrenchments. On the 22d, Hood having fallen back from his line of defence along Peach-tree creek to his final interior position of redoubts, forming the outer line of the defences of Atlanta proper, resolved to stake all upon a single die, and putting force enough into his intrenchments to hold them, massed all the rest of his army, and hurled it with terrible force against Sherman's left. At first a part of the

Union lines gave way, for McPherson's position was not fully established; but they soon rallied, and grew stronger under the assaults of the enemy. Six times did Hood fling his massed columns on the Union lines, attacking in turn the Fifteenth, Sixteenth, and Seventeenth corps, but at night, after one of the bloodiest and most skilfully fought battles of the war, victory perched on the Union banners. Thirty-two hundred and forty of the enemy's dead, a vast number of his wounded, and ten hundred and seventeen unhurt prisoners fell into the hands of the Union troops. Hood's entire loss could not have been less than twelve thousand. Five thousand stand of arms, and eighteen stand of colors were captured. The Union loss, by official count, was seventeen hundred and twenty-two; but among the slain was Major-General James B. McPherson, the commander of the Army of the Tennessee, and one of the ablest and most skilful officers in the Union service. His loss was a great national misfortune; and none felt it more deeply than General Sherman. On receiving intelligence of his death, he was affected to tears, and in his report he alludes to it in terms which show how tenderly he loved him. "He was," he says, "a noble youth, of striking personal appearance, of the highest professional capacity, and with a heart abounding in kindness, that drew to him the affections of all men."

General Sherman had on the 21st sent General Garrard with a cavalry force to break the Augusta railroad, and destroy the bridges over the Yellow and Ulcofauhatchee rivers in the vicinity of Covington, Georgia; and on the 23d he returned, having completely accomplished that work, and, in addition, burned a train of cars, 2,000 bales of cotton, and large amounts of stores at Covington and Conyer's station, and brought in 200 prisoners. General Sherman now planned a more extensive expedition, having for its object the destruction of the Atlanta and Macon as well as the West Point railroad, his intention being to isolate Atlanta from all its communications, and thus compel its surrender. The expedition was to consist of two columns, one of 5,000 cavalry, under the command of General Stoneman, a cavalry officer of high reputation, the other of 4,000 mounted troops, under command of General McCook. They were to move off in different directions, one towards McDonough, the other towards Fayetteville, and having done what they could separately, unite at or near Lovejoy's station, and destroy the Macon road thoroughly for many miles. General Stoneman asked permission, after this was accomplished, to take his own proper command, and go on to release the Union prisoners, then suffering at Andersonville. General McCook performed his part of the work speedily and well, but from some unexplained cause, General Stoneman failed completely, and was himself taken prisoner with several hundred of his men, and McCook was placed in a critical position, and compelled to fight his way out. The whole expedition proved a failure, and lost to the commanding general a very considerable portion of his cavalry, which he could not well afford to lose.

On the 28th of July, Hood, having been led by the purposed movements of the Union troops of the Fifteenth corps to believe that he could catch the right flank of the army "in air," again massed his forces, and assaulted that part of the Union lines with the utmost desperation, repeating his assaults six times, but found the Union forces perfectly ready for him on each occasion, his men only reaching their lines to be killed or hauled over as prisoners. His loss in that battle was fully 5,000, while Logan, whose corps was the one principally engaged, lost less than 600. In the three battles of the 20th, 22d, and 28th of July, Hood had thus nearly one half of his force thrown *hors du combat*, for Johnston states in his report that the troops he transferred to him on the 17th of July consisted of about 41,000 infantry and artillery, and 10,000 cavalry. He received, however, about this time a considerable reinforcement of the Georgia militia, who, though of little value for purposes of assault, were serviceable as garrison troops, and mingled with his veterans, who had no appetite for further offensive warfare, lay safely ensconced behind the impregnable defences of Atlanta.

General Sherman now extended his lines southwestward towards East Point, in the hope of drawing the enemy out, from the fear of having his communications severed; but Hood extended his fortified line correspondingly, and refused to abandon his works. It began to be evident that Atlanta could only be captured by another flank movement of the whole army, a matter of great difficulty, as it involved the apparent raising of the siege, and the dependence of his army for supplies on the stores accumulated at Marietta, from which he must necessarily be separated by the Chattahoochie river, and a considerable distance of travel over bad roads. He therefore resolved to try first the expedient of a bombardment of the city, and, if unsuccessful in that, to try again the flanking process. Just at this juncture, he learned that the rebel General Wheeler with the greater part of Hood's cavalry had gone northward to attack his communications between Allatoona and Chattanooga, and as he had abundant supplies below that point, he welcomed this movement as taking the rebel cavalry out of the way, and leaving him a fair field. He now dispatched Kilpatrick with 5,000 cavalry to break the West Point and Macon railroads so thoroughly as to render them impassable. This, General Kilpatrick attempted to do, but in the haste with which he operated, he did not disable the roads sufficiently to prevent their speedy repair, and General Sherman found it necessary to move his whole army. Accordingly, on the night of the 25th of August he commenced the movement, sending the Twentieth corps, now under the command of General H. S. Williams, back to the Chattahoochie, and with it all surplus wagons, ambulances, and incumbrances of all kinds, as well as all the sick and wounded, who were carefully placed within the strongly intrenched position there. Schofield remained in position, and the Army of the Tennessee moved westward towards Sandtown and Camp creek, as if about to cross the Chattahoochie, while the the Army of the Cumberland proceeded in the same direction, though not so far. Hood congratulated his troops that the siege of Atlanta was raised, and that the Union army, alarmed for its communications, menaced by Wheeler, was about to turn back to rescue them. On the night of the 27th, Sherman's troops had reached the West Point railroad, in the vicinity of East Point and below, and the 28th was devoted to the destruction of that road, twelve and a half miles of which were so effectually obliterated, that there was no danger of their being renewed for months, and on the 29th, the army was directed to move on the Macon road, and when opportunity occurred, destroy that in the same way. They marched in three columns, and on the 29th, 30th, and 31st, had considerable skirmishing with Lee's and Hardee's corps, which Hood had sent to oppose them as soon as he found that it was his communications instead of their own that the Union troops were bent on occupying. General Howard had some fighting (he was now in command of the Army of the Tennessee) on the afternoon of the 30th with the rebel cavalry; and on the 31st, Lee and Hardee attacked him in his temporary intrenchments, near Jonesboro, and were repulsed with a loss of not less than twenty-five hundred. On the 1st of September, the Macon railroad was destroyed for several miles, and General J. C. Davis, supported by Howard and Blair, assaulted Lee and Hardee, and defeated them, capturing one brigade and two four-gun batteries. The next day they pursued the enemy as far as Lovejoy's station.

Meanwhile, on the night of the first of September, Hood blew up his ammunition trains, and retreated southward from Atlanta, which was occupied the next day by the Twentieth corps. The remainder of the army came back by easy marches to Atlanta, and General Sherman, having determined to make Atlanta a strictly military post, directed the removal of all the civilians from it, sending those who were loyal northward, and turning the disloyal over to General Hood, with such precautions for the prevention of suffering as could be devised.

Hood, smarting under a sense of being thoroughly outgeneralled, was exceedingly restive, and determined to revenge himself on his skilful antagonist. The loss of Atlanta was a severe one to the leaders of the self-styled Confederacy, and they, too, were determined that they would not only win it back, but would recover Northern Georgia and East and Middle Tennessee. The rebel president, in a speech delivered at Macon in the latter part of September, declared that this should be accomplished, and gave his instructions to General Hood for effecting it. On the 24th of September, Hood suddenly transferred his army, which had been encamped near

TENNESSEE
GEORGIA
RINGGOLD
VARNELL'S STA.
TUNNEL HILL
DALTON
TILTON
RESACA
NEWTOWN
CALHOUN
ADAIRSVILLE
KINGSTON
ROME
CASSVILLE
CASSVILLE STA.
CARTERV.
ETOWAH R.
EUHARLEE
ALLATOONA
ACKWORTH
BIG SHANTY
Kenesaw Mt.
BURNT HICKORY
VAN WERT
NEW HOPE CH.
DALLAS
MARIETTA
ROSWELL
VININGS STA.
BUCKHEAD
DECATUR
ATLANTA
CHATTAHOOCHEE R.
EAST POINT
ROUGH & READY
RED OAK
FAIRBURN
ABBREVIATIONS & C.
TH.....THOMAS
MC.P.....MAC PHERSON
SCH.....SCHOFIELD
HO.....HOWARD
H.....HOOKER
REBELWORKS
SCALE

Lovejoy's station on the Macon railroad, to Newnan on the West Point road. Sherman kept a watchful eye upon his movements, and reconnoitred frequently in his vicinity. On the 27th of September, he discovered that he was moving towards the Chattahoochie; and on the 1st of October, that he had crossed that river and concentrated his forces at Powder Springs, near Dallas, Ga. On the 3d of October, General Sherman, who had previously strengthened his garrisons along the railroad, started in pursuit, and on the 5th, when Hood's advance assaulted Allatoona, he was on Kenesaw mountain, signalling to the garrison at Allatoona, over the heads of the enemy, to hold out till he relieved them. The rebels were repulsed at this point with heavy loss, and finding themselves pressed in the rear by Sherman's forces, they moved westward, and crossing the Etowah and Oostanaula rivers by forced marches, attacked Dalton on the 12th, which was surrendered by the cowardly officer in command. Finding himself still pressed by Sherman, Hood obstructed Snake Creek gap, and crossing through the gap in Pigeon mountain, entered Lafayette, whither Sherman followed and sought to bring on a battle. This Hood was not anxious for, and he accordingly retreated southward to Gadsden, Ala., where he intrenched himself, taking possession of Will's Creek gap in Lookout mountain. Sherman followed him to Gaylesville, but no further.

It was generally supposed that this was the end of Hood's raid upon the Union lines of communication, and that he would retreat still further south, towards central Alabama and Mississippi. But Sherman had better comprehended his strategy, and was prepared to meet it by a stroke of counter-strategy, evincing his possession of the highest order of military genius. He knew that

Dick Taylor had moved up to Tuscumbia, Alabama, and reasoned that Hood would join him, and the two, serving under Beauregard would strike a blow ere long for the recovery of Middle Tennessee; and if successful, then for East Tennessee also. But he felt that Tennessee would be safe in charge of his trusty lieutenant, General Thomas, to whom he could assign a force sufficient to grapple with Hood, Taylor, or Beauregard; while for himself he had projected a campaign which would speedily cripple the power of the rebels. Turning eastward then from Gaylesville, he announced to his army that he should follow Hood no longer, but let him go north as far as he pleased. "If he will go to the river," he said, "I will give him his rations." Giving his instructions to General Thomas, and dividing his army so as to spare him a part of the Army of the Cumberland and the Army of the Ohio, he moved southeast towards Atlanta by the 1st of November, causing the railroad track to be removed from Atlanta to Chattanooga, and sent to the latter city,—the property of value at Atlanta and along the line having been first sent to Chattanooga, which thenceforward became the outpost of the Union armies in that direction. On the 4th of November he began his preparations for his new movement, and the same day telegraphed his intentions to Washington, in the following words: "Hood has crossed the Tennessee. Thomas will take care of him and Nashville, while Schofield will not let him into Chattanooga or Knoxville. Georgia and South Carolina are at my mercy—and I shall strike. Do not be anxious about me. I am all right." The campaign he had projected was neither more nor less than this. With the four corps, and the fine cavalry force still under his immediate command, an army of not far from sixty thousand infantry and artillery, and about ten thousand cavalry, he purposed cutting loose from all bases, and constituting a strictly movable column, with thirty or forty days' rations, and his train reduced to the smallest possible dimensions, to move south-eastward, through the heart of the enemy's country, upon Savannah; and thence, should circumstances favor, northward through South Carolina and North Carolina, to compel the surrender or evacuation of Richmond. The project was one of the most magnificent ever conceived by a military commander. The distances were great, and the obstacles which might be interposed unknown; yet, impelled by a will "that could greatly dare and do," while adopting all needful precautions against surprise or disaster, he moved forward boldly to the execution of his plan. As a preliminary step, he deemed it necessary to destroy all the public buildings in Atlanta. He then moved forward in two columns, General Howard commanding the right and General Slocum the left, while his cavalry covered his flanks, and a part of it now in advance, and now far in rear, mystified the enemy continually as to his intentions.

General Howard's column moved through East Point, Rough and Ready, Griffin, Jonesboro, McDonough, Forsythe, Hillsboro, Monticello, and bridging the Ocmulgee entered Milledgeville on the 20th of November. Here General Sherman made his headquarters for a few days, while Howard moved on through Saundersville, Griswold, towards Louisville, the point of rendezvous, with the left wing. That wing, under the command of General Slocum, had meantime passed through Decatur, Covington, Social Circle, Madison; made a feint of an attack upon Macon; passed through Buckhead and Queensboro, and dividing, one detachment moved towards Augusta, and the other to Eatonton and Sparta.

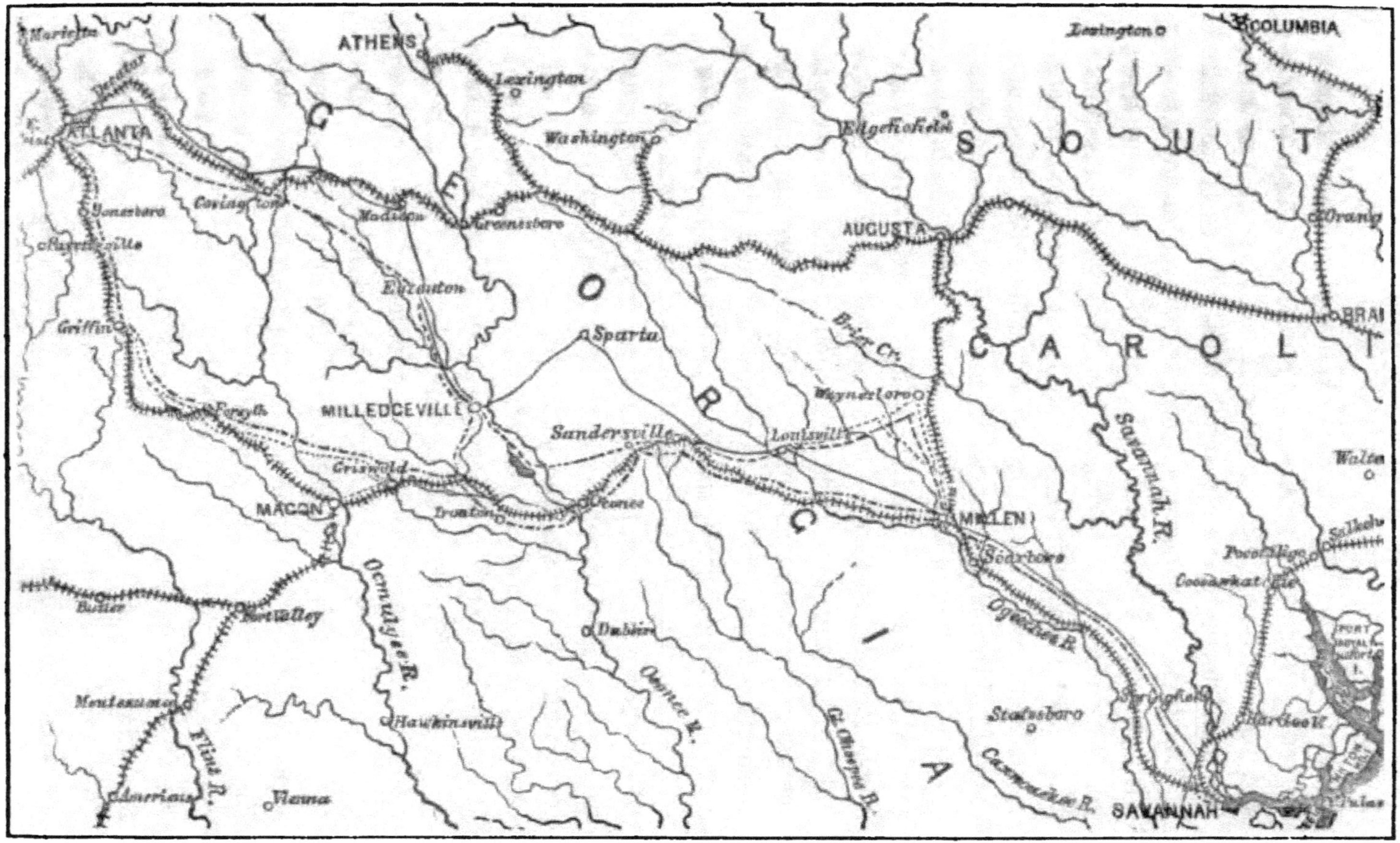
COLUMBIA
Lexington
ATHENS
Lexington
Washington
Edgefield
ATLANTA
Marietta
Decatur
Covington
Jonesboro
Madison
Greensboro
AUGUSTA
Eatonton
Griffin
Sparta
Brier Cr.
Waynesboro
MILLEDGEVILLE
Forsyth
Sandersville
Louisville
Griswold
MACON
Irwinton
Oconee
MILLEN
Scarboro
Savannah R.
Pocotaligo
Coosawhatchie
Butler
Fort Valley
Ocmulgee R.
Dublin
Oconee R.
Ogeechee R.
Montezuma
Hawkinsville
Flint R.
Americus
Vienna
Gt. Ohoopee R.
Statesboro
Canoochee R.
Springfield
SAVANNAH
G E O R G I A
S O U T
C A R O L I

Uniting again, they entered Warrenton, and thence moved to Louisville, where they joined the right wing; and passing down the left bank of the Ogeechee to Millen, and thence to the Savannah canal, where on the 9th of December, by means of scouts, they communicated with General Foster and Admiral Dahlgren, who had been awaiting their arrival. In this whole march of about 300 miles neither of the main columns had encountered any serious opposition. There had been occasional skirmishing, but with very slight results. The cavalry had had one or two conflicts with Wheeler's cavalry, but had repulsed them after a brief fight. The rebels had concentrated what troops they could, including militia and conscripts, into their service to oppose the daring march of Sherman; but they were not able to assemble enough of these to oppose any considerable resistance to his progress, and from his feints upon Augusta and Macon they were led to throw them into those cities, where they were completely out of his way. Bragg, who was in command of these troops, was thus beguiled into remaining at Augusta, and thus when Savannah was actually assailed could not come to its relief. On the 13th of December, General Sherman carried Fort McAllister by storm. By some strange oversight on the part of General Hardee, who was in command at Savannah, it had a garrison of only one hundred and fifty men. By the capture of this fort, General Sherman could communicate directly with the fleet. On the 16th he summoned the city of Savannah to surrender. General Hardee replied, refusing, and announcing his determination to hold the city to the last. Thereupon Sherman commenced investing the city, and bringing heavy siege-guns into position, he was prepared to commence its bombardment, his lines inclosing it on all sides, except the north and east, where the river and the Union causeway leading to Charleston were not yet fully commanded by his fire. On the afternoon of the 20th the rebel ironclads moved up the river, and commenced a furious fire on the Union left, supported by several of the rebel batteries. This fire was continued all night, and under cover of it Hardee escaped with his entire force, burning the navy yard partially, and destroying such stores as he could not remove. The two rebel ironclads were blown up during the night. The next morning (Dec. 21st), General Sherman entered the city, which was entirely uninjured. The captures included over one thousand prisoners, one hundred and fifty guns, thirteen locomotives, one hundred and ninety cars, a large supply of ammunition and materials of war, three steamers, and thirty-three thousand bales of cotton safely stored in warehouses. Over twenty thousand slaves, freed by the expedition, accompanied it to Savannah. The entire losses of the expedition were less than four hundred men. It had destroyed over two hundred miles of railroad, and thus effectually broken the enemy's communications with Hood's or Beauregard's army in Alabama and Tennessee. Kilpatrick was sent at once on an expedition with cavalry and infantry to destroy thoroughly the Gulf railroad, which he succeeded in doing for forty or fifty miles. Having reduced Savannah to order, and conciliated the inhabitants by his wise measures, General Sherman issued the following congratulatory order to his troops:

"HEADQUARTERS, MILITARY DIVISION OF THE MISSISSIPPI,
IN THE FIELD, SAVANNAH, Ga., Jan. 8, 1865.

"*Special Field Orders, No.* 6.

"The general commanding announces to the troops composing the Military Division of the Mississippi that he has received from the President of the United States and from Lieutenant General Grant, letters conveying the high sense and appreciation of the campaign just closed, resulting in the capture of Savannah and the defeat of Hood's army in Tennessee.

In order that all may understand the importance of events, it is proper to revert to the situation of affairs in September last. We held Atlanta, a city of little value to us, but so important to the enemy, that Mr. Davis, the head of the rebellious faction in the South, visited his army near Palmetto, and commanded it to regain it, as well as to ruin and destroy us by a series of measures which he thought would be effectual.

That army, by a rapid march, first gained our railroad near Big Shanty, and afterwards about Dalton. We pursued, but it marched so rapidly that we could not overtake it, and General Hood led his army successfully far towards Mississippi, in hopes to decoy us out of Georgia. But we were not then to be led away by him, and purposed to control events ourselves. Generals Thomas and Schofield, commanding the department to our rear, returned to their posts, and prepared to decoy General Hood into their meshes, while we came on to complete our original journey.

We quietly and deliberately destroyed Atlanta and all the railroad which the enemy had used to carry on war against us; occupied his State capital, and then captured his commercial capital, which had been so strongly fortified from the sea as to defy approach from that quarter.

Almost at the moment of our victorious entry into Savannah came the welcome and expected news that our comrades in Tennessee had also fulfilled, nobly and well, their part; had decoyed General Hood to Nashville, and then turned on him, defeating his army thoroughly, capturing all his artillery, great numbers of prisoners, and were still pursuing the fragments down into Alabama. So complete a success in military operations, extending over half a continent, is an achievement that entitles it to a place in the military history of the world.

The armies serving in Georgia and Tennessee, as well as the local garrisons of Decatur, Bridgeport, Chattanooga, and Murfreesboro, are alike entitled to the common honor, and each regiment may inscribe on its colors at pleasure the words "Savannah" or "Nashville."

The general commanding embraces in the same general success the operations of the cavalry column, under Generals Stoneman, Burbridge, and Gillem, that penetrated into Southwestern Virginia, and paralyzed the efforts of the enemy to disturb the peace and safety of the people of East Tennessee. Instead of being put on the defensive, we have, at all points, assumed the bold offensive, and completely thwarted the designs of the enemies of our country.

By order of

Maj.-Gen. W. T. SHERMAN.

L. W. DAYTON, Aid-de-Camp.

But his work was not yet completed, South Carolina was to be humbled, the surrender of Charleston, the "nest of the rebellion," compelled, Columbia to be captured, and North Carolina to be occupied. His troops refreshed and recruited, and largely reinforced, he moved about the 14th of January, northward, the Fifteenth and Seventeenth corps going by transports to Beaufort, S. C., and thence joined by Foster's command, moving on the Savannah and Charleston railroad, and the Fourteenth and Twentieth corps, crossing the Savannah river a few later. Delayed at first by the overflowing of the swamps from the heavy rains, and the terrible condition of the roads, he struck the railroad between Branchville and Charleston, early in February, compelled the enemy to evacuate Branchville on the 11th of February, and broke up the South Carolina railroad, for sixty or seventy miles, thus preventing any reinforcement from the West, and moved north, entering Orangeburg on the 16th of February, and Columbia, the capital of South Carolina, on the 18th, Beauregard having evacuated it in great haste on his approach. Charleston being flanked by this movement, its evacuation was compelled without a fight, and Hardee retreated, after setting fire to the cotton, ammunition, &c., which caused a conflagration which laid two-thirds of the business portion of the city in ashes. On the morning of February 18th, the Union troops from Morris Island entered the city, and the stars and stripes once more floated over the ruins of Fort Sumter.

From Columbia the Seventeenth and Twentieth corps moved in two columns upon Winnsboro, thirty miles north on the Columbia and Charlotte railroad, the Seventeenth destroying the railroad, and twisting the rails so that they could not be used again. From Winnsboro, where they found many of the refugees from Charleston and Columbia, General Sherman sent Kilpatrick's cavalry still northward towards Chesterville, to keep up the delusion of Beauregard, who believed that he was moving on Charlotte, and was laboring very diligently to obstruct his progress in that direction; but Sherman him-

---

* The burning of a considerable portion of Columbia, which Wade Hampton charged upon General Sherman, was really the work of degraded camp followers, who had become drunk on whiskey furnished by the inhabitants. General Sherman exerted himself to the utmost to extinguish the flames, and about twenty of the soldiers of the right wing were killed or seriously injured in the effort to arrest the conflagration.

self with his main army moved directly eastward, crossing the Catawba or Wateree nearly east of Winnsboro, and moving his left wing directly towards Cheraw, while the right threatened Florence. It was while in the vicinity of the Catawba that intelligence came of the evacuation of Charleston as the result of Sherman's flanking movement, and great were the rejoicings of the army thereat. A heavy rain which came on at this time, and damaged General Howard's pontoons, occasioned some delay, and enabled the rebels to concentrate their forces at Cheraw and its vicinity. Thus far the Union army had encountered no serious opposition in its whole march from Savannah, and, indeed, had hardly seen any rebel troops; but now there seemed a prospect that the rebels would make a stand, and the Union leader, as cautious as enterprising and daring, made all preparations to avoid a surprise or repulse. The left wing had moved to Chesterfield, northwest of Cheraw, while the right (Howard's), passing through Camden, and delayed one day by the injury to their pontoons, had found, on approaching within thirteen miles of Cheraw fom the southwest, the enemy's pickets in their front, and indications of a battle in reserve not far distant. They moved forward, however, after putting themselves in communication with the left wing, and on the 3d of March, after a short and not very severe battle, captured and occupied Cheraw, taking twenty-five pieces of cannon, and a large quantity of small-arms and ammunition. The rebel force which opposed their progress proved not to be as large as was at first supposed, consisting of a division of Wade Hampton's cavalry, and the infantry which had been in Charleston. They fled most precipitately across the Great Pedee, and could not get their cannon across, but succeeded in burning the bridge. On the next day (March 4th) the army celebrated Mr

Lincoln's second inauguration, firing a salute from the Blakely guns captured from the enemy. A part of these cannon, and a large amount of commissary stores, sufficient to supply nearly two corps of Sherman's army, had been brought from Charleston to Cheraw, as a place of safety. After leaving Columbia, the rapidly increasing mass of refugees, black and white, who followed the army, were organized into an emigrant train, and put under the charge of the officers and men who had escaped from the rebel prisons at Salisbury and elsewhere on the route. Under the direction of their escort they foraged for themselves, and being supplied liberally with horses and mules, wagons and other vehicles, of which large numbers were taken along the route, they moved on with very little expense or trouble to the army. General Sherman had won the good-will of the negroes, both during this and his Savannah campaign, by his thoughtful interest in their welfare. On the route to Savannah, as well as in this campaign, he took great pains to make them understand that they were free, and to aid them in securing and maintaining their freedom. Consulting at Savannah their preachers and most intelligent men, as to the course best adapted to conduce to their future elevation and independence, he established colonies of them on the Sea-islands and the coast, where they could have their lands in fee-simple, and cultivate the Sea-island cotton and rice, and have schools and churches established for them; and during his campaign northward he advised those who could to go to Charleston after its evacuation, and procure work, and commence the life of freemen. To those who followed the army in the emigrant train, he was uniformly kind, and on several occasions explained to them very clearly their new condition and responsibilities. The poor, ignorant, but truly loyal freedmen, looked upon him as almost a divinity; and it was to them, at all times, a sufficient reason for doing or abstaining from doing any thing, if they learned that "Massa Sherman" wished it.

On the afternoon and night of the 6th of March, the Union army crossed the Great Pedee river in safety, and swept forward the next day,—the main army, in four columns, moving on Laurel Hill and Montpelier, North Carolina, and the cavalry, under Kilpatrick, guarding the extreme left, and approaching Rockingham, North Carolina, where they came in contact with Butler's division of Wade Hampton's cavalry, which they repulsed with considerable loss. The four columns, with the cavalry, in moving from the Pedee, covered a belt of country forty miles in width. On the 8th the central columns entered Laurel Hill, N. C., and found the people of North Carolina much more favorably inclined towards the Union than those of South Carolina. The army now refrained from destroying every thing in their line of march, as they had done in South Carolina, and fraternized to some extent with the inhabitants. On the 9th of March they crossed the Little Pedee, or Lumber creek, as it is called in the higher part of its course, and, owing to the snaggy condition of the stream, built bridges across, rather than use their pontoons. A long and heavy rain delayed somewhat their approach to Fayetteville, but that place was reached on the 11th of March. On the 10th the rebel General Hampton approached, before daylight, Kilpatrick's headquarters, at Monroe's plantation, and at first captured his guns, and a considerable number of prisoners; but Kilpatrick rallied his men, repulsed the enemy, recaptured his men and guns, and drove Hampton off with severe loss. Sherman here communicated with Schofield at Wilmington, and reported his army in fine condition, and his movement thus far without serious loss. Indeed his losses up to this time had been mostly in foragers, who had been pounced upon by Wade Hampton's cavalry, and murdered and mutilated in cold blood, after surrendering. Of these victims to brutality, there were nearly one hundred. General Sherman had some sharp correspondence with the rebel general on the subject, and declared his determination to retaliate unless these cowardly murders were stopped; and Hampton, though making a blustering reply, killed no more. Up to the date of his arrival at Fayetteville, the results of this campaign of Sherman had been: fourteen cities captured, hundreds of miles of railroads and several thousands of bales of cotton destroyed; eighty-five cannon, four thousand prisoners, and twenty-five thousand horses, mules, and cattle taken, and fifteen thousand refugees, black and white, set free. After a delay of two days at Fayetteville, General Sherman again moved forward, the rebel General Bragg having meantime attacked Schofield at Kingston, and been defeated with heavy loss. General Sherman had fixed upon the vicinity of Goldsboro, as the place where he would form a junction with Schofield, and the 22d of March as the time—before leaving Savannah—and having brought his army thus far in time, he was disposed to move with moderation, to allow Schofield time to reach the rendezvous. On the 15th of March Johnston attacked Kilpatrick's cavalry at Moore's cross-roads, about four miles from Averysboro, and at first pushed it back, with some loss; but a division of the Fourteenth corps coming up, the Union troops held their position. The next day, March 16th, the Twentieth and Fourteenth corps attacked the rebels, who were in large force, near Averysboro, and after a sharp battle drove them from the field, with the loss of their guns, and leaving their dead and wounded on the field.

Sherman, who had met with but small loss, now moved forward towards Goldsboro; but it was a necessity of Johnston's position that he must, if possible, defeat and cripple his great antagonist before he could form a junction with Schofield, as that once effected, his own force would be so greatly inferior, that there could be no hope of success for him. Accordingly, bringing his entire force (he had about forty thousand effective men), by a forced march, into position at Bentonville, on the 19th of March, he massed them, and flung them upon the Union lines of Slocum's (left) wing with the utmost fury. Morgan's division of the Fourteenth corps was in advance of the line of Union defences, and this was driven back and doubled upon itself by the sudden attack, with the loss of three guns. General Slocum promptly brought up the remainder of the Fourteenth corps and the Twentieth to the support of his lines, and sent to General Sherman for the co-operation of the right wing. Meanwhile the rebels charged fiercely again and again upon the Union troops, making at one time three charges in thirty-five minutes, and with such desperation, that the whole ground in front of the Union lines was strewn with their dead and wounded, and many of them had fallen within the breastworks over which they had thrown themselves in their fury. But the veterans of the Fourteenth and Twentieth corps had withstood too many headlong charges from the rebels to give way; they stood firm as a rock, and repelled every charge with grape and canister, and a most deadly musketry-fire, till at length, exhausted with their efforts, and finding that they could not make any impression on Sherman's troops, they withdrew sullenly to their lines. The next day, March 20th, was spent in intrenching and strengthening the position the Union troops had taken; and the right wing having come up, moved forward, and flanked the enemy's position, keeping up a brisk artillery fire upon them meanwhile. Finding that their communications with Raleigh were threatened, the rebels attempted to fall back on Smithfield, but were pressed so closely by the Union forces, that they lost seven guns, and more than two thousand prisoners were captured from their army, while the deserters came in by hundreds.

General Sherman, who had sent some of his staff to Goldsboro on the 22d, came in himself with his army on the 23d, having previously issued the following order.

"HEADQUARTERS, MILITARY DIVISION OF THE MISSISSIPPI,
IN THE FIELD, NEAR BENTONVILLE, N. C.,
March 22, 1865.

"*Special Field Orders, No.* 35.

"The general commanding announces to the army, that yesterday it beat, on its chosen ground, the concentrated armies of our enemy, who has fled in disorder, leaving his dead, wounded, and prisoners in our hands, and burning his bridges on his retreat.

"On the same day Major-General Schofield, from Newbern, entered and occupied Goldsboro, and Major-General Terry, from Wilmington, secured Cox's bridge crossing and laid a pontoon bridge across Neuse river, so that our campaign has resulted in a glorious success. After a march of the most extraordinary character, nearly five hundred miles, over swamps and rivers deemed impassable to others, at the most inclement season of the year, and drawing our chief supplies from a poor and wasted country, we reach our destination in good health and condition.

"I thank the army, and assure it that our Government and people honor them for this new display of the physical and moral qualities which reflect honor upon the whole nation.

"You shall now have rest, and all the supplies that can be brought from the rich granaries and storehouses of our magnificent country, before again embarking on new and untried dangers.

"W. T. SHERMAN,
"Major-General Commanding."

General Sherman reported to General Grant that his entire losses in killed, wounded, and prisoners, from the time of leaving Savannah till he encamped with his army around Goldsboro, were less than twenty-five hundred men.

After disposing his army in camp at Goldsboro, and giving orders for their immediate supply with shoes and clothing, General Sherman hastened to City Point, for an interview with General Grant and the President. He arrived on Monday evening, March 27th, and returned the next day. The campaign was ended, and though a new one might commence within a week, General Sherman was disposed to allow his soldiers all the time for rest and recovery from fatigue possible, before entering upon it. Between his army, augmented by the corps of Schofield and Terry, and the fine army of Grant, the rebellion was evidently destined to be crushed as between the upper and nether millstone. The two armies were separated by only one hundred and fifty miles, and a railroad, which could be rapidly put in order, connected them. Other forces were pressing upon the rebel communications from the west, and within a few weeks, at furthest, the toils would be woven so thickly about the army and the leaders of the rebellion, that escape would be impossible. It was a time when waiting with uplifted arm ready to strike, was better, perhaps, than fighting, and the two great captains could wait as well as fight.

The delay was not, however, of long duration. By the utmost diligence the army was refitted and supplies gathered in, so that on the 10th of April his columns were all again in motion. Smithfield was entered on the 11th, with only slight skirmishing, Johnston retreating across the Neuse, and burning the bridges behind him; the Neuse was crossed the next day, and the intelligence of Lee's surrender having come to the army, they pressed on through deep mud and horrible roads, and entered Raleigh on the 13th, and the cavalry advanced to Durham Station, the infantry of the right wing following as fast as they could. In order to cut off Johnston's retreat, General Sherman, unaware that Stoneman had already captured Salisbury, now made preparations to move his army diagonally across the railroad, which at Greensboro' turns sharply southwestward. By this movement he would save a very considerable march for his troops. On the 14th he received from General Johnston a letter desiring an interview, with a view to a capitulation. General Sherman replied, agreeing to meet him at a point intermediate between the two armies on the 17th at noon, provided no change was made in the *status* of the two armies. This was agreed to, and at this meeting General Johnston acknowledged the hopelessness of the contest and the liberal terms granted to General Lee, but asked that some provisions might be inserted in his terms of surrender which would enable him to allay the natural anxieties and fears of his soldiers, and to maintain his control over them until they could be got back to the neighborhood of their homes, thereby saving the State of North Carolina from serious devastation. He also desired to embrace in the surrender the other rebel armies still in existence—Taylor's, Kirby Smith's, etc. General Sherman met him very frankly, and expressed his gratification at the sentiments he uttered; but finding that he had not then the power to bind the rebel army of Texas, the negotiation was postponed till the next day, when Johnston asked that Breckinridge might be present; to this Sherman, after some hesitation, acceded. The result of the next day's deliberations was the drawing up of the following memorandum, to be submitted for approval to the higher authorities on both sides, a truce to exist meanwhile. The delay was of advantage to Sherman, as it enabled him to finish his railroad to Raleigh and bring up supplies.

MEMORANDUM or basis of agreement, made this 18th day of April, A. D. 1865, near Durham's Station, and in the State of North Carolina, by and between General Joseph E. Johnston, commanding the Confederate Army, and Major-General William T. Sherman, commanding the Army of the United States in North Carolina, both present:

First. The contending armies now in the field to maintain their *statu quo* until notice is given by the commanding general of either one to his opponent, and reasonable time, say forty-eight hours, allowed.

Second. The Confederate armies now in existence to be disbanded and conducted to the several State capitals, there to deposit their arms and public property in the State arsenal, and each officer and man to execute and file an agreement to cease from acts of war, and abide the action of both State and Federal authorities. The number of arms and munitions of war to be reported to the chief of ordnance at Washington city, subject to future action of the Congress of the United States, and in the mean time to be used solely to maintain peace and order within the borders of the States respectively.

Third. The recognition, by the Executive of the United States, of the several State Governments, on their officers and Legislatures taking the oath prescribed by the Constitution of the United

States; and when conflicting State Governments have resulted from the war, the legitimacy of all shall be submitted to the Supreme Court of the United States.

Fourth. The re-establishment of all Federal courts in the several States, with powers as defined by the Constitution and the laws of Congress.

Fifth. The people and inhabitants of all States to be guaranteed, so far as the Executive can, their political rights and franchise, as well as their rights of person and property, as defined by the Constitution of the United States and of States respectively.

Sixth. The executive authority of the Government of the United States not to disturb any of the people so long as they live in peace and quiet, abstain from acts of armed hostility, and obey laws in existence at any place of their residence.

Seventh. In general terms, war to cease, a general amnesty, so far as the executive power of the United States can command, or on condition of disbandment of the Confederate armies and the distribution of arms and resumption of peaceful pursuits by officers and men as hitherto comprising the said armies. Not being fully empowered by our respective principals to fulfil these terms, we individually and officially pledge ourselves to promptly obtain necessary authority, and to carry out the above programme.

W. T. SHERMAN, Major-General,
Commanding the Army of the United States
in North Carolina.

J. E. JOHNSTON, General,
Commanding Confederate States Army
in North Carolina.

The terms thus proposed were inadmissible, and by the unanimous voice of the Cabinet, General Grant concurring, were disallowed. The provisions of it, if granted, would have proved unjust to many of those who had contributed most largely to the national success, and might have resulted in serious trouble and disaster to the interests of a permanent peace. It was, also, an assumption of the power of the military leaders to adjust the civil questions growing out of the war, which, if permitted, would have proved fatal to the authority of civil government, and had been expressly forbidden to General Grant about two months previous. Of this, however, General Sherman was not aware; and the authority which had been deputed to him to deal with the question of the *status* of freedmen, etc., at Savannah, led him to suppose that he was not transcending the limits which were allowable in this case. In military ability and genius he was far superior to both Johnston and Breckinridge, but in diplomacy the crafty ex-Vice-President outwitted him.

Yet, blunder as this agreement undoubtedly was, it afforded no just ground for the aspersions which, for a brief period, were cast upon the reputation of the gallant general and hero. No more loyal heart than that of William T. Sherman beats on this continent, and none more desirous of the nation's success and prosperity. It was his over-anxious desire for peace, from his ample knowledge and experience of the horrors of war, his wish to close at one stroke the conflict already protracted over four years, and his belief—erroneous, indeed, but honestly entertained—that in a general pacification important matters would right themselves, which led him to enter into this conditional agreement; and while we dissent from the measure, we cannot but admire the motives which prompted him to initiate it.

General Grant hastened to Raleigh, and explaining the objections to the measure, requested General Sherman to give notice to General Johnston of the rejection of the memorandum and the resumption of hostilities at the end of forty-eight hours. Before the expiration of that period, General Johnston solicited another interview; and General Grant, fully persuaded of General Sherman's ability and patriotism, wisely left to him the negotiations; and on the 26th, General Johnston surrendered to him on the terms made by General Grant to General Lee. In all, about 29,000 men were surrendered by this capitulation, which embraced every thing east of Dick Taylor's command, which extended to the Chattahoochie.

The surrender made, General Sherman hastened to Savannah and Hilton Head, to arrange for permanent garrisons at Augusta and other points within the limits of his command, and returned to Morehead City on the 4th of May. During his absence he had seen the published orders of General Halleck (who had certainly transcended his authority) and of Secretary Stanton, which directed his subordinate officers to pay no regard to his truce. That this measure was ill-advised, all parties now admit; and that it excited his indignation, which found vent in his report of May 9th, is not surprising. The matter was subsequently, through the intervention of General Grant, so far harmonized that the parties were on terms of courtesy towards each other, but hardly of cordiality.

After the review of his troops at Washington, on the 23d and 24th of May, General Sherman obtained a short leave of absence, the first in many months, and visited New York, West Point, and the other Northern and Western cities. An attempt was made by the Democratic party in Ohio to nominate him for Governor, but he promptly declined, expressing his firm determination not to be a candidate for any political honors, and heartily indorsing General Cox, the Republican candidate, who had been an officer in his own army. On the 27th of June, 1865, he was appointed by the Government to the command of the new military division of the Mississippi, embracing the Department of the Missouri (including the Northwest States and Territories, and Arkansas and the Indian Territory). His headquarters are at St. Louis.

In person, General Sherman is tall, slender, but vigorous, and capable of extraordinary endurance of fatigue. His eyes are gray, his hair and whiskers sandy, with a reddish tinge. His temperament is highly nervous, and he is one of the most restless of men, constantly in motion, and as constantly smoking; he requires but little sleep, and is a close and somewhat abstracted thinker. His manners are usually somewhat stern, or, as a New Englander would say, gruff; partly, perhaps, from his quick, nervous way of speaking, and partly from the imperiousness of his will, which brooks no opposition, and a naturally harsh temper—a fault which he freely admits, though he seldom controls it. He is careless in his dress, and has no aspirations to be a military dandy. He has a mind well cultivated by reading and study, and is especially familiar with ancient and modern history. He possesses decided ability as a writer, expressing himself with great terseness and force, and often condensing a whole volume of military law in a single sentence. His style is, however, somewhat marred by his habit of using short, jerky sentences. In conversation he is very rapid and vehement, his sentences short, and uttered in an imperious way. His decisions are so quick as to seem to be intuitions, but are very rarely wrong.

Innumerable anecdotes are told of him which illustrate these traits of his character. Just at the commencement of his Atlanta campaign, while he was straining every nerve to push forward supplies for his army, the Christian Commission telegraphed him, asking for transportation for two of their delegates, eminent clergymen of New York, to visit his army with stores, tracts, &c. "Certainly not," was the prompt reply, "crackers and oats are more necessary for my men than ministers and tracts." Though in general entertaining a dislike for much of the female nursing in the camps and hospitals, he had taken a fancy to a Mrs. Bickerdyke, a resolute, daring, strong-limbed, and strong-lunged woman, who had really accomplished a vast amount of good by her care for the interests of the private soldiers, especially those who were sick or wounded, and would grant her requests almost uniformly, even when he denied others the same favors. Mrs. Bickerdyke was a sworn enemy to indolent and unfaithful army surgeons, and often procured their dishonorable discharge when they were incompetent or neglectful of their duties. One of these surgeons who found himself summarily discharged from the service through her influence, went to General Sherman and asked to be reinstated, alleging that his character had been misrepresented. "Who got you discharged?" asked the general. "I was unjustly discharged," said the surgeon, evasively. "But who got you discharged?" persisted the general. "Why, I suppose it was that woman, that Mrs. Bickerdyke." "Ah!" said Sherman, puffing at his cigar, violently; "well, if it was Bickerdyke, I can't do any thing for you. She ranks me."

To him, there are no such things as impossibilities. In March, 1864, finding that only ninety car-loads of rations daily were forwarded from Nashville to Chattanooga, he insisted that the number must be quadrupled, and going to Louisville, he extended the Louisville and Nashville railroad three miles to the Ohio river within two days, brought the Jeffersonville railroad to the north bank of the river, seized a ferry-boat, and had it fitted up for transporting locomotives and cars, had inclined planes erected, impressed as many locomotives and cars as he wanted from the Illinois, Indiana, and Ohio railroads, and rushed them through to Nashville. In less than a month the railroad agents were running two hundred and seventy cars per day through to Chattanooga, but, not satisfied with this, he required a report daily of the additions made to the rolling-stock, and on the 28th of April had his three hundred and sixty cars daily running to Chattanooga. On his march from Savannah to Goldsboro, a distance of five hundred miles, the roads for great portions of the distance had to be corduroyed, and bridges built over many of the streams, yet he required and secured a march of from twelve to fifteen miles a day with his immense army, a greater rapidity of movement for a large infantry force, in so long a march, than was ever recorded in history. No wonder that when he reached Goldsboro twenty thousand of his men were without shoes.

General Sherman is idolized by his men. They know that he cares for them, and harsh and stern as he may be to speculators, cotton-buyers, or even civilians or officers who come to his headquarters when he is out of humor, no private soldier ever comes to him to have a wrong redressed who does not have a patient hearing and a just decision. His foresight and comprehension of all the possible moves of the enemy, and his skill in providing for them, are remarkable, and exhibit in the strongest light his military genius. His patriotism is undoubted and fervent. Knowing what the Southern people are, and what they have done, he expostulates with them in strong terms, but never attempts to palliate their conduct, or to intimate that any thing short of submission will secure to them the restoration of their former privileges.

A letter of his, written in the summer of 1864 to a lady in Baltimore, whom he had known years ago "playing as a school-girl on Sullivan's Island beach," expresses his sentiments on this subject so eloquently, that we cannot refrain from quoting it. In justification of the war, he says:

"All I pretend to say is, on earth as in heaven, man must submit to some arbiter. He must not throw off his allegiance to his Government or his God without just reason and cause. The South had no cause—not even a pretext. Indeed, by her unjustifiable course, she has thrown away the proud history of the past, and laid open her fair country to the tread of devastating war. She bantered and bullied us to the conflict. Had we declined battle, America would have sunk back, coward and craven, meriting the contempt of all mankind. As a nation, we were forced to accept battle, and that, once begun, it has gone on till the war has assumed proportions at which even we, in the hurly-burly, sometimes stand aghast. I would not subjugate the South in the sense so offensively assumed, but I would make every citizen of the land obey the common law, submit to the same we do—no worse, no better—our equals, and not our superiors."

He adds: "God knows how reluctantly we accepted the issue; but once the issue joined, like, in other ages, the Northern race, though slow to anger, once aroused, are more terrible than the more inflammable of the South. Even yet my heart bleeds when I see the carnage of battle, the desolation of homes, the bitter anguish of families; but the *very moment the men of the South say, that instead of appealing to war they should have appealed to reason, to our Congress, to our Courts, to religion, and to the experience of history, then will I say, Peace! Peace!* Go back to your point of error, and resume your place as American citizens, with all their proud heritages."

With all his impatience of restraint, General Sherman has always manifested his recognition of the maxim, that "unhesitating obedience is the first duty of the soldier." Though often tried sorely in this regard, he has never failed to obey any order from his superiors in command, however distasteful, with the utmost promptness. His fealty to Lieutenant-General Grant is honorable to both. It is related that a distinguished civilian, who visited him at Savannah, desirous of ascertaining his real opinion of General Grant, began to speak of him in terms of depreciation. "It won't do; it won't do, Mr. ——," said Sherman, in his quick, nervous way; "General Grant *is a great general.* I know him well. He stood by me when I was crazy, and I stood by him when he was drunk;* and now, sir, we stand by each other always."

In short, while we acknowledge, as he does also, most frankly, that General Sherman is not wholly free from faults, we think he has fairly won the right of being reckoned as one of the half-dozen great captains of the nineteenth century, and that none of his compeers have cause to feel ashamed of his company.

---

* Alluding to the reports so maliciously circulated of Sherman's insanity and Grant's intemperance.

III.

Major-General George H. Thomas.

Among the few men of Southern birth and education, who, at a period of wide-spread delusion and infatuation, were not beguiled into following the *ignis-fatuus* of the State Rights heresy, men who, like Milton's Abdiel, in the midst of the rebellious host of fallen angels, were

"Faithful among the faithless found,"

Major-General Thomas stands conspicuous alike in the purity of his character, the intensity of his devotion to the national cause, his undaunted bravery, and successful generalship.

Born in Southampton county, Va., in the very heart of the Old Dominion, and of a family possessing far more than ordinary claims, both in wealth and social position, to rank among the F. F. V.'s, he was never, for a moment, influenced by the twaddle which men in high position were not ashamed to utter, of the necessity of "going with their State," but promptly acknowledged, and firmly held to his allegiance to the national flag and the national cause, as paramount to all State ties, and, from the first dawn of the rebellion, threw all the energies of his great soul into the work of suppressing it.

He was born, as we have said, in Southampton county, Va., July 31, 1816. His father, John Thomas, was of English, or more probably, remotely of Welsh descent; his mother, Elizabeth Rochelle, of an old Huguenot family, and both wealthy, respectable, and highly connected.

His early education was obtained at the best schools of that portion of Virginia, and at the age of nineteen years he accepted the position of deputy clerk of the county, under his uncle, James Rochelle, then county clerk, and commenced the study of the law. In the spring of 1836, through the influence of family friends, he received an appointment as cadet, and entered the Military Academy at West Point the following June. In June, 1840, he graduated twelfth in a class of forty-five, and was appointed second lieutenant in the 3d Artillery on the 1st of July. In November of the same year he joined his regiment in Florida, eighteen months before the termination of the first Florida war. A year later (November 6, 1841) he was brevetted first lieutenant "for gallant conduct in the war against the Florida Indians." In January, 1842, the regiment was ordered to the New Orleans barracks, and in June of the same year to Fort Moultrie, Charleston harbor. In both these migrations, Lieutenant Thomas accompanied them. In December, 1843, he was ordered to duty, with company C of his regiment, at Fort McHenry, Md. On the 17th of May, 1843, he was promoted to a first-lieutenancy, and in the spring of 1844, joined company E at Fort Moultrie.

As there were indications of approaching war with Mexico, Lieutenant Thomas was sent with his company to Texas in July, 1845, with orders to report to General Zachary Taylor. They arrived at Corpus Christi the same month, in company with the Third and Fourth regiments of infantry, being the first United States troops that occupied the soil of Texas. Company E and its lieutenant marched with the army of occupation from Corpus Christi to the Rio Grande, and with one company of the First Artillery and six of the Seventh U. S. infantry, was left to garrison Fort Brown, opposite Matamoras; while General Taylor, with the main body of his army, fell back to Point Isabel, to establish a depot of supplies there.

On the 2d of May the Mexicans invested Fort Brown, and the garrison sustained a bombardment until the afternoon of the 8th, when the Mexican troops abandoned the siege, and went to reinforce General Ampudia at Resaca de la Palma, that general having been on that day driven from Palo Alto by General Taylor, while marching to the relief of Fort Brown. On the 9th, General Taylor defeated the Mexicans at Resaca de la Palma, and drove them across the Rio Grande, near the fort, the garrison contributing to this decisive victory by pouring an unintermitting fire of shot and shell into the disordered masses of the retreating enemy, as they rushed in confusion to the river to escape the advancing columns of General Taylor. After the evacuation of Matamoras, Lieutenant Thomas was detached from his company with a section of his battery, and for nearly four months assigned to duty with the advance guard, first at Reynosa, and afterwards at Camargo. In September he rejoined his command, and marched to Monterey, and for his gallant conduct at the battle of Monterey, Sept. 23d, 1846, was brevetted captain. About the 1st of November he took command of Company E as senior lieutenant, retaining it till February 14, 1847. In December, 1846, he was again placed in the advance with Quitman's brigade, and entered Victoria about January 1, 1847. During this month General Scott, having assumed command of the army in the field, ordered General Taylor to select a division, and with it occupy the country he had conquered. General Taylor selected, among other troops, companies C and E of the Third Artillery, and returned to Monterey about the last of January. Soon after, Santa Anna advanced upon him with a force quadruple that of Taylor, and on the 21st of February the bloody but decisive battle of Buena Vista was fought, and resulted in the complete defeat of Santa Anna, and the dispersion of his army. In this battle Lieutenant Thomas greatly distinguished himself, receiving the highest encomiums of his commander, and on the 23d of February he was brevetted major for his gallant and meritorious conduct.

In August, 1848, he recrossed the Rio Grande into Texas, having been among the first to enter and among the last to leave the Mexican territory. In September, 1848, he was placed in charge of a commissary depot at Brazos Santiago, and in December was granted a six months' leave of absence, the first he had had since entering the service. In June, 1849, he rejoined his company at Fort Adams, Newport, R. I., and on the 31st of July was placed in command of company B of the Third Artillery, with which he was ordered in September to proceed to Florida, to put down an Indian outbreak there. He remained on duty in Florida till December, 1850, when he received orders to go to Texas, but on reaching New Orleans found later orders directing him to report for duty at Fort Independence, Boston-harbor. He remained at Fort Independence till March 28th, 1851, when he was relieved by Captain Ord, and assigned to duty at West Point as Instructor of Artillery and Cavalry. He remained at West Point about three years, having in December, 1853, been promoted to a full captaincy.

On leaving West Point, Captain Thomas took command of a battalion of artillery, and sailed for California, *via* Panama. On his arrival at Benicia barracks he was assigned to Fort Yuma, Lower California, and reaching that place July 15th, with two companies of artillery, he relieved Major Heintzelman. The next year Congress authorized an increase of four regiments in the army, two of infantry, and two of cavalry, and Captain Thomas received the appointment of junior major in the Second Cavalry, and, on the 18th of July, 1855, left Fort Yuma to join his regiment at Jefferson Barracks, Missouri. In the following spring the regiment was ordered to Texas, where he was on duty from May 1st, 1856, to November 1st, 1860. During this time he was for three years in command of the regiment, and in August, 1859, headed the escort which accompanied the Texas Reserve Indians to their new home in the Indian Territory. In the autumn of 1859, and the winter, spring, and summer of 1860, he was engaged in an examination of the country on the headwaters of the Canadian and Red rivers, and the Conchas, and collected much valuable geographical information concerning those regions which had previously been entirely unexplored. He had, during his last expedition, a rencounter with a party of predatory Indians, whom he defeated, and recaptured from them all the animals they had stolen from the settlements. In this skirmish he was slightly wounded in the face. In November, 1860, he obtained a short leave of absence, the second in more than twenty years. In April, 1861, he was ordered to Carlisle Barracks, Pennsylvania, to remount the Second Cavalry, which had been dismounted and ordered out of Texas, by the traitor Twiggs. When he arrived, two companies had already been mounted, and sent to Washington; four more were sent forward at once, and the remaining four were assigned to duty under his command, in the department of Pennsylvania. On the 25th of April, Major Thomas was promoted to a lieutenant-colonelcy, and on the 5th of May appointed colonel of the Fifth U. S. Cavalry. In the same month he was assigned to the command of a brigade in General Patterson's army, in Northern Virginia, and afterwards held the same position under General Banks.

On the 17th of August he was appointed a brigadier-general of Volunteers, and on the 26th was relieved from duty with the army of Northern Virginia, and ordered to report to Brigadier-General Robert Anderson, commanding the Department of the Cumberland. On his arrival at Louisville, September 6th, he was at once assigned to the command of Camp Dick Robinson, fifteen miles southeast of Nicholasville, Kentucky, which he reached September 15th, and relieved Lieutenant Nelson, U. S. N. (afterwards Major-General Nelson, U. S. V.). Here were about six thousand troops collected by Nelson, and Thomas soon greatly increased the number, and having organized them, sent four regiments of infantry, a battalion of artillery, and Woolford's cavalry, under command of Brigadier-General Schoepf, to Rockcastle hills, thirty miles southeast, to establish Camp Wildcat, and resist the advance of the rebels, who, under General Zollicoffer, had entered Kentucky through Cumberland Gap. On the 26th of October the battle of Wildcat was fought, and Zollicoffer defeated, and driven back to Cumberland Gap by the Union troops, under the personal command of General Schoepf. Immediately after this battle, General Thomas moved his headquarters to Crab Orchard, and began preparations for an advance into East Tennessee; but General Buell, who commanded the department, being desirous of driving the rebel General A. S. Johnston from Bowling Green, where he had concentrated a large force, ordered General Thomas to move, with all his force, except three regiments, to Lebanon, Kentucky, and put himself in a state of readiness for an active campaign. General Thomas obeyed promptly, and at Lebanon organized the First division of the Army of the Cumberland. His troops had, however, but just arrived there, when intelligence came that Zollicoffer had advanced to Monticello, and was threatening Somerset. He immediately sent General Schoepf a battery of artillery and two regiments of infantry, to prevent him from crossing the Cumberland river, and two days afterwards ordered two more regiments and another battery to reinforce him; but Zollicoffer had meanwhile succeeded in crossing the river, and established himself on the north side, opposite Mill Spring. On the 31st of December he took the field in person, with six regiments of infantry, one of cavalry, a battery of artillery, and four companies of engineers, to march against Zollicoffer, and dislodge him from his position, if he did not come out to meet the Union forces.

The march was a most laborious one, occupying nineteen days, the roads being almost impassable, but General Thomas at last succeeded in reaching Logan's cross-roads, about ten miles north of Mill Spring, though two of the regiments of infantry had fallen behind. He halted at this point for these to come up, on the 18th of January, and at the same time made arrangements to communicate with General Schoepf, at Somerset, and undertake a combined movement upon the enemy's intrenchments. This movement was to be made on the 26th. The rebel commander meantime having been informed that only two regiments had reached Logan's cross-roads with General Thomas, resolved to surprise and overwhelm him before the others could come up. He accordingly moved on the evening of the 18th, reaching Thomas's camp about daylight, and driving in the pickets in some confusion.

General Thomas was not long in forming his troops and advancing upon the enemy. The rebels assaulted with great desperation, but without effect; and the two regiments which were behind having come up, a simultaneous assault was made upon the rebel front, right, and rear, and, after a sharp struggle, they broke and fled, retreating in great disorder towards their intrenchments. They were pursued promptly to the river, and General Thomas gave orders to storm their intrenchments early the next morning; but during the night they fled, abandoning their fortifications, artillery, ammunition wagons, cavalry, horse, and camp equipage, provisions, and small-arms. General Zollicoffer was killed in the battle. Many of the wealthy rebels in Middle Tennessee were so terrified by this defeat that they removed, with their slaves and property, to Alabama and Mississippi, regarding Tennessee as unsafe. General Thomas now concentrated his force at Somerset, and prepared for an expedition into East Tennessee, the possession of which he regarded as of the first importance. He had nearly accumulated the necessary supplies and subsistence for the expedition, when General Buell again recalled him, ordering him to move with all dispatch to Lebanon, and thence to Munfordsville, where he was then concentrating his forces for an attack on Bowling Green. Before the troops could be assembled there, however, the rebels had lost Forts Henry and Donelson, and had abandoned Columbus, Bowling Green, and Nashville, and retreated further south. General Thomas was met on his way to Munfordsville by orders to go on with his division to Louisville, and there take steamers for Nashville. He arrived at Nashville on the 2d of March with his division, in readiness to take the field. General Buell constituted that division the reserve of the Army of the Cumberland,

and it did not reach Pittsburg Landing till after the rebels had retreated to Corinth. On the 25th of April, 1862, Brigadier-General Thomas was appointed and confirmed Major-General of Volunteers, and on the 1st of May his division was transferred, by General Halleck, to the Army of the Tennessee, and he was assigned to the command of the right wing of that army, consisting of five divisions—viz., Brigadier-General T.W. Sherman's, Brigadier-General W. T. Sherman's (subsequently commander of the Army of the Tennessee and of the Military Division of the Mississippi), Brigadier-General S. A. Hurlbut's, Brigadier-General T. J. McKean's, and Brigadier-General Thomas A. Davies' divisions.

On the evacuation of Corinth by the rebels, General Thomas's command was stationed along the Memphis and Charleston railroad from Iuka, Mississippi, to Tuscumbia, Alabama, for its protection. On the 10th of June he was retransferred to the Army of the Ohio, his old associates, and ordered to concentrate his command at Decherd, Tennessee. Leaving his command temporarily in charge of General Schoepf, he went on to McMinnville to take charge of the divisions of Generals Nelson and Hood, then at that place. On the 3d of September, General Buell sent him orders to join him at Murfreesboro. On arriving there, he found that General Buell had moved on to Nashville, whither he followed promptly, and reached that city on the 8th of September, when he was at once put in command of the post, while General Buell pushed on towards Kentucky. On the evening of the 13th General Thomas received orders to follow; and, leaving Negley's and Palmer's divisions as a garrison at Nashville, he moved on the 15th and overtook General Buell on the 19th near Cave City, and was at once made second in command of the whole army. In that rapid race to Louisville and back, which followed, in which Bragg always managed to be a little ahead, General Thomas took his full share of the labor and responsibility. He reached Louisville on the 26th of September. On the 29th the army was divided into three army corps, under Generals McCook, Crittenden, and Gilbert, and General Thomas was still second in command; and when on the 1st of October the army moved from Louisville in pursuit of Bragg, now retreating with his ill-gotten prey from Kentucky, General Thomas took command of the right wing. In the battle of Perryville the left wing was principally engaged,—the right wing, from the position of the two armies, being unable to come into action, except in the way of skirmishing on the part of its cavalry. When General Rosecrans assumed command, the name of the army was again changed to the "Army of the Cumberland;" and on the 5th of November, General Thomas was placed in command of the centre, the 14th army corps, consisting of five divisions,—the 1st, 3d, 8th, 12th, and 13th, under the command of Generals Fry, Rousseau, Negley, Dumont, and Palmer. With his corps he reached Nashville early in November, and on the 26th of December advanced towards Murfreesboro. During the series of battles and skirmishes which preceded the battle of Stone river he was cool, active, and vigilant, cheering on his men by his example, and sharing their dangers. In the battle of Stone river, on the first day, it was his corps that arrested the progress of Bragg's legions, flushed with victory, when, having routed and trampled down McCook's corps and forced back Negley's division of Thomas's, they were held firmly at bay by Palmer's veterans, while General Thomas was aiding the commander in forming a new and impregnable line. Firm as a rock, they stemmed the torrent of advancing rebels at a time when every moment was of infinite value to the success of the day and the retrieval of the disaster. Again and again were Bragg's masses hurled upon them, but, though sadly thinned, their lines were unbroken. It was a portion of Thomas's corps that on the 2d of January punished so effectually the rash attempt of Breckinridge to advance and turn the Union left, and in forty minutes strewed the line of their advance and retreat with two thousand dead and wounded rebels; and when on that dark Saturday night, January 3d, 1863, Bragg's dispirited legions fled from Murfreesboro, it was Thomas's corps which advanced and drove them the next morning towards Manchester. Well did General Rosecrans speak of him in his report as "true and prudent; distinguished in counsel, and on many battle-fields celebrated by his courage."

The two armies for the next five months lay twenty miles apart watching each other, both considerably and about equally reinforced, but neither strong enough for an offensive movement. At length, late in June, General Rosecrans having brought his cavalry up towards his standard of perfection, and accumulated supplies at his secondary base, moved forward, and by a series of brilliant strategic movements, in which General Thomas bore a distinguished and honorable part, dislodged the rebels from Shelbyville, Manchester, Tullahoma, Winchester, and Decherd, and compelled them, by mountain passes and devious routes, to seek refuge and safety in Chattanooga. Then repairing the railroads, and constructing bridges to make the route safe and easy for troops and supplies, he moved forward again to capture Chattanooga by a flank movement. For this purpose, General Rosecrans marched his army in three, or, including his cavalry, in four columns, moving by different routes;—McCook crossing the Tennessee near Stevenson, and passing down the west side of Lookout mountain to Valley Head and Alpine, and thence ascending towards Chattanooga by way of McLemore's cove; Thomas crossing at Bridgeport, and threatening Chattanooga along the railroad; while Crittenden, crossing at and above Bridgeport, and at the same time threatening Chattanooga from the opposite bank of the Tennessee by a detachment of his corps, caused Bragg to evacuate it speedily, and then, leaving a small garrison there, passed over east towards Ringgold, the cavalry meantime making an extensive detour westward, and crossing the river near Athens, Tennessee. The object of these movements had been attained in part, for Bragg had been compelled to abandon Chattanooga, or risk the loss of his communications; but he was receiving large reinforcements, which gave him greatly the preponderance in numbers over the Union army, and having retreated but a short distance southward, he now proposed, by rapid movements, to attack Rosecrans' scattered corps before they could form a junction, and thus win back his stronghold.

Rosecrans was fully aware of his critical situation, and understood that he must fight a desperate battle at heavy odds, for the possession of the prize he had captured. By dint of extraordinary exertion, he succeeded in bringing up McCook's corps from the south, and Crittenden's from the east, to unite with Thomas, who was already in a strong position in McLemore's cove; but McCook's corps were sorely jaded by their long and difficult march, and had had no time to rest. Meanwhile Bragg, though annoyed at the failure of his plan for defeating Rosecrans' army in detail, approached it with great confidence, having a force outnumbering his as three to two. On the first day of the battle, victory inclined to neither side. The attack, in which all of Bragg's army did not participate, was made upon Thomas's corps, and though outnumbered, they stood like a wall; and though, in the course of the day, the other corps were brought into action, yet the heaviest blows had been given and received by Thomas's veterans. It is said that when Longstreet's corps, fresh from Virginia, flung themselves upon Thomas's command, they would call out, "You are not fighting conscripts now!" and as Thomas's men charged back, they would shout in turn, "You are not fighting with Eastern store-clerks!" On the second day (September 20th), Thomas's corps was still in front, supported by one division (Johnson's) of McCook's corps, and one (Palmer's) of Crittenden's, while the remainder of McCook's corps was posted on Thomas's right, and the remainder of Crittenden's placed in reserve, near the point of junction of the two, to support either, as circumstances might require. The battle commenced early, and the rebels came up in solid masses, pressing heavily on Thomas's lines, and seeking for some weak point which they might penetrate. They sought in vain for hours: every attack was repulsed, with heavy loss. The fighting had been continuous from about sunrise till one o'clock, when the misconception of an order of General Rosecrans afforded to the rebels the opportunity they had so long sought of penetrating the Union lines, and they were not slow to avail themselves of it. They advanced rapidly and heavily, and pouring their columns in at the gap, cut off a part of Crittenden's and McCook's corps from Thomas, and forced them back in confusion. Seven brigades were thus lost for the day, by an army already far inferior in numbers to the enemy, and Thomas's command was flanked. General Rosecrans and Generals McCook and Crittenden were with the portion thus cut off, and were unable again to reach that portion of the battle-field where Thomas still held his ground, grim and defiant, against the hosts which sought to swallow him up. Hitherto he had been regarded by the generals commanding the armies in which he had fought, as a brave, trustworthy, prudent officer,—one who would be found in his place, doing his duty, but not as a man of genius or high strategic ability; but, in this time of peril he developed qualities and improvised combinations which would have done honor to any general of modern times. We have said he was flanked by this disastrous break, and the rush of the enemy into the gap; we may add, that General Rosecrans, as well as Generals McCook and Crittenden, believed the day lost, and so telegraphed from Chattanooga. But Thomas had no idea of losing the day. Wheeling his troops within the jaws of Frick's gap, where the mountain-walls, precipitous and bold, prevented another flank movement, he stood like a lion at bay, and with the remnant of that army fought hour after hour. Thrice he was compelled to change his position and shorten his lines, falling somewhat further back into the jaws of the gap, and when at last his men, exhausted by two days of hard fighting, without relief, food, or rest, were compelled to stand up against the whole force of the rebel army, now more than two to their one,—a force hurled upon them with all the rage of wolves disappointed of their prey,—Thomas called up Granger's reserve, held back till then, and the three fresh brigades under the immediate command of General Steedman of Ohio, repulsed them three times in the space of forty minutes with most frightful slaughter, and compelled them to withdraw, leaving the field to Thomas and his unconquered heroes. During the night General Thomas fell back three miles, and took up a stronger position near Rossville, where he formed his troops in line of battle, and remained during the whole of the next day (Monday, September 21st); but no enemy appearing, they marched in the evening to Chattanooga, and entered it in order, and without loss of material beyond that lost on the 20th. General Rosecrans had, on reaching Chattanooga, immediately put the town in a state of defence, had placed the train in safety, and reorganized the retreating troops, so that on Monday morning they were sent to support General Thomas; and Generals McCook and Crittenden had returned to Rossville, and rendered assistance in placing the troops in the new lines of defence there. But without detracting in the least from the merits of General Rosecrans, and his other corps-commanders, who on this occasion were rather the victims of unfavorable circumstances than personally blameworthy, the fact remains, that but for the undaunted courage, and extraordinary military ability of General Thomas on that day, we should have lost our army, lost Chattanooga, and the whole hard-won fruits of the blood and toil of the Army of the Cumberland for the previous year. It was an honorable and deserved encomium which General Rosecrans paid to him in his report, when he said: "To Major-General Thomas, the true soldier, the prudent and undaunted commander, the modest and incorruptible patriot, the thanks and the gratitude of the country are due for his conduct at the battle of Chickamauga."

On the 19th of October, an order was received from the War Department, relieving General Rosecrans from the command of the Army of the Cumberland, and appointing General Thomas his successor. Meantime, a part of the Army of the Ohio, then under the command of General Burnside at Knoxville, Tennessee, had arrived at Chattanooga. Two corps from the army of the Potomac, under command of General Hooker, and the Army of the Tennessee, under General W. T. Sherman, were ordered to Chattanooga; and General Grant was assigned to the command of all these armies, as well as the other forces on the Mississippi, the whole constituting the grand Military Division of the Mississippi. At the same time, with these changes of commanders, General Thomas was appointed a brigadier-general in the regular army, for his gallant conduct at the battle of Chickamauga, his commission dating from October 27th, 1863.

On assuming command of the Army of the Cumberland, General Thomas found that army in a critical condition. The enemy had captured some of their supply trains, and had obtained possession of a portion of the Nashville and Chattanooga railroad,—thus necessitating the transportation of all the supplies for this large army, and the reinforcements which it was receiving, over sixty miles of the worst road in the United States, across the Cumberland mountains and Walden's ridge, a road in which from six to eight miles a day was the greatest distance which the trains could accomplish, and even that distance at a terrible sacrifice of draft animals. The army was placed upon half rations, and the cavalry horses (an arm of the service of the greatest importance in that region) were dying by scores daily for want of forage. Added to this, the rebel force, strengthened by still further reinforcements, was daily growing bolder, and threatened to bombard Chattanooga.

In this emergency General Thomas did all in his power to improve the condition of his command. The defences of Chattanooga were strengthened, excursions made by the cavalry in search of forage; pontoons prepared, guns mounted; and all that could be accomplished before the other armies came up, was done. With the coming of General Grant, and the arrival of the two corps from the Army of the Potomac and the Army of the Tennessee, affairs assumed a more encouraging appearance. By a bold and skilful stroke, the distance which supplies were transported by wagon-train was reduced from sixty miles to ten; Hooker's command seized and held the railroad to Wauhatchie; Sherman was busy with his boats and pontoons near the mouth of North Chickamauga creek; and Grant was arranging in silence and quiet his plans for driving Bragg's forces from the front of Chattanooga. At length the full time had come; Bragg had sent his insolent letter, requiring the removal of non-combatants from Chattanooga, as he was about to shell the city. Hooker's command had by a dexterous movement, supported by General Thomas, driven the enemy from Lookout mountain, and planted the Union flag on the bold brow of that lofty eminence; Sherman had crossed the Tennessee and Chickamauga creek, captured the first works of the enemy at the isolated extremity of Mission ridge, and sent his cavalry eastward to cut the railroad lines; and Thomas's army, hitherto spectators, were in their turn to be called upon for work. On the 24th of November they sallied forth from Chattanooga, and by a bold and rapid dash possessed themselves of the strong works of the enemy on Orchard knob, fronting Chattanooga, and commanding a part of the rebel fortifications on Mission ridge. To this point General Grant advanced the same day with the whole of General Thomas's army, and a part of the Army of the Tennessee, and Howard's corps from the Army of the Potomac. On the 25th, after Sherman had made his persistent attacks on Fort Buckner, and Hooker had moved southward to take Fort Breckinridge in the rear, General Gordon Granger's Fourth corps, of Thomas's army (the consolidated Twentieth and Twenty-first corps, McCook's and Crittenden's), was ordered to assault Fort Bragg, and in obedience to the order, made that wonderful charge up Mission ridge which will live in history as one of the most extraordinary and daring assaults ever attempted. The soldiers of the corps were bound to retrieve their reputation, and to wipe away any disgrace which might attach to them for their retreat at Chickamauga, and nobly they acccomplished their purpose. After the defeat and flight of Bragg, the Army of the Cumberland, increased to 60,000 men, and brought up to the highest state of efficiency by its able commander, remained in the vicinity of Chattanooga, though detachments from it occasionally reconnoitred the enemy's position, and on two or three occasions had some severe fighting. When General Grant was appointed lieutenant-general, and promoted to the command of the armies of the United States, General Sherman was, at his request, placed in command of the grand Military Division of the Mississippi, and General Thomas was thus subordinated to an officer who was not only his junior in years and military experience, but who had, in 1862, been a division commander under him. Many of our generals would have objected to serve under such circumstances, and would have asked to be relieved from their commands; but General Thomas was too pure a patriot and too good a soldier to take offence at General Sherman's promotion over his head. He knew well Sherman's military abilities, had confidence in his plans for the coming campaign, and while doing his duty by his own command, rendered all the service in his power to General Sherman, and obeyed promptly and implicitly his orders.

When, on the 7th of May, 1864, the grand army of General Sherman was put in motion for Atlanta, General Thomas's army constituted the centre; and at some periods of the campaign, when the position required the transference of the Army of the Ohio to the right or left, it acted as both centre and right or left wing. The campaign, though one of extraordinary hardship and endurance, was one of comparatively few battles, the principal being the battle of Buzzard's Roost gap, Resaca, Dallas, Kenesaw mountain, the three battles of the 20th, 22d, and 28th of July, near Atlanta, and the battle near Jonesboro. In all these General Thomas took an active part;—at Buzzard's Roost, making the demonstration in front; at Resaca, pressing upon the enemy's lines and ousting him from his position. In the actions about Dallas, he attacked and drove the enemy from his position at New Hope church. At Kenesaw mountain, besides receiving and repulsing the assault of the enemy at the Kulp house, he led one of the assaulting columns against the impregnable position of the rebels on the mountain. On the 20th of July, his army alone sustained the shock of Hood's furious attack, and, after a severe battle, drove the enemy back to his intrenchments, with very heavy loss. The action of the 22d was confined mainly to the armies of the Tennessee and Ohio, but General Thomas had his army ready to close up and hold all that had been gained. The battle of the 28th was fought by the Army of the Tennessee, and Palmer's corps of the Army of the Cumberland. At Jonesboro, it was Davis's Fourteenth corps of his army that assaulted and drove the enemy southward, capturing almost an entire brigade, while Slocum's (the Twentieth) occupied Atlanta. After the capture of Atlanta, when Hood had succeeded in rallying his beaten and shattered forces, and moved northward to cut General Sherman's lines of communication, General Thomas was dispatched after him to prevent him from accomplishing any considerable mischief. When General Sherman had determined upon his expedition towards Savannah, he placed all the troops he could spare under General Thomas's command, with orders to entice Hood westward, and fight him, if he would fight, in the neighborhood of Nashville. The policy suggested by Sherman was admirably carried out by Thomas. Hood and Beauregard followed the course of the Tennessee river as far as Athens, Tenn., while Breckinridge was sent from Central Georgia north towards Knoxville; and Hood believed he could form a junction of the two forces somewhere near Nashville. As Hood moved north from Athens, Thomas fell back slowly but steadily, at the same time summoning reinforcements from all quarters to concentrate at Nashville. Hood moved forward, reckless as usual, and confident of an easy victory, which should fulfil Jefferson Davis's prediction that within sixty days Tennessee should again be in the possession of the Confederate government.

Meanwhile two divisions of infantry, a part of the Sixteenth corps, under Major-General A. J. Smith, were on their way from Missouri to join General Thomas; and several one-year regiments, and detachments from places of minor importance, were arriving at Nashville; and on the 23d of November, General Gordon Granger, under previous orders, withdrew the garrisons of Athens, Decatur, and Huntsville, Alabama, and sent them by way of Stevenson towards Nashville. Five of these regiments were ordered to Murfreesboro' to strengthen the garrison there under command of the gallant Rousseau. Schofield, with the larger part of General Thomas's available forces, was at Pulaski, Tenn., on the 23d of November; but finding Hood approaching, he, in accordance with General Thomas's orders, evacuated that place and fell back to Columbia, which he reached on the 24th. On that day and the 25th the enemy skirmished with Schofield's troops, but only with dismounted cavalry, until the morning of the 26th, when his infantry came up, and pressed Schofield's lines strongly during that day and the 27th, though without assaulting; and finding that they were bent upon crossing Duck River, which flows a short distance in rear of the town, the Union commander withdrew on the night of the 27th to the north bank of Duck River, and took up a new position, where he could more effectually prevent them from crossing, and thus flanking his position. During the 28th of November he held this position undisturbed. About 2 A.M. on the morning of the 29th, the enemy succeeded in forcing back a part of the Union cavalry, and effecting a crossing at two points, in small numbers. As this was likely to interfere with his line of retreat, General Schofield immediately made arrangements to fall back towards Franklin, disposing his troops in such a way as to cover his trains and keep the roads open. The march was rapid, and there was heavy fighting over the whole route. General Schofield himself remained with his artillery till nearly night on the banks of Duck River, resisting the enemy's crossing, and kept the larger portion of them south of the river till dark. He then pushed forward, past the enemy, attacking them wherever they were in the way, and driving them; and having made a night-march of twenty-five miles with his entire army, he reached

Franklin, and got into position at an early hour on the morning of the 30th of November, posting his men in front of the town, and having the Harpeth River, which here sweeps in a semicircle in rear of the town, covering both flanks, while his trains were being sent off with all due expedition to Nashville. General Thomas had ordered, this very day, Steedman's garrison from Chattanooga to join him at Nashville; and it came up on the 1st of December, losing a few troops by the attack of the enemy's cavalry upon the train.

Had Hood, who pushed his troops to the utmost, attacked Schofield at Franklin as soon as he came up, and before the Union general had had time to form his troops, and to throw up those defences which the army at the West had learned were so invaluable, the effect might have been disastrous; for his force largely outnumbered Schofield's, and they were not hampered by the necessity of protecting their trains. But his men were nearly spent by their rapid march, and he delayed the attack till afternoon. By this time Schofield's position, most admirably chosen, had been rendered nearly impregnable. Soon after noon Hood commenced assaulting the Union lines, and hurled his troops against them again and again with much the same result—a most bloody repulse each time. Once, and only once, did he succeed in making an impression on Schofield's lines. Finding Stanley's corps at one point a little weaker than the rest, he massed his troops against it in overwhelming numbers, forced it back from its first line, and a few of his troops had clambered up the barricades of the second line, when Stanley, calling up a fresh brigade, and springing lion-like into the fight, drove back the rebels with terrible slaughter, and though himself grievously wounded, saved the day. It was ten o'clock at night when

Hood, having finally become satisfied that he could not carry the Union intrenchments, abandoned the mad attempt. His losses had been frightful; Cleburne, the bravest of his major-generals, and Brigadier-Generals Williams, Adams, Gist, Strophel, and Granberry had been slain; Major-General Brown and Brigadiers Carter, Monigel, Quarles, Cockerill, and Scott were wounded; and Brigadier-General Gordon a prisoner—thirteen general officers *hors du combat!* Nor were the losses among his troops less extraordinary: 1,750 were buried upon the field, 3,800 were so severely wounded as to be sent to the hospitals in Franklin, and 702 were prisoners; making an aggregate of 6,252. The Union loss was 189 killed, 1,033 wounded, and 1,104 missing—an aggregate of 2,326.

No sooner was the battle definitely ended than Geneneral Schofield gave the order for marching; and the early morning of the 1st of December saw the wearied and wayworn heroes entering Nashville, after a night-march of eighteen miles.

There had been great interests involved in this race of the two armies of forty-three miles, from Columbia to Nashville. If Hood could have overtaken and passed Schofield, or defeated and routed him, he would have accomplished his purpose of regaining Tennessee; for he would have divided Thomas's army, and could have overwhelmed the position at Nashville, probably, by sheer weight of numbers, and not only Tennessee but Kentucky would have been at his mercy. But General Thomas was as skilful in his selection of officers as General Grant: he knew that he could trust implicitly the energy, daring, rapidity of movement, and skilful strategy of Schofield; that though it might require almost superhuman exertions to accomplish it, Hood would not be suffered to win the race; and hence, through that trying week from Nov. 23 to Dec. 1, he was, though straining every nerve to bring up his forces, calm, cool, and collected; and when Hood, on the 2d of December, appeared before the fortifications of Nashville with his advanced guard, he was already, to all intents and purposes, beaten. Schofield's army, though sorely jaded, were in good condition, requiring only rest for a day or two before another struggle; A. J. Smith's large and finely disciplined divisions had come in by transports on the 30th of November; Steedman, with his division from Chattanooga, had arrived on the 1st of December. The citizens of Nashville capable of bearing arms, and the railroad, quartermaster's, and commissary's employés, forming together a force of nearly ten thousand, had been trained and disciplined under General Donaldson; while Wilson's cavalry, which for want of horses had hitherto been inferior to that of the enemy, was now rapidly being mounted.

General Thomas's forces now somewhat outnumbered Hood's, and he had the strong works in front of Nashville, works perfected during the previous few weeks, and the gunboats, which protected the river, and which would effectually guard his flanks, to protect his troops against assault. Hood had sent Forrest's cavalry to try to cross the Cumberland at various points, and make a raid into Kentucky; but the gunboats so effectually guarded the river, that that rough rider could find no place of passage. Nashville lies in a bend of the Cumberland, much as Franklin does on the Harpeth; and having the gunboats to guard his flanks, General Thomas had only need to stretch his works across the bend, and station his cavalry on the north side to guard the railroad lines. Hood had had a surfeit of prompt assaults, and in this instance, the only one in his career where a sudden assault could have done him any service, he hesitated, skirmished a little, and finally sat down to besiege the city, taking position on a line of hills about four or five miles south of the city. This sealed his fate. General Thomas tempted him in every possible way to attack him—bombarding his lines, making feints of attack, or stirring him up by shells on his flanks from the gunboats. It was all in vain. Hood was evidently of the opinion that he could starve Thomas out or compel him to evacuate the city by merely investing his works on the south front.

At length, finding that Hood could not be coaxed or driven into an attack, General Thomas determined to assume the offensive himself. On the afternoon of the 14th, there being indications of a thaw, he issued his special field orders to his commanders, detailing his plan of battle, and assigning to each his part. The right of his line rested on the Cumberland, covered by gunboats, and consisted of the Sixteenth army corps, Major-General A. J. Smith commanding, on the extreme right. The Fourth army corps (Stanley's), Brigadier-General T. J. Wood temporarily commanding, formed the right centre; the Twenty-third army corps, Major-General Schofield commanding, the left centre; while a provisional organization of white and colored troops, under command of Major-General Steedman, occupied the extreme left, which, like the right, was covered by gunboats. General Steedman had also the command of the interior line, extending along the inner fortifications, and which was manned by the garrison of Nashville and the quartermaster's troops.

His plan of action was to demonstrate boldly on his left (Hood's right), where the enemy was strongest, and thus attract still more of Hood's troops to that wing, while his actual attack would be made by massing his troops on Hood's left, which was his weakest point, and thus, with the aid of the gunboats, push and roll back his left wing upon the centre, and having got well in upon his flank and rear, crush his centre also, for his first day's work. For the second day, he proposed to hurl his forces upon his right till that should be overpowered and give way, when he would envelop his army, and either capture it entire, or so bruise and crush it that Hood should be glad to make his escape from Tennessee on any conditions.

This programme was carried out almost without variation. In accordance with General Thomas's orders, General Steedman, before dawn, deployed on the left a heavy line of skirmishers, consisting principally of colored troops; and soon after daylight he pushed his line up to and across the Murfreesboro' turnpike. After a stout but brief resistance the enemy's pickets fell back, and Steedman pursued until he came face to face to a battery planted on the further side of a deep rocky cut of the Chattanooga Railroad, which was too long for his line to flank, and impossible for it to cross. Here they met with considerable loss, as they could not charge the battery; but their attack had been so eager and vehement that it had accomplished its purpose, Hood believing that the Union army was there in force, and drawing from his already enfeebled left, troops to strengthen still further his right. This proved a costly and grievous mistake for him; for, a few minutes later, A. J. Smith's corps, followed by Wood's, and supported and covered by the cavalry, swept like an avalanche upon the enemy's left, rolling it up, storming its batteries, and flanking his positions, and compelling him to fall back upon his centre.

Desiring to gain still further on Hood's flank, General Thomas sent Schofield, who had thus far been chafing in reserve, around Smith's right, to still further outflank the enemy, and gain, if possible, the rear of the new and strong position to which he had fallen back. The fighting for this purpose was stubborn, and it was not till near nightfall, when the Fourth corps, under General Wood, charged and carried Hood's most advanced position, that the task of the day seemed likely to be accomplished. Sixteen pieces of artillery and about 1,200 prisoners, besides large quantities of small-arms and about 40 wagons, were the fruits of this day's fighting. As General Thomas left the position he had occupied during most of the day, he said to an officer of his staff, "So far, I think, we have succeeded pretty well. Unless Hood decamps to-night, to-morrow Steedman will double up his right, Wood will hold his centre, and Smith and Schofield again strike his left, while the cavalry work away at his rear."

Hood, finding his fortifications, on which he had bestowed so much labor, no longer tenable, abandoned them during the night; and shortening his lines, planted himself squarely across the Granny White and Franklin turnpikes, to cover his trains, which he had already commenced hurrying to the rear. His new position, which, with a view to the emergency, he had selected and fortified several days before, was a very strong one, his front line being scarcely three miles in length, occupying the wooded crests of closely connecting hills; and the two keys to his position, the Granny White and Franklin pikes, were strongly fortified. Here, then, he stood, ready to deliver the final battle, which was to decide whether he should retain his foothold in Tennessee, or whether, with his troops routed and demoralized, he must make a rapid flight towards the Tennessee River in mid-winter, with Thomas's victorious legions at his heels, taking prisoners and supplies at every swoop, and utterly ruining the proud army which had advanced so boldly into the very heart of the Union territory.

At dawn the Union troops were in motion ; over, into, and through Hood's abandoned lines, and on towards his new position, till his heavy curtain of skirmishers and the booming of his artillery checked for a few moments the ardor of their advance. Thomas had sent a heavy force of his cavalry, by a considerable *detour*, to strike Hood's rear, and commenced again demonstrating on the enemy's right with Steedman's and Wood's corps, shelling the batteries on the Overton Hills and the rebel lines on Overton Knob, simply with the intent of holding Hood in position there. Smith and Schofield, with Croxtin's and Hatch's cavalry brigades, were held back, skirmishing and feeling the enemy's position at all points on the right, but not allowed to go into action, though their troops were like hounds straining at the leash. It was near four o'clock P.M., and as yet nothing had been done. At length Thomas heard the welcome sound of the prolonged fire of rifles, and the rapid reverberation of the Spencer carbine, sweeping round the rebel flank and creeping up along Hood's rear, telling that Wilson's cavalry were at their work, and instantly gave the order to Smith and Schofield to advance ; but they had heard and interpreted it as soon as he, and before his order could reach them both had given the word for an assault ; and with bayonets levelled and cheers that made the rebels shake in their shoes, both corps swept forward, up to, over and around the rebel works ; while Wood and Steedman, catching up the inspiration, rushed gallantly at the works in their front ; and after a short but intensely fierce engagement the entire line carried all before it. The rebel resistance, while it lasted, was as desperate as in any battle of the war; but in thirty minutes it was all over—the day was lost, and they, panic-stricken, were hurrying pell-mell down the Granny White and Franklin turnpikes, throwing every thing aside in their mad haste to get away. Muskets, blankets, knapsacks, every thing was abandoned, if they might but escape from the grasp of the Yankee troops, which seemed to surround them everywhere.

The pursuit was continued relentlessly for a fortnight, and though Hood succeeded in forming a strong rear-guard of about 4000 infantry and all his available cavalry under command of General Forrest, this was the only organized portion of his troops, the remainder being a mere demoralized mob, who, shoeless, hungry, and hard-bestead, pushed on in despair through the deep mud towards the further banks of the Tennessee.

The killed and wounded numbered not less than 10,000 during the two days; and 13,189 prisoners, besides 2,207 rebel deserters, were captured there or picked up in the pursuit. Eighty cannon, with gun-carriages and caissons, 3,079 small-arms, and numerous battle-flags, were among the trophies of this great victory. The Union loss, in killed, wounded, and prisoners, was less than 10,000.

On the 8th of December, Forrest, who had been demonstrating against the Union force at Murfreesboro' for several days, was attacked by General Milroy at General Rousseau's order, and defeated and routed; while Breckinridge, who had led about 6,000 troops into East Tennessee, was completely routed and driven from the region by General Stoneman.

Hood having finally succeeded in reaching Alabama

with his shattered remnant of an army, General Thomas was about to send his troops into winter-quarters; but General Grant disapproving, he exerted himself to the utmost in filling up his ranks, and organizing the finest cavalry force ever called into the field on this continent. Schofield was presently sent to Wilmington, and after the capture of that important point joined Sherman at Goldsboro'. Wilson, with a cavalry force of about 15,000, swept through Selma, Montgomery, West Point, Columbus, and Macon; and a detachment of his cavalry hunted most perseveringly, and finally captured, Jefferson Davis, the rebel chief. Gordon Granger, who had been with his Thirteenth corps at Stevenson and its vicinity during the Nashville battle, was sent to Mobile, to aid in its reduction; and A. J. Smith's corps followed it; and the two, with the aid of a division of colored troops, under General Steele, and the naval squadron under command of Admiral Thatcher, succeeded in the capture of that rebel stronghold. Stoneman, with a fine cavalry force, moving eastward from Knoxville on the 14th of March, captured the rebel ports in Southwestern Virginia, threatened Lynchburg, and on the 12th of April entered Salisbury, N. C.; and seizing there an immense quantity of rebel stores and supplies, effectually blocked all further progress on the part of Johnston.

The gallantry of General Thomas at Nashville, and the efficiency of his pursuit, won for him the rank of major-general in the regular army, in January, 1865. On the reduction and reorganization of the army at the close of the war, he was appointed, by general order of June 27, 1865, commander of the military division of the Tennessee, embracing the four departments of Tennessee, Kentucky, Georgia, and Alabama, commanded severally by Generals Stoneman, Palmer, Steedman, and C. R. Wood.

General Thomas, being from a State in rebellion, has had no political influence at his back to advocate his claims to advancement or to extol his victories in Congress, and he is of too modest and retiring a disposition ever to push them himself. Hence he has not received in the past the honor to which his great merit entitled him; but he has been content to work his way upward, and let his countrymen judge of what he had been able to do for his country; and in the end, modest merit has triumphed.

In person, General Thomas is tall, standing about six feet two in his stockings, and finely proportioned. His complexion is fair, though now bronzed by exposure, his hair brown, his beard sandy, his eye blue and keen, his countenance so frank, open, and winning, that it attracts at once. He is thought personally to resemble Washington, with whom he has also many traits of character in common. He is greatly beloved by his soldiers, who speak of him as "Pap" Thomas, and feel the sort of confidence in his knowledge, his military skill, and his goodness which a young child feels for its father. It would be very hard to persuade those who have served under him, from Mill Spring onward, that any other general in the army was quite equal to "Pap" Thomas.

If a blameless life, pure and noble aspirations, remarkable modesty, an amiable and even temper, great patience and perseverance, and untiring energy and persistency, with a calm, clear head, close observation, and a thorough mastery of his profession, are the qualities to make a good general, then George H. Thomas is entitled to rank among the great and good generals of our time.

IV.

Major-General Philip Henry Sheridan.

General Sheridan is by nearly ten years the youngest officer among our "Great Captains," having been born in 1831. The exact place of his birth is involved in some uncertainty, the army registers crediting Massachusetts with being the birth State of the hero; while his friends generally concur in stating that he was born in Perry county, Ohio. His parents certainly resided in that county when he was but little beyond infancy.

The influence of his friends was sufficient to secure young Sheridan an appointment as cadet at West Point, from the congressional district to which he belonged, and in 1848, having passed with honor the preliminary examination, he was admitted into the Military Academy; and though at first he was not remarkable for proficiency, and remained a second year in the fourth class, he improved rapidly in scholarship as he went on, and exhibited superior excellence in the more active duties of the course. He graduated in 1853 with honor, having as classmates the lamented McPherson, Major-General Schofield, Generals Terrill, Sill, and Tyler, and the rebel General Hood. On his graduation, he entered the army as brevet second-lieutenant of infantry, and was attached to the first regiment U. S. A. He was at once ordered to join his regiment, then serving in Texas, and early in the autumn took his position in his company at Fort Duncan. Here he was employed constantly in service against the Apaches and Camanches, the robber Indian tribes of the Southwest. On one occasion, he and two of the soldiers belonging to the fort were attacked a short distance from it by a band of Apaches, when Sheridan, springing instantly upon the bare back of the fiery Mustang from which the Indian chief had just dismounted, galloped to the fort, called the soldiers to arms, and seizing his pistols without dismounting, rode back to the rescue of the two men he had left behind, and who, armed with rifles, were still fighting. Riding up to the Apache chief, he instantly shot him dead ; and then, his comrades having come up, rode down and killed most of the other savages. For this brilliant affair he was entitled to distinction, but the commanding officer (since a rebel general) was prejudiced against him for his Northern birth, and declared him guilty of a breach of discipline in being away from his command.

This petty persecution was followed by others, till Lieutenant Sheridan felt himself compelled to seek a transfer to some other department. This was accomplished in the spring of 1855, by his assignment to a full second-lieutenancy in the Fourth infantry regiment, then serving in Oregon. He returned to New York, in order to sail thence to the Pacific coast; and while waiting for the recruits who were to go out with him, was for two months in command of Fort Wood, in New York harbor. In July, 1855, he sailed for San Francisco; and on arriving there, was at once selected to command the escort which accompanied the expedition for surveying the route for the proposed branch of the Pacific railroad to connect San Francisco with the Columbia river. This accomplished, he was sent on expeditions into the Yakima Indian country, to put down the threatened warlike demonstrations of that tribe. He succeeded in gaining the esteem and confidence of the Indians, and exerted his influence successfully in keeping them on friendly terms with the whites. He was subsequently selected to adjust difficulties with other tribes of Indians, and accomplished his mission so admirably as to receive high commendation from the lieutenant-general. He continued in these important duties, building posts among the Indian tribes, and greatly beloved by them, till 1861; when, on the resignation of several Southern officers in order to join the Southern rebellion, Lieutenant Sheridan was advanced to the rank of first-lieutenant, and ordered to return to the East. On the increase of the regular infantry of the United States army, he was promoted to the rank of captain in the regular army, with a commission dating from May 14, 1861, and assigned to the Thirteenth regiment of infantry.

In September, 1861, Captain Sheridan was ordered to join his regiment at Jefferson barracks, near St. Louis, Mo., and appointed to audit the claims arising from the operations of the army during the campaign in Missouri; and this accomplished, he was appointed chief quartermaster and commissary of the army then organizing for operations in Southwestern Missouri. This proved a laborious duty, but with his indomitable energy he succeeded in accomplishing it; and in March, 1862, he was appointed chief quartermaster of the Western Department, General Halleck's entire command of sixteen divisions, with the rank of major. His service in this position was short, for the necessity for good cavalry commanders was such, that his superior officers were compelled to consent to his service in the field in that capacity; and on the 27th of May he was commissioned colonel of the 2d regiment of Michigan Volunteer Cavalry, and immediately ordered to the duty of joining in the expedition to cut the railroads south of Corinth, to prevent the escape of the rebels southward on the evacuation of Corinth. The expedition proved successful, though exposed to some perils, from which they were relieved by the adroit management of Colonel Sheridan. Immediately on their return they were sent out again to pursue the rebels, who, at this time, were retreating from Corinth, and in the pursuit Colonel Sheridan's regiment encountered the rebel left wing, and resisted and repelled the attack of two regiments of infantry, two of cavalry, and a battery of artillery, capturing and bringing off the guns of Powell's rebel battery.

On the 6th of June, Colonel Sheridan led a cavalry reconnoissance below Boonesville; and at Donaldson's cross-roads met and signally defeated a force of rebel cavalry, under the notorious Forrest. On the 8th of June, in command of two cavalry regiments (his own and the 2d Iowa), he started in pursuit of the enemy, drove them through the town of Baldwin, which he captured, and to Guntown, where he engaged a force much larger than his own, but with success, and before the close of the engagement received orders to fall back to Boonesville, from whence he accompanied the main army back to Corinth.

On the 11th of June, 1862, he was put in command of a cavalry brigade, and on the 26th, ordered to take up a position at Boonesville, twenty miles in advance of the main army, and cover the front of the army, at the same time watching the operations of the rebels whom he confronted.

While at this place, on the 1st of July, 1862, he was attacked by a rebel force of nine regiments, comprising nearly 6,000 men, under command of General Chalmers. After skirmishing for some time he fell back towards his camp, which was situated on the edge of a swamp, an advantageous position, where he could not readily be flanked, and could hold the enemy at bay for some time. Finding that the enemy, with their greatly superior numbers, were likely to surround him, he had recourse to strategy. Selecting ninety of his best men, armed with revolving carbines and sabres, he sent them around to the rear of the enemy by a *detour* of about four miles, with orders to attack promptly and vigorously at a certain time, while he would make a simultaneous charge in front. The plan proved a complete success. The ninety men appeared suddenly in the enemy's rear, not having been seen till they were near enough to fire their carbines, and, having emptied these, they rushed with drawn sabres upon the enemy, who, supposing them to be the advance guard of a large force, were thrown into disorder; and, before they had time to recover, Sheridan charged them in front with such fury that they fled from the field in complete disorder, utterly routed. Sheridan pursued, and they continued their flight, utterly panic-stricken, to Knight's mills, twenty miles south from Boonesville, throwing away their arms, knapsacks, coats, and every thing which could impede their flight.

General Grant reported this brilliant affair to the War Department, with a recommendation that Colonel Sheridan should be promoted. This recommendation was granted, and his commission of brigadier-general bore date July 1, 1862.

At this time the rebels in his front had but one stream (Twenty Mile creek) from which to water their live-stock, and from his post at Boonesville General Sheridan frequently made sudden dashes in that direction, and captured large quantities of their stock, often two or three hundred at a time. In August, 1862, he was attacked by a rebel cavalry force under Colonel Faulkner, near Rienzi, Mississippi, but after a sharp engagement the rebels were defeated and retreated in haste, Sheridan pursuing them to near Ripley, and, charging upon them before they could reach their main column, dispersed the whole force, and captured a large number of prisoners. Early in September, 1862, General Grant having ascertained that the rebel General Bragg was moving towards Kentucky, detached a portion of his own forces to reinforce the Army of the Ohio, then under command of General Buell. Among these were General Sheridan, and his old command, the Second Michigan Cavalry. As General Grant expected, General Buell gave Sheridan a larger command, assigning him to the charge of the third division of the Army of the Ohio. He assumed command of this division on the 20th of September, 1862. At this time General Bragg was approaching Louisville, which was not in a good condition for defence, and General Sheridan was charged with the duty of defending it. In a single night, with the division under his command, he constructed a strong line of rifle-pits from the railroad depot to the vicinity of Portland, and thus secured the city against the danger of surprise. On the 25th of September, General Buell arrived at Louisville, and soon commenced a reorganization of the Army of the Ohio, now largely reinforced. In this reorganization, General Sheridan was placed in command of the eleventh division, and entered upon his duties on the 1st of October.

Buell soon took the offensive again, and began pushing the rebels, who had already commenced a retreat, but were embarrassed by the amount of plunder they had collected. On the 8th of October, the rebels made a stand near Perryville, Ky., for the double purpose of checking the pursuit and allowing their trains to move forward out of harm's way. The battle which followed, though a severe one, was not decisive, owing to some defects in the handling of the forces, and Bragg was allowed to make good his retreat with most of his plunder and with but moderate loss: but in it Sheridan played a distinguished part, holding the key of the Union position, and resisting the onsets of the enemy again and again, with great bravery and skill, driving them at last from the open ground in front by a bayonet charge. This accomplished, he saw that they were gaining advantage on the left of the Union line, and moving forward his artillery, directed so terrible a fire upon the rebel advance that he drove them from the open ground on which they had taken position. Enraged at being thus foiled, they charged with great fury upon his lines, determined to carry the point at all hazards; but, with the utmost coolness, he opened upon them at short range with such a murderous fire of grape and canister, that they fell back in great disorder, leaving their dead and wounded in winrows in front of the batteries. The loss in Sheridan's division in killed and wounded was over four hundred, but his generalship had saved the Union army from defeat. On the 30th of October, General Rosecrans succeeded General Buell as commander of the Army of the Ohio, which, with enlarged territory, was thenceforward to be known as the Army of the Cumberland, and in the reorganization General Sheridan was assigned to the command of one of the divisions of McCook's corps, which constituted the right wing of that army. He remained for the next seven or eight weeks in the vicinity of Nashville, and then moved with his corps, on the 26th of December, 1862, towards Murfreesboro. During the 26th, his division met the enemy on the Nolensville road, and skirmished with them to Nolensville and Knob gap, occupying at night the latter important position. The next morning a dense fog obscured the horizon; but as soon as it lifted, Sheridan pressed forward and drove the enemy from the village of Triune, which he occupied.

The next three days were spent in skirmishing, and in gradually drawing nearer, over the almost impassable roads, to Murfreesboro, the goal of their hopes. At length, on the night of the 30th of December, the army was drawn up in battle array on the banks of Stone river; and to the right wing was assigned the duty of repelling the first onset of the enemy, and holding it at bay, while the left wing should swing round upon Murfreesboro. Sheridan's position was on the extreme left of the right wing, joining the centre. To his right were Davis's and Johnson's divisions; on his left, Negley, in command of one of Thomas's divisions. The record of that fearful battle, the next day, belongs, properly, to history. The enemy, at dawn, falling *en masse* upon the extreme end (Johnson's division) of the right wing, rolled it up, and drove back in utter discomfiture brigade after brigade, till Johnson's and Davis's divisions were crumbled in pieces, and the victorious rebel column swept down in irresistible force upon Sheridan's command, hoping to roll that back also, but were met with a resolution and determination which checked for the time their further progress. His support on the right (Davis's division) being gone, Sheridan wheeled in the face of the foe, and changed front, so as to avoid being flanked on the right. On came the enemy, only to be beaten back; but relying on their great superiority of numbers, they returned to the charge four times; and at length the rebels, having crushed Negley's division on his left, and in spite of another change of front threatening to outflank and surround him, and slain two of his brigade commanders, and nearly every colonel in the division, he found himself compelled to fall back, but did so in perfect order. This tenacity in holding his position against such overwhelming odds aided materially in enabling General Rosecrans to retrieve the disaster of the day, and on the subsequent days turn this defeat into a glorious victory. Falling back in good order, they did not disturb the lines of Rousseau's division, but united with and strengthened it to hold the rebels finally in check, while General Rosecrans formed a new and impregnable line. During the subsequent days, though holding an important position, Sheridan's division were not seriously engaged.

General Rosecrans, in his report of this battle, pays the following high compliment to Sheridan's generalship: "Sheridan, after sustaining *four successive attacks*, gradually swung his right round southeasterly to a northwestern direction, *repulsing the enemy four times*, losing the gallant General Sill of his right, and Colonel Roberts of his left brigade; when, having exhausted his ammunition, Negley's division being in the same predicament and heavily pressed, after desperate fighting they fell back from the position held at the commencement, through the cedar woods, in which Rousseau's division, with a portion of Negley's and Sheridan's, met the advancing enemy and checked his movements."

For his gallantry in this battle, General Rosecrans suggested, and the President recommended Sheridan's promotion to the rank of major-general, his commission to date from December 31st, 1862. He was at once confirmed by the Senate.

In March, 1863, General Sheridan commanded a scouting expedition, in which he fully reconnoitred the enemy's position, took a considerable number of prisoners, and defeated several bodies of rebel troops which were sent out to meet him, and returned with a loss of only five killed and five wounded. For some months he was engaged in bringing his men into the highest state of drill and discipline, while awaiting a forward movement.

The advance, so long expected, took place on the 23d of June, 1863, and to Sheridan's division was assigned the duty of driving the rebels out of Liberty Gap, a strong mountain pass which was one of the keys to the rebel position. He was successful in this enterprise and soon occupied Shelbyville, which had been evacuated by the enemy as untenable after the capture of the gap. He did not remain long here, however, but pushed forward to Winchester, Tennessee, which, by a flank movement, he had compelled the enemy to abandon. The subsequent movements of the Army of the Cumberland in approaching Chattanooga were slow, in consequence of the necessity of repairing the railroad and bringing forward supplies, and there were no incidents of importance till about the beginning of September, when the Army of the Cumberland crossed the Tennessee at different points,—Sheridan's division moving to Bridgeport, and crossing on a pontoon bridge, and thence passing by way of Trenton to Winston gap of Lookout mountain, thus flanking the rebel position at Chattanooga, and compelling them to evacuate that position. Though General Rosecrans had put a small garrison into Chattanooga, he well knew that he could only hold it by fighting Bragg's army, which had retreated towards Lafayette; and General Sheridan, who had been ordered to make a reconnoissance, ascertained, on the 12th of September, that the rebels had been largely reinforced, the paroled prisoners of Vicksburg, one corps from Lee's army, and considerable bodies of troops from Charleston and Mobile having joined them. These additions made their force materially larger than that of General Rosecrans, which also, owing to the topographical difficulties encountered, was scattered. By great efforts, however, he succeeded in concentrating them, and on the 19th and 20th of September was fought the battle of Chickamauga—a battle attended with great loss of life and manifold disasters, but which, after all, left in the hands of the Union army the substantial fruits of victory, inasmuch as they held Chattanooga, the prize for which both armies were contending. In this great battle, General Sheridan bore an honorable part. On the first day, his division, moving up promptly at the word of command, saved Wood's division from disaster, and retrieved the fortunes of the day. On the 20th, as at Stone river, the breaking of Brannan's and Wood's divisions imperilled Sheridan's, and though a part of it charged gallantly against the on-coming foe, it was at last flanked and compelled to fall back by the enemy; but owing to the thorough discipline enforced by its commander it rallied in good order in Dry valley, and taking a circuitous route came up by the Lafayette road in season to support General Thomas effectively in the long and desperate struggle of the afternoon and evening. It has always been a noticeable feature of General Sheridan's military character, that he possessed in an extraordinary degree the power of rallying, reforming, and leading on his men to victory when they were broken and discomfited. We shall see other instances of this in his history.

A change of commanders followed soon after. General Thomas succeeded General Rosecrans; the two corps commanded by Generals McCook and Crittenden were consolidated into one, under the command of General Gordon Granger; and two corps of the Army of the Potomac, under General Hooker, and the army of the Tennessee, under General Sherman, were added to the force at Chattanooga, and the whole force placed under the command of General Grant. General Sheridan commanded an enlarged division in General Granger's corps.

Meantime Bragg still threatened the Union forces in Chattanooga, and at last sent a message that he was about to bombard the city. General Grant, who had been watching all his manœuvres as keenly as a tiger watches its prey, ascertained that he had sent Longstreet with 20,000 men to reconquer East Tennessee, and at once sprang upon him;—sending Hooker's force to drive him from Lookout mountain, throwing forward Thomas's army to seize Orchard knob and the forts in front of Chattanooga, moving Sherman across the Tennessee to carry his position at the termination of Mission ridge, and assault persistently and determinedly the strong fort and rifle-pits on Tunnel hill (a cavalry expedition meantime cutting the East Tennessee railroad), and, when Sherman had drawn by his repeated assaults the greater part of Bragg's forces to Fort Buckner, hurling Gordon Granger's corps upon Fort Bragg, the strongest and most formidable of the defences of Mission ridge. Each body of troops did its work splendidly; but of all the movements in this grand combination, that of Granger's corps against Mission ridge was the most brilliant and heart-stirring. Between three and four o'clock P. M., at the signal, the firing of six guns, that magnificent corps, almost wholly composed of veterans, sprang at once to arms, and in five minutes were on their way across the plain swept by the fire of fifty cannon and five thousand muskets,—not a man flinching, not a straggler falling back from the firm lines that moved with the precision of machinery towards the mountain. With a shout they enter and clear the first rifle-pits, flinging the captured rebels back into the storm of iron and leaden hail through which they have just passed. With another shout they commence the ascent of the mountain, a difficult task even without opposition,—tenfold more difficult now, when the air is filled with missiles which rain pitilessly upon them: up, up to the second rifle-pits, which they clear with a bound, tumbling their occupants down the steep mountain-side; and up, up again, though the ascent is almost perpendicular, till almost breathless they reach the summit, and bounding upon it, realize from the swift retreat of the foe that the field is won.

In this grand assault, General Sheridan and his division were nobly conspicuous. He had felt keenly the breaking of his division at Chickamauga, though it was so nobly atoned for in their subsequent support of General Thomas, and riding in the advance, he called in thunder tones to his division, "Show the Fourth corps that the men of the old Twentieth are still alive and can fight. Remember Chickamauga." Ever in the front, and always coolest in the moment of the greatest peril, he took a flask from one of his aids, filled the pewter cup, and raising his cap to the rebel battery, drank it off with a "how are you?" never checking for a moment the speed of his advance. The rebels most ungenerously responded by firing the six guns of one of their batteries at the daring rider, and showering him with earth, but doing no other damage. Cheering his men forward to the charge, he now put spurs to his noble steed, and ere many minutes passed was on the summit, dashing after the rebels. For a few minutes there was sharp fighting, and General Sheridan's horse was killed under him, and he leaped at once upon a rebel cannon; but as he could not keep up with his men on this, he soon found another horse, and pushed on down the eastern slope of Mission ridge, after the now fast-flying enemy, pushing them as far as Mission mills, where, the next day, other troops took up the pursuit. Two days later, he was on his way with his division, under General Sherman's command, to raise the siege of Knoxville, and this accomplished, returned to Chattanooga. In February, he was again sent into East Tennessee, in command of two divisions of troops, to drive the rebels out of East Tennessee, which he accomplished, though not without great exposure and suffering.

In March, 1864, General Grant having been promoted to the rank of lieutenant-general, and appointed to the command of all the armies of the United States, summoned the principal generals in the Western departments to a special conference at Nashville. General Sheridan, among others, was present at this conference, and at its conclusion was ordered to report at Washington. At the beginning of April he was appointed to the command of the cavalry corps of the Army of the Potomac, relieving General Pleasonton, who was ordered to report to General Rosecrans for duty in Missouri.

His corps thoroughly organized, and each of its three divisions placed under the command of daring and capable generals, General Sheridan reported himself ready for duty; and when the first movement commenced on the 4th of May, 1864, the cavalry corps was actively engaged in protecting the flanks of the Army of the Potomac, and reconnoitring the position and movements of the enemy. In the performance of this duty they encountered the rebel force in considerable numbers; and actions of some importance occurred at Craig's church, at Parker's store, and at Todd's tavern. The cavalry were also held responsible for the safety of the army trains and the ambulances containing the sick and wounded, for the first four or five days of the campaign. On the 9th of May they were relieved from this duty; and General Meade directed him to select the best mounted troops of his command and start off on an expedition to the rear of Lee's army, and cut off his communications and supplies, allowing him full discretion as to the best plan of effecting the object of the expedition. General Sheridan at once made preparation for this important movement, selecting the staff-officers who were to accompany him, ordering the issuing of three days' rations to his men, and leaving behind every thing in the way of a train except the ammunition-wagons and two ambulances. The baggage actually indispensable was carried on pack-mules. Thus freed from incumbrances, he moved, on the same day on which General Meade's order was given, towards Fredericksburg; but before reaching that city turned off towards Childsburg, and after a short rest moved thence to Beaver Dam station, on the Virginia Central road, crossing the North Anna river at the fords. At Beaver dam they found a rebel provost-guard, with more than three hundred Union prisoners, who had been captured the day before at Spottsylvania; these they promptly released, taking the rebel guard prisoners. Thence moving towards Richmond, a detachment was sent to Ashland station, on the Fredericksburg road, where they destroyed rail road-track, trains, station-houses, and other rebel government property, and then after a sharp fight rejoined the main column. On the 11th of May, Sheridan's command had reached a point within six miles of Richmond. Here they encountered the rebel cavalry under the command of Lieutenant-General J. E. B. Stuart in person; and a severe battle took place, in which General Stuart was killed, and some rebel guns captured. The next morning, before daybreak, a detachment was sent towards Richmond to reconnoitre, and penetrated to the second line of the defences of that city, within less than two miles of the capital, and having captured a rebel courier, withdrew. Early in the morning of May 12, Sheridan's advance approached Meadow bridge on the Chickahominy, where they again encountered the enemy, who had destroyed the bridge and constructed defences commanding the railroad bridge, over which the Union troops must cross. Nothing daunted, Sheridan's gallant troopers dashed across; and though compelled to traverse about half a mile of swampy ground, rushed on the rebel works, and carried them after a most determined resistance.

Meantime, another rebel force had come up in his rear and surrounded his command. Cool and calm as the Union commander habitually was in the most trying circumstances, here was a position to task his finest energies in generalship. To attempt to retreat would inevitably be fatal; to go forward was to encounter a rebel force greatly outnumbering his own, and to cross a difficult river (the Chickahominy) under their concentrated fire. His decision was quickly made. It was, to reconstruct the Meadow bridge over the Chickahominy, and cross it with his force and train. This he accomplished, though under fire all the time, keeping the rebels at bay with his artillery the while, and repelling their charges by fierce counter-charges. Once or twice his men were slowly pressed back, but he encouraged them, and, fighting under his eye, they soon regained their position. At length the bridge was completed, and his ammunition train was to be taken across it; and, if the rebel fire continued, it could scarcely escape destruction from explosion, a destruction which would imperil his force and render their capture or death inevitable. But not for a single moment did his self-possession forsake him. When the train was ready for advancing, he ordered up an ammunition-wagon, supplied his men who had fallen back with fresh cartridges, and, placing himself at their head, said: "Boys, you see those fellows yonder? They are green recruits just from Richmond. There's not a veteran among them. You have fought them well to-day, but we have got to whip them. We can do it, and we will!" The men responded with a rousing cheer, and with the order, "Forward!—Charge!" in his clear ringing tones, he led them on in a charge which sent the rebels flying back to their works; and his artillery opened upon them, adding greatly to their terror. Under cover of this charge the train crossed in perfect safety. Pressing hard upon the now beaten and demoralized foe, amid a most terrific thunder-storm, in which it was difficult to distinguish between the artillery of heaven and the thunder of his guns, he drove them back to Mechanicsville, and finally to Cold Harbor, capturing a considerable number, and encamped with his wearied command near Gaines' Mills. The next day he moved on to Bottom's bridge, and the day following to General Butler's headquarters, not being molested in any of his movements. He then opened communication with Yorktown, and thence with Washing ton. Other expeditions may have resulted in a larger destruction of property, the capture of more prisoners, or the traversing a larger region of territory, but none during the war has carried greater terror into the hearts of the enemy, or more gallantly extricated itself from a position of extraordinary difficulty.

The next few days were spent in co-operation with the great army, now on its way towards the Chickahominy. General Sheridan's headquarters were at the White House, on the Pamunkey; but he was for the most part at the front, directing the movements of the cavalry protecting both wings of Grant's army, and several times engaged in sharp conflicts with the rebel cavalry, now under the command of Fitzhugh Lee. On the 31st of May he took possession of Cold Harbor, his troops having orders to hold it until relieved by the infantry. This was done, though with considerable loss, for more than twenty-four hours, when the infantry force came up; and General Sheridan then moved forward and guarded the flank of Grant's army in its movement to and across the James. This accomplished, he set out on the 8th of June for a second cavalry expedition into the heart of the rebel country. This time his object was to penetrate northward and westward of Lee's lines, and cut the Virginia Central railroad at some point which should effectually prevent the movement of supplies or troops from the Virginia and Tennessee railroad towards Richmond. Gordonsville and Charlottesville were the objective points at which he aimed; and had his movements been properly sustained by those of General Hunter, he would have succeeded to the utmost of his hopes. As it was, however, he accomplished very much in the way of embarrassing the enemy. Crossing the Pamunkey, he moved at once to Aylett's station; thence the next day to the Fredericksburg railroad at Chesterfield station, where he seriously damaged the railroad; thence to Childsburg, Newmarket, and Mount Pleasant, and crossed E. N. E. creek at Young's bridge. On the morning of the 10th of June he moved forward again; and having crossed both branches of the North Anna river, encamped at Buck Childs, a small village three miles north of Trevilian station, on the Virginia Central railroad. It had been his intention to destroy the railroad from this point west for some distance, and then, marching through Everittsville, to cut the railroad extensively between Gordonsville and Charlottesville, and march at once upon Charlottesville. On arriving at Buck Childs, however, he found the rebel cavalry in his front, and immediately prepared to give them battle. Recalling his old tactics at the West, he sent a part of his force to attack the rebels in rear, while he assailed them in the early morning of June 11th in front. The fighting was desperate, but he at last drove them back from line after line of breastworks, through an almost impassable forest, to the station at Trevilian; and here his detached troops attacking them in rear, their route was complete, and Sheridan established his headquarters that night at Trevilian.

The next morning, the railroad from Trevilian station to Louisa Court-House was completely destroyed, the ties burned, and the rails twisted and bent so as to be utterly unserviceable. This occupied from daybreak to 3 P. M., of the 12th of June. The rebels, meantime, had concentrated in considerable force at Gordonsville, and advancing towards Trevilian, commenced the construction of rifle-pits at a distance of about four miles, to resist the movements of Sheridan. After a careful reconnoissance, General Sheridan found the enemy too strongly posted to be effectively assailed by his light artillery, especially as his ammunition was getting low, and therefore declined a general assault. On the extreme right, however, the Union troops assaulted and carried the enemy's lines again and again, but were eventually driven from them by the long-range guns of the rebel infantry; and finding his ammunition giving out, and being unable to obtain forage for his horses, General Sheridan determined to withdraw; but he carried out this determination in a characteristic way. Returning to Trevilian station, he ordered supper, inviting his generals to sup with him; and having given orders for the removal of the wounded who could be moved, and detailed surgeons to stay with those who were most severely injured, and perfected his order of march, he partook quietly of his tea, and then set about the withdrawal of his force from a position in which nearly the entire cavalry of the rebel army confronted it. While the train and the rear divisions were moving off with the wounded, he ordered forty rounds of canister to be fired at the rebel position; and when the enemy, sorely cut up by this fire, attempted to take the battery by a bold, sudden dash, he charged upon them with a regiment of cavalry, at the same time pouring in a full round of canister at very short range, and hurled them back, while the gun was withdrawn, and then, when they were retreating, moved quietly back; and all his men being, by day-dawn, well out of Trevilian station, he marched the next day fifteen miles, to Troyman's store, without the slightest opposition, and the day following (June 14th) reached the vicinity of Spottsylvania Court-house, which a month before had been the scene of such bloody and terrible battles. Here he remained a day, and on Wednesday evening reached Guiney's station, on the Fredericksburg and Richmond railroad, where he established his headquarters for the time, but soon moved to White House, and thence marched to the James, to join General Grant. While moving towards the James, they were attacked by the enemy on the 23d of June, at Jones's bridge, over the Chickahominy, and on the 24th, near St. Mary's church, the rebels being on both occasions in strong force, and fully confident of their ability to overwhelm him. Sheridan acted entirely on the defensive, but produced such terrible havoc among the enemy with his artillery, fighting at short range, that they were in the end very willing to withdraw. During the afternoon and night of June 25th, General Sheridan crossed the James river, five miles above Fort Powhatan, on a pontoon bridge, protected on either side by gunboats, without loss, the enemy being kept at bay by the gunboats.

During the next thirty days, his cavalry were engaged in cutting the railroads to the south and southwest of Petersburg; and on the 27th of July, crossed the James at Deep Bottom, and on the 28th, fought a severe battle with the rebels near Malvern Hill, holding their position for some hours against a greatly superior force.

Meantime the third rebel invasion of Maryland and Pennsylvania, *via* the Shenandoah valley, was in progress, and the national capital was more seriously threatened than ever before; and Chambersburg, Pennsylvania, Hagerstown and Frederick, Maryland, were occupied by the rebel General Ewell, and Baltimore endangered. This movement was intended to call off General Grant from the siege of Richmond, where the pressure of his grip was becoming unendurable; but he was not to be thus lured from his prey; he could and did spare one corps, the Sixth, to the defence of Washington; but the other forces for the defence of that region must be drawn from other sources. The Nineteenth corps, from the Department of the Gulf, was on its way thither, and the very considerable force in Western Virginia, Eastern and Western Pennsylvania, and Maryland, though partly composed of militia, was, if rightly handled, amply sufficient to hold the territory around Washington, and drive back the invader to Southern Virginia. It was, however, the misfortune of these troops to be included in four distinct military departments, the commanders of which, jealous of their respective prerogatives, did not co-operate harmoniously with each other. Washington and Baltimore, and the country adjacent, formed the Department of Washington; Eastern and Central Pennsylvania and Northern Maryland, the Department of the Susquehanna; Northwestern Virginia and Western Pennsylvania, the Department of West Virginia; and the region of the Shenandoah, and eastward to the Bull Run mountains, the Middle Department. It was one of those inspirations which have stamped General Grant as one of the ablest military minds of the century, which led him to propose the combination of these four departments into one grand military division, to be called the Middle Military Division, and subsequently the Military Division of the Shenandoah. In the extent of its territory, this division was hardly inferior to any of the others, and in the difficulty of its management, it yielded the palm to none. For its command, which required military genius of a very high order, General Grant, with his usual sagacity, selected General Philip H. Sheridan. Though the junior in years of every major-general in the division, he had already exhibited a skill and tact in handling troops, a combination of caution and audacity, a celerity of movement, and a fertility of resource, which indicated him as the man for the place.

On the 7th of August he received his command, and on the same day established his headquarters at Harper's Ferry. Concentrating his troops at once along the Potomac, in the immediate vicinity of the Shenandoah Valley, whither General Early, now in command of the rebel forces, had withdrawn with his troops and plunder, General Sheridan gradually pressed the rebels back from the important positions of Martinsburg, Williamsport, &c., garrisoning these as fast as they were relinquished, and establishing complete and prompt communications between his headquarters and the advanced posts. He then began to make feints of an advance, in order to test the enemy's strength and position. Early, who prided himself on his astuteness, fell back gradually, for the purpose of luring Sheridan on; but Sheridan would not move till he was ready, and understood too fully Early's plots, and the objects to be accomplished, to make any premature movements. As Early retired, however, he gradually occupied every important position, seizing and securing Winchester on the 12th of August, and throwing out a cavalry detachment to Front Royal, where they encountered and defeated, after a sharp struggle, the rebel cavalry. This accomplished, he fell back in turn, abandoning Winchester, and awaiting at Harper's Ferry and its vicinity the concentration of his forces. As he expected, this brought the rebel troops northward again, and several sharp skirmishes took place, Sheridan's cavalry, under General Torbert, meantime reconnoitring thoroughly the enemy's position, and taking note of all his movements. Finding that there was some danger of their moving southward to join General Lee, a movement which was to be prevented at all hazards, General Sheridan again advanced, as if to give them battle, and thus arrested their progress, and then again with drew towards Charlestown to attract them nearer to the Potomac. General Early thought Sheridan was afraid, and that by good management he might flank him, and entering Maryland again, reap another harvest of plunder. Accordingly, he moved east to Berryville, and issued a long general order to his troops, forbidding straggling and depredations upon the inhabitants of the Shenandoah Valley.

General Early had entirely misconceived the character and abilities of his opponent, as he soon found to his cost. His movement to Berryville was made on the 16th of September, and it found Sheridan fully prepared to act. General Grant, by his heavy blows upon Lee's forces at Richmond and Petersburg, was effectually preventing that general from sending any aid to Early, and Sheridan's force was sufficient to handle his opponent very roughly. On the 18th of September his cavalry met and defeated the rebels at Darksville, on Opequan creek, north of Winchester, while his infantry had driven the main rebel force from Perryville towards Winchester, where they had been joined by the rebel cavalry, retreating from Darksville.

Sheridan had now his antagonist in the very position which he desired. He had crowded him west of Opequan creek, and by the location of his own army was between him and his true line of retreat towards Richmond, southeast through the gaps in the Blue ridge. If now, by quick and heavy blows, he could rout and drive him southwestward, he would effectually cripple him, for the time at least. The battle began at daylight on Monday morning, September 19th, by the attack of Wilson's cavalry on the rebels on the west bank of the Opequan. By some misunderstanding the infantry were not brought into the action till near noon, and though the resistance of the rebels was stubborn and continued until 5 P. M., they were finally completely routed, driven through, or, as General Sheridan very forcibly expressed it in his dispatch, "sent whirling through Winchester," and pursued relentlessly till they reached their defences at Fisher's Hill, thirty miles below Winchester, where they succeeded in rallying for another stand. In this disastrous battle and retreat three of their ablest generals were killed and four more severely wounded. Among the latter was Fitzhugh Lee, the commander of the rebel cavalry of the Army of Virginia. They lost, also, between 3,000 and 4,000 in killed and wounded, nearly 5,000 prisoners, fifteen battle flags, and five pieces of artillery.

With the celerity which has always marked his movements, Sheridan now brought up his entire force to assault the strong position of the rebels on Fisher's Hill. The works were too formidable to be carried by an attack in front alone, and therefore, while keeping up a feint of a front attack, the Eighth corps (General Crooks') was sent far to the right, and sweeping about the enemy's left, flanked him, attacked him in rear, in a gallant charge, driving him out of his intrenchments; while the Sixth corps attacked at the same time in the centre, front, and the Nineteenth (Emory's) on the left; Averill with his cavalry ranging the while along the base of South Mountain. Confused and disorganized by attacks at so many different points, the enemy broke at the centre, and the Sixth corps separating his two wings, he fled in complete disorganization towards Woodstock. Artillery, horses, wagons, rifles, knapsacks, and canteens were abandoned and strewn along the road. Eleven hundred prisoners and sixteen pieces of artillery were captured; the pursuit was continued until the 25th, and did not conclude till the enemy had been driven below Port Republic, and many of them had scattered in the mountains, sick of the conflict and determined to abandon it. The loss of the enemy from the 19th to the 25th of September, in killed, wounded, prisoners, and missing, was not less than 10,000.

This victory occasioned great rejoicing throughout the North. Salutes were fired on the 26th of September at all military posts in the United States; and the brave and skilful commander of the Army of the Shenandoah was appointed by the President a brigadier-general in the regular army, to fill the vacancy occasioned by the death of the lamented McPherson.

While General Sheridan made his headquarters at Port Republic, he sent his cavalry under General Torbert forward to Staunton; which place they captured, and destroyed all the storehouses, machine-shops, and other buildings, owned or occupied by the rebel government, and also the saddles, small-arms, hard bread, and other military stores found in the place. They then proceeded to Waynesboro, also on the Virginia Central railroad; tore up seven miles of the railroad track, destroyed the depot, the iron bridge over the Shenandoah, a government tannery, and other stores. General Sheridan also improved the time of holding possession of the Shenandoah valley to destroy all the grain, hay, and forage to be found there, excepting what was necessary for the subsistence of his own army; and thus effectually crippled both Early's army and Lee's, both of which had depended upon this fertile valley as the granary from which to draw most of their supplies of grain and forage. The whole valley being thus rendered untenable by the rebel army, and the guerilla movements, which had been encouraged by the inhabitants, who had harbored them, sternly repressed, General Sheridan moved leisurely northward, and on the 6th of October made his headquarters at Woodstock. South of this point, over two thousand barns filled with wheat and hay, and over seventy mills stocked with wheat and flour, had been destroyed; and a vast herd of stock, and more than three thousand sheep, had been reserved for the supply of the army. The Luray valley, as well as the Little Fort valley, were subjected to the same devastation,—the inhabitants of both, like those of the Shenandoah, having, while professedly loyal, engaged in guerilla operations and the murder of Union soldiers.

On the 8th of October, the rebel General Rosser, a cavalry officer of considerable ability, who had just been promoted to the rank of major-general, thinking that he had found an opportunity to achieve a reputation, began to harass Sheridan's rear. He did, indeed, gain a reputation by this movement, but it was not an enviable one; for Sheridan, facing about, offered battle, and finding him reluctant to accept it, ordered his cavalry to attack by daylight on the morning of the 9th, one division charging along the Strasburg pike, while another, moving by a back road, took the enemy in flank. The rebels, after a short resistance, were severely beaten, and eleven pieces of artillery, several caissons, a battery forge, forty-seven wagons, and over three hundred prisoners, captured by the Union troops. The rebel cavalry fled in great terror on being charged by Sheridan's cavalry, and were pursued "on the jump" for twenty-six miles, the pursuit being continued beyond Mount Jackson, and across the south fork of the Shenandoah.

General Early was not yet fully satisfied with the punishment he had received, and on the 12th of October, having crept up quietly under cover of the forest on

Little North mountain, he appeared in force on the wooded slope south of Cedar creek, and commenced a heavy and rapid artillery fire on Sheridan's lines. He had not, however, approached so stealthily that General Sheridan was unaware of his movements, and with a promptness which showed that he was not surprised, he returned the artillery fire, shot for shot, and then ordering forward his troops, sprang upon the foe, and after a sharp action of three hours, terminating in a cavalry charge, drove Early once more in confusion up the valley.

Having thus disposed of General Early, General Sheridan made a flying visit of inspection to his various outposts, and employed a part of his cavalry meantime in making a thorough devastation of Luray valley from Front Royal to Sperryville, the inhabitants of that valley having harbored and aided the guerrillas and bushwhackers, who were murdering the operatives along the Manassas Gap railroad, which General Sheridan was putting in repair. In this expedition sixty-five hundred head of cattle and five hundred horses were captured, and thirty-two large flouring-mills, thirty distilleries, four blast-furnaces, and over fifty barns were destroyed. By holding Front Royal, General Sheridan was enabled to open communication, by way of the Manassas Gap railroad, with Washington, and thus transport his supplies and troops more expeditiously than he could do by way of Harper's Ferry. This railroad was opened on the 15th of October, and General Sheridan passed over it to Washington.

It was while he was thus absent, that Early planned another attack upon the Union army, which was well-nigh successful, and which, in all respects, proved one of the most remarkable battles of the war.

After the battle of the 12th, General Early had fallen back to his stronghold on Fisher's Hill, where the dense forest screened his movements from the view of the Union troops; and here, on the 18th of October, he had been reinforced by about twelve thousand fresh troops, half, or more than half of them without arms, but organized and officered, and ready for battle so soon as they should be able to obtain arms from prisoners or the slain upon the battle-field. This accession made his force twenty-seven thousand. He had learned of Sheridan's visit to Washington, and believed that the Sixth army corps had gone also, and that, with Sheridan, it was on its way to join Grant's army. With this impression, he regarded the occasion as an auspicious one to make one more attack, and effectually revenge himself on the army which had thrice defeated him, and twice sent his legions in wild confusion southward, almost to the sources of the Shenandoah. In fact, the Sixth corps was still with the Eighth and Nineteenth forming the Army of the Shenandoah; and General Sheridan, whom he so justly dreaded, was on his way back from Washington to his command, and, on the night of the 18th, had reached Winchester. Had Early known these facts, it is very questionable whether he would have attempted the daring enterprise in which he so nearly succeeded, only to fail most signally.

The Union position was an echelon of three lines, posted on three separate crests of moderate height in the vicinity of Cedar creek, near the point where it crosses the Strasburg and Virginia turnpike, a short distance northeast of Strasburg. The Army of Western Virginia formed the left wing, and occupied the most advanced position on the eastern crest; the Nineteenth corps held the centre, half a mile in rear of this; while the Sixth corps occupied the right crest, which was also furthest in the rear. The fronts and the flanks, to some extent, of the Army of Western Virginia and the Nineteenth corps, were protected by breastworks of logs and earth, with batteries in place, and the right was guarded by Torbert's cavalry. In front, the position was impregnable, except by a surprise, and to turn either flank was an enterprise so rash and dangerous, that it was considered impossible by most of the officers. In Sheridan's absence, the command devolved on General Wright, commanding the Sixth corps, as the senior corps commander.

With a rashness which could have only been inspired by desperation, since at every point of his progress, except the last, discovery would have been inevitable ruin, Early resolved to attempt, by a nocturnal movement, to turn the left flank of the Union army. To do this, it was necessary to descend into the gorge at the base of the Massanutten mountain, cross the north fork of the Shenandoah, which was then fordable, and for miles to skirt Crook's position (the Army of Western Virginia), passing, at some points, within four hundred yards of his pickets. Three days previous a brigade of Union cavalry had held the road along which the rebels now passed, and would have rendered such an enterprise impossible, but by some strange oversight it had been withdrawn. But even without this, the hazards which Early ran might well have been sufficient to deter a bold man. At almost any point of his march, had he been discovered (and once he was on the very verge of discovery), his army would have been cut in two by the Union infantry, and the cavalry would have prevented his retreat to Fisher's Hill, when he would have inevitably lost half his force, and the Union loss would have been trifling.

His management of his advance was admirable: his canteens had been left behind in camp, lest they should betray the movement by their clatter against the shanks of the bayonets, and every precaution was taken to move with the utmost stillness and quiet. At dawn they were lying formed for battle, within six hundred yards of the Union camps, enveloping completely Crook's flank. Just at break of day, with the well-known rebel battle-yell, and a sudden and terrific rattle of musketry, they flung themselves on the camp of the Army of Western Virginia, and within fifteen minutes that body of veteran troops, surprised, broken, and panic-stricken, were hurrying back, a mass of fugitives, upon the centre, where the Nineteenth corps, forewarned, had sprung into the trenches, but found themselves almost immediately attacked in flank and rear, while the rebel General Gordon had seized a position which completely commanded their camp. Early had sent his cavalry and light artillery to the right, to menace the Sixth corps (or, as he supposed, the Nineteenth); and this corps now occupied with that force, whose strength, at that early hour, could not be ascertained, could not come to the help of the imperilled Nineteenth. For an hour and more of desperate determined fighting that corps held its position; but Gordon's men reaching onward along and beyond its flank, turned it, and fell upon its rear, and in it's turn, it was compelled to abandon its position, and retreat towards Winchester, or rather towards Middletown, on the Winchester road.

The Sixth corps had by this time found what was the force in its front, and had turned them over to Torbert's cavalry, who were amply sufficient to take care of them, while it came up to the support of the Nineteenth corps; but it, too, was flanked in its turn, and though it moved slowly and in good order, was compelled to retreat to a position where it could fight to better advantage. The train had been, by skilful management, removed out of harm's way, and was well on the road to Winchester, but the army had been driven off the pike, and it was necessary to fall back until it could again obtain a position upon it, and thus secure its communications.

Five hours had passed since the first attack, and the Army of the Shenandoah was, for the first time, defeated; not routed, but badly beaten. Their camps were in the possession of the enemy, and their fortified positions; they had lost twenty-four guns and twelve hundred prisoners, and they had retreated full three miles, and their stragglers a dozen or more. It was about ten o'clock when Sheridan came up the pike at full speed, his noble horse completely flecked with foam, swinging his cap and shouting to the stragglers, "Face the other way, boys. We are going back to our camps. We are going to lick them out of their boots." The effect was magical. The wounded by the roadside raised their voices to shout; the fugitives, but now hurrying forward to Winchester, turned about at sight of him who had always led them to victory, and followed him back to the battle-ground as hounds follow their master.

Still riding rapidly, he reached the main army, ordered it to face about, form line, and advance to the position it had last quitted. They obeyed without hesitation, and for two hours he rode along the lines, studying the ground and encouraging the men. "Boys," he said, in his earnest animated way, "if I had been here this never should have happened. I tell you it never should have happened. And now we are going back to our camps. We are going to get a twist on them—we are going to lick them out of their boots!" For two hours more there was silence, but rapid preparation. The Sixth corps held the turnpike and its vicinity. The Nineteenth was formed on its right, in double line, under cover of a dense wood. Rude temporary breastworks were thrown up in an incredibly short time, and the old animation and valor pervaded every heart. The panic was over. Then came a message from Sheridan to Emory (commanding the Nineteenth corps), that the enemy were advancing against them in column. They came, and were received with so deadly a fire of artillery and musketry that they awaited no second fire, but fell back at once out of sight, and Emory sent word to the commanding general that the attack had been repulsed. Sheridan's delight at this was evident. "That's good, that's good," he said eagerly. He then sent word to Emory that, if they renewed the attack, he must meet them by a counter-attack, drive them back, and follow them up. At half-past three, orders came for the entire line to advance, the Nineteenth corps to move in connection with the Sixth, and the right of the Nineteenth to swing towards the left, so as to drive the enemy upon the pike. The enemy's left was now his strong position, being supported by successive wooded crests, while his right ran out to the pike, across undulating open fields, which offered no natural line of resistance. Sheridan's plan was to push them off these crests by this swinging movement of his right, and then, as they were doubled up on the turnpike, hurl his cavalry upon them across the Middletown meadows. Like most of his plans, it was entirely successful; the crests were carried by a charge of infantry, and Gordon's division, which during the morning had so perseveringly flanked the Army of the Shenandoah, was itself flanked in turn by the Nineteenth corps, and broke in confusion.

The fighting which followed was desperate, and the rebels held their position with great tenacity; while the Union soldiers, who had neither eaten nor drank any thing since the previous day, and had been fighting since five in the morning, were greatly exhausted; but they forgot their hunger, their thirst, and their weariness—forgot every thing but that they were Sheridan's soldiers, and that they must drive the enemy back. Again they charged on the rebel second line, over stone walls, over steep hill-sides, and through thickets; Sheridan himself dashing along the front, cheering them with his confident smile and his assurances of success, and giving his orders in person to brigade, division, and corps commanders. The result could not be doubtful; the second charge carried the enemy's second line with the same rush and with greater ease than the first, and the cavalry swept on in magnificent line and pushed the routed foe into more hopeless confusion and speedier flight than in the battle of the 19th of September. Desperate were the efforts of the rebel officers to rally their men and make another stand; but they were utterly in vain, and Early's army was again "sent whirling" up the valley. The fighting soon swept far ahead of the tired infantry, who resumed their position in their old camps; while the cavalry pushed Early's jaded legions on and still on through Strasburg, past Fisher's Hill, till they reached Woodstock, sixteen miles distant. The rebels abandoned every thing in their flight—cannon, small-arms, knapsacks, great-coats, baggage-wagons, caissons, ammunition-wagons, and ambulances. The twenty-four cannon captured from the Union troops in the morning were retaken, and besides them twenty-five more of Early's own. Besides these, there were fifty wagons, sixty-five ambulances, sixteen hundred small-arms, several battle-flags, fifteen hundred prisoners, and two thousand killed and wounded left upon the field. The Union losses during the day had been heavy, especially in the morning, being in all about thirty-eight hundred, of whom eight hundred were prisoners. From this last and stunning defeat, Early's army never recovered. In all the records of modern history there are but three examples of such a battle, lost and won on the same field, and in the same conflict—Marengo, Shiloh, and Stone river; and in the two former the retrieval was due mainly to reinforcements brought up at the critical time, while the third was not so immediately decisive; but here, as is well remarked by Captain De Forest (to whose graphic and eloquent description of the battle in "Harper's Magazine" we acknowledge our indebtedness), "the only reinforcement which the Army of the Shenandoah received or needed to recover its lost field of battle, camps, intrenchments, and cannon was one man—SHERIDAN."

Lieutenant-General Grant's opinion of this remarkable battle may be gathered from the dispatch sent by him to Secretary Stanton, on the evening of the 20th of October. It was as follows:

HON. E. M. STANTON, Secretary of War:

I had a salute of one hundred guns fired from each of the armies here, in honor of Sheridan's last victory. Turning what bid fair to be a disaster into a glorious victory, *stamps Sheridan, what I have always thought him, one of the ablest of generals.*

U. S. GRANT, Lieutenant-General.

General Sheridan also received an autograph letter of thanks from the President, and on the 14th of November a general order, announcing General McClellan's resignation as major-general in the regular army, appointed General Sheridan to the same rank, to fill the vacancy, to date from the 8th of November, as an acknowledgment of his ability and generalship in the campaign in the valley of the Shenandoah, and especially in the battle of the 19th of October.

For six weeks after this battle there were occasional skirmishes of greater of less severity, between Torbert's cavalry or some portions of it, and the rebel cavalry officers Rosser and Lomax; but Early, though moving uneasily up and down the valley from Mount Jackson or New Market to Fisher's Hill, carefully avoided any thing like a general engagement, and in December sent a part of his forces to strengthen General Lee. Meantime the guerrilla warfare continued with all its vexatious annoyances and stealthy murders, and General Sheridan found it necessary to desolate the valley of the Blue Ridge by his cavalry, as he had done the valleys west of it. In two expeditions undertaken for this purpose, property to the amount of nearly seven and a half millions of dollars was either captured or destroyed; vast herds of cattle, sheep, and swine, and large numbers of horses and mules brought in. Driven from the region, the guerrilla bands have since concentrated near the upper Potomac, and at Piedmont, New Creek, and other points, have done some mischief; but their power has been greatly crippled by the stern and thorough measures adopted by General Sheridan. In December the Sixth corps was returned to the Army of the Potomac; and the Army of the Shenandoah for nearly two months acted principally as an army of observation. About the first of March, General Sheridan moved with his magnificent cavalry force up the valley towards Staunton; and after the capture of that town moved forward to Fisherville and Waynesboro, and near the latter place attacked and defeated Early, capturing twelve hundred and fifty-two prisoners (including eighty-seven officers), five cannon, one hundred wagons, over one hundred horses and mules, &c., &c. Early himself escaped with difficulty, some of his staff-officers and his personal baggage being captured. He was pursued as far as Greenwood Station, where more cannon, and ordnance, and commissary supplies were captured. Sheridan next entered Charlottesville, where he remained two days bringing up his trains, and dispatched from thence his First division to destroy the James River canal, at Scottsville, and thence to Duguidsville, fifteen miles below, which they accomplished. The Third division were sent at the same time to burn the bridges and tear up the railroad track on the Lynchburg railroad. He himself moved to Columbia on the James river, destroying the canal and its locks all the way; and turning thence to the Virginia Central railroad, broke up its track thoroughly for fifteen miles, and destroyed all bridges over the James and its tributaries. On the 18th he reached the north bank of the Pamunkey near White House, where he remained for a short time with his troops. He desolated the country through which he passed completely, and destroyed property which the rebels themselves estimated at fifty millions of dollars. The destruction of the James River canal and the Lynchburg railroad were terrible blows to Lee's army at Richmond, as by far the greater part of their supplies were brought in by these routes.

On the 25th of March, Sheridan's army moved from White House across the James river, at Wilcox's landing, reaching their destination at night. After two days spent in recruiting and preparing for another campaign, General Sheridan was ordered to move, on the 29th, with his cavalry, *via* Reams' Station, to Dinwiddie Court-house, and from thence either strike at Burkesville Junction, or, if it should seem best, support the infantry, one or two corps of which would in that case be put under his command—the Fifth corps down the Halifax road, and the Second down the Vaughan road, to cross Hatcher's Run at the point which had been held since the movement in February. The Sixth and Ninth corps were moved westward to connect with the new line thus to be formed, and parties of the Twenty-fourth and Twenty-fifth corps were brought from the Army of the James to aid in strengthening the lines. It was deemed best by Lieutenant-General Grant that Sheridan should, under the circumstances, support directly the infantry attack; and accordingly, on Thursday, March 30, he connected his right, near Dinwiddie, with the left of the Fifth corps, on the Boydton road. The enemy was found to be strongly intrenched at Five Forks, an important position about six miles west of the crossing of the Boydton plank-road, over Hatcher's Run. They also held in some force the White Oak road, by which the Five Forks were approached from the east.

On the 31st of March, the Fifth corps, or rather Crawford's and Ayres' divisions of it, attempting to advance on this road, were driven back in disorder by the sudden and overwhelming attack of the rebels, and did not rally till they reached Griffin's division of that corps on the Boydton road. Here, Miles' division of the Second corps having attacked the enemy in flank, drove them back; and the Fifth corps, Griffin leading, having rallied, advanced, and at sunset occupied nearly the same position as in the morning.

But this retreat had opened the way for the rebels to

throw themselves with great fury upon Sheridan's cavalry, lying west of Dinwiddie; and at one time they had nearly cut off Merritt's command, and imperilled the entire cavalry force. General Sheridan, commanding in person, succeeded in checking the enemy's advance; and, having dismounted his cavalry in front of Dinwiddie Court-house, he fought a desperate battle with them, lasting till late in the evening; and the enemy, unable to drive his troops, whom they greatly outnumbered, finally lay down sullenly upon their arms, apparently determined to fight it out the next day.

Lieutenant-General Grant had ordered General Warren, commanding the Fifth corps, to report to General Sheridan; and on the evening of this battle sent a dispatch to Sheridan, saying that Warren would report to him about midnight. As he did not appear, General

Sheridan, at 3 A.M., April 1st, sent a messenger with a note asking him to attack the enemy in rear at daylight, and he would attack them in front. He believed that by this means they might capture the whole force in his front. General Warren did not make his appearance; but General Sheridan attacking boldly, the rebels were driven in confusion across Chamberlain's Run, and Sheridan pursued, determined to carry their stronghold. About 8 A.M. he met Warren's advance near J. Boisseau's house, four or five miles north of Dinwiddie, and directed them to hold fast in their position, and be ready to move to the front when required. He himself passed on with his cavalry, and surrounded the rebel intrenchments on the south, southwest, and west; and in the afternoon ordered up the Fifth corps to attack from the east. They moved very slowly, and it seemed to General Sheridan that General Warren was not desirous of bringing them into the fight; and when at last they were formed, that he did not seek to inspire his men with confidence in their ability to succeed. The movement was, nevertheless, successful, the rebels being driven from their strong position, routed, their left flank doubled up in confusion by the attack of the Fifth corps; while Merritt's cavalry, dashing on to the White Oak road, capturing their artillery and turning it upon them, and riding into their broken ranks, so demoralized them that they made no serious stand after their line was broken, and Sheridan captured between 5,000 and 6,000 prisoners. At the close of the day's fighting, General Sheridan relieved General Warren of command, and put General Griffin in command of the corps.

Having disposed his forces so as to hold the White Oak road, General Sheridan, on the morning of April 2d, ordered Miles' division of the Second corps, which had also been directed to report to him, to move up the White Oak road towards Petersburg, and attack the enemy at the intersection of that with the Claiborne road, where they were massed in considerable force, and he himself followed with two divisions of the Fifth corps. Miles was successful, and drove the enemy towards Sutherland's Depot, and was about to attack him there, when, at General Meade's instance, General Humphreys, of the Second corps, again assumed command of Miles' division. General Sheridan then, taking his two divisions of the Fifth corps, returned to Five Forks, and marched out the Ford road towards Hatcher's Run, with a view to cut off the enemy's retreat, the cavalry having been already dispatched to cross Hatcher's Run, and break up the rebel cavalry.

This movement proved successful. The Fifth corps reached the Southside Railroad at Ford's Depot, and marched rapidly eastward towards Sutherland's, in flank and rear of the enemy, who confronted Miles. Finding themselves thus attacked, the rebels fled northward, and escaped along the main road by the Appomattox River, pursued by Sheridan's troops, who succeeded in engaging them slightly about dusk.

During that night Petersburg and Richmond were evacuated, and the next morning the pursuit of the retreating rebels was taken up in earnest by both cavalry and infantry. At Deep Creek they made a stand, and a severe fight took place, ending in the rout of the rebels and the capture of large numbers of prisoners, five pieces of artillery, and many wagons.

Encamping on the night of the 3d at Deep Creek, General Sheridan pressed forward in pursuit to Jetersville, having sent his division of cavalry to strike the Danville Railroad, between Burkesville and Jetersville.

Here he ascertained that Lee, with his entire army, was at Amelia Court-house, and ordered the Fifth corps at once to intrench till the main army could come up.

On the morning of the 5th of April, Davies' cavalry brigade, making a reconnoissance, captured a train of 180 wagons, with five pieces of artillery and a large number of prisoners. Some heavy fighting ensued, but the rebels were finally repulsed.

The Second corps having come up, and the Fifth corps being returned to General Meade's command, at his request, General Sheridan, on the morning of the 6th of April, sent his cavalry towards Deatonsville to ascertain Lee's exact position, and attack him if he was attempting to escape. The cavalry officer found Lee attempting to escape by way of Farmville, and attacked at once, capturing sixteen pieces of artillery, 400 wagons, and a large number of prisoners, and cutting off three divisions of the enemy's infantry from their line of retreat. The infantry (the Sixth corps were coming up with orders to report to Sheridan) could not reach the ground in season, and the rebels fought with the energy of despair. Two divisions of the Sixth corps (Wheaton's and Seymour's) finally reached the ground, and with a part of the Second corps soon began to drive the enemy, who had previously broken a part of the line of the cavalry. They were driven as far as Sailor's Creek.

On the morning of the 7th, the cavalry pressed on to Farmville, and there again encountered the enemy, who fought desperately, and being driven over the Appomattox, made a stand there, and fought again, but without decisive result. On the morning of the 8th, General Sheridan ascertained that a large railroad train, laden with supplies for the rebels, was at Appomattox Station, and that General Lee was hastening thither with his troops, in the hope of obtaining the means of reaching Lynchburg. By making a forced march with his cavalry, he succeeded in reaching Appomattox, and capturing and sending eastward the train just as the rebel army came up; and then dashing upon the famished rebel soldiers, drove them back to Appomattox Court-house, capturing many prisoners, twenty-five pieces of artillery, a hospital-train, and a park of wagons. He then notified the lieutenant-general that the enemy had reached the last ditch, and urged that the infantry should be brought up with all speed. The next morning Lee surrendered his army.

After the surrender, Sheridan returned with his cavalry to Richmond and Washington, and was ordered at once to Texas with a large force, to bring the rebel General E. Kirby Smith to terms. Smith surrendered, however, about the time of his arrival; and on the 27th of June, 1865, General Sheridan was appointed commander of the military division of the Gulf, embracing the departments of Florida, Mississippi, Louisiana, and Texas.

In person, Major-General Sheridan is small, about five feet five inches in height, of dark complexion and hair, with a piercing blue eye, and an energetic, determined face. In private life he is social and genial, with a ready command of language. His manner is fascinating, and wins for him at once the love and confidence of his subordinates. He is, with all his dashing qualities, calm, cool, cautious, fertile in resources, careful of his men, and thoroughly self-possessed at all times. No officer in the army can rouse his troops to so high a pitch of enthusiasm, or hold them there so firmly, as "Little Phil Sheridan."

V.

Vice-Admiral David Glascoe Farragut.

HEROES have not been wanting in the history of maritime warfare, at any time in these last three hundred years. Holland points, with pride, to her gallant De Ruyter and Van Tromp, who made the little republic among the marshes and canals that yield tribute to the Zuyder Zee, famous the world over. England glories in her Blake, her Collingwood, and most of all, in her Nelson, the model naval hero of all her history; and we cannot suppress our admiration of the daring of the reckless John Paul Jones, the matchless patriotism of Lawrence, and the gallant bearing and extraordinary success of Perry, Bainbridge, Decatur, and the elder Porter, while in the present war the heroic Foote, Dupont, Winslow, D. D. Porter, and Rogers have covered their names with glory.

But among all these illustrious names there is none which so thoroughly awakens our enthusiasm, or so readily calls forth our applause, as that of our illustrious Vice-Admiral. With all of Nelson's courage and daring, he has more than his executive ability and fertility of resource, a wider, and more generous intellectual culture, and a more unblemished, *naïve*, frank, and gentle character.

He bears in his veins some traces of the best blood of Spain, his father, George Farragut, having been a native of Citadella, the capital of the island of Minorca, and a descendant of an ancient and honorable Catalonian family. The father came to this country in 1776, and united most heartily in our struggle for independence, attaining during the war the rank of major. After the conclusion of the war, Major Farragut married Miss Elizabeth Shine, of North Carolina, a descendant of the old Scotch family of McIven, and settled as a farmer at Campbell's station, near Knoxville, Tennessee. Here, on the 5th of July, 1801, his illustrious son was born. The father seems to have been not altogether contented with a farmer's life in that mountainous region, for not long after, we hear of him as a sailing-master in the navy, and an intimate friend of the father of Commodore David D. Porter, who then held a similar rank. Young Farragut inherited his father's love for the sea, and though brought up so far inland, among the Cumberland Mountains, he had hardly reached the age of nine and a half years, when the longing for a sailor's life possessed him so strongly, that his father consented; and after some little delay, a midshipman's warrant was procured for him.

His first cruise was under the command of Captain (then master-commandant) Porter, who, in July, 1812, was promoted to the rank of captain, and soon after sailed in the Essex for the South American coast and the Pacific. To this famous frigate the young midshipman was ordered, before her departure, and he remained on her through the eventful two years that followed, when she drove the British commerce out of the Pacific. When, on the 28th of March, 1814, the British frigate Phœbe, 36 guns, and sloop-of-war Cherub, 28 guns, without scruple attacked the Essex in the harbor of Valparaiso, in violation of the rights of a neutral nation (a precedent which the British government seem to have forgotten of late), there ensued one of the fiercest naval battles on record. Though fighting against hopeless odds, the two British vessels having twice the number of guns and men of the Essex, Commodore Porter, with the reckless daring which was so marked a trait of his character, refused to strike his colors till his ship had been three or four times on fire, and was in a sinking condition, with her rigging shot away, the flames threatening her magazine, and 152, out of her crew of 255, killed, wounded, or missing. The battle had lasted two and a half hours. On his surrender, the Essex Junior, a whaling-ship which he had converted into a sloop-of-war, but which had been unable to take any part in the battle, was sent home with the prisoners on parole. The young midshipman, then a boy under thirteen, was in the hottest of the fight, and was slightly wounded during the action. Before the loss of the Essex, he had served as acting-lieutenant on board the Atlantic, an armed prize.

On his return to the United States, Commodore Porter placed him at school at Chester, Pa., where he was taught, among other studies, the elements of military and naval tactics; but in 1816 he was again afloat and on board the flag-ship of the Mediterranean squadron, where he had the good fortune to meet, in the chaplain, Rev. Charles Folsom, an instructor to whom he became ardently attached, and to whose teachings he attributes much of his subsequent usefulness and success. Mr. Folsom was appointed consul at Tunis, not long after, and thither young Farragut accompanied him. In a letter recently published, Mr. Folsom speaks thus of his intercourse with the young hero: . . . "All needed control was that of an elder over an affectionate younger brother. He was now introduced to entirely new scenes, and had social advantages which compensated for his former too exclusive sea-life. He had found a home on shore, and every type of European civilization and manners in the families of the consuls of different nations. In all of them my young countryman was the delight of old and young. This had always been among his chief moral dangers; but here he learned to be proof against petting and flattery. Here, too, he settled his definition of true glory—glory, the idol of his profession—if not in the exact words of Cicero, at least in his own clear thought. Our familiar walks and rides were so many lessons in ancient history, and the lover of historic parallels will be gratified to know that we possibly sometimes stood on the very spot where the boy Hannibal took the oath that consecrated him to the defence of his country."

This pleasant period of instruction passed all too quickly, and the boy, now grown to man's estate, after some further service in the Mediterranean, was, on the 1st of January, 1821, at the age of nineteen and a half years, promoted to the rank of lieutenant, and ordered to duty on the West India station. In 1824 he was assigned to duty at the Norfolk navy-yard; and with the exception of a two years' cruise in the Vandalia, on the Brazil station, remained at Norfolk till 1833. Here he married a lady of highly respectable family, and during the long years of suffering through which she was called to pass, from a hopeless physical malady, he proved one of the most tender and affectionate of husbands, never wearying of administering all the relief and comfort to the sufferer in his power. When death at last terminated her protracted distress, he mourned her tenderly and long. He subsequently married another lady of Norfolk, Miss Virginia Loyall, the daughter of one of the most eminent citizens of that city. The issue of this marriage is a son, now a cadet at West Point, who bears the honorable name of LOYALL FARRAGUT. That he may do honor to such a name and attain in another field to a reputation as untarnished and a distinction as lofty as his father's, must be the wish of all who know either sire or son.

In 1833, Lieutenant Farragut was made executive officer (lieutenant-commander) of the sloop of war Natchez, and again ordered to the Brazilian coast, and in 1838 transferred to the West India or home squadron. In 1841 he was commissioned as commander, and ordered to the sloop-of-war Decatur, on the Brazil squadron. In 1842 he received three years' leave of absence, and at its expiration was again ordered to the Norfolk navy-yard, where he remained till 1847, when he took command of the sloop-of-war Saratoga, of the home squadron. In 1850 he was again assigned to duty at Norfolk, where in 1851 he was appointed assistant inspector of ordnance. After serving in this capacity for three years he was sent to California, in 1854, as commander of the Mare Island navy-yard. In 1855 he was commissioned captain; and from 1858 to May, 1860, he was in command of the steam sloop-of-war Brooklyn, in the home squadron. During all these years of service, Captain Farragut had been a diligent student, ever seeking the opportunity of increasing his professional and general knowledge. While inferior to no officer of the navy in his acquaintance with every thing appertaining to naval science or warfare, he is superior to most of them in the wide range of his general culture, especially in the languages. He speaks with fluency and correctness most of the languages of Europe, as well as Turkish and Arabic.

In 1860 he had spent nearly nineteen years afloat,—eighteen years and four months on shore duty, and ten years and ten months either waiting orders or on leave of absence. Forty-eight of his fifty-eight years had been spent in the naval service.

In April, 1861, came the rebellion. Captain Farragut was at his home in Norfolk, surrounded by those who were sympathizers with the rebellion, and who were already maturing plans for the seizure of the government property, and its conversion to rebel uses. No more loyal heart ever beat than his, and in frank and manly terms he denounced the whole proceedings of the traitors, and gave expression to his abhorrence of them. This roused all the demoniac hatred of the plotters of treason, and they told him at once, in tones of menace, that he could not be permitted to live there, if he held such sentiments. "Very well," was his prompt reply, "then I will go where I can live and hold such sentiments." Returning to his home, he informed his family that they must leave Norfolk for New York in a few hours. They immediately made their preparations, and the next morning, April 18, 1861, bid adieu to Norfolk. Arriving at Baltimore, he found the mob in possession of the city, and with difficulty secured a passage by steamer and canal-boat to Columbia, Pennsylvania, from which point he reached New York with his family by railway. Securing a residence for his family at Hastings, on the Hudson, he repaired at once to Washington and asked to be employed in the service of his country. But though fully appreciating his loyalty and ability, the government had no ship for him to command. The treachery of the former Secretary of the Navy had sent most of our ships to distant foreign ports, and of the very few that were left, the best had been seized or destroyed at Norfolk, and the remainder, to which they were making additions as rapidly as possible, were in command of his seniors in the service. The Navy Department were, however, anxious to give him employment, and in default of any thing else he served for a time as a member of the Naval Retiring Board, which shelved the incompetent officers of the navy, and promoted the active, loyal, and deserving.

Meantime, the government had resolved on the capture of New Orleans, and entered with zeal upon the work of fitting out a squadron, as well as an army for its reduction. The squadron was to consist of a fleet of armed steamers, and twenty bomb-schooners, each carrying gigantic mortars, throwing fifteen-inch shells.

The bomb-fleet was to be under the command of Commander David D. Porter, but he was to report to Flag-Officer Farragut, who was to have charge of the entire squadron. Selecting the Hartford as his flag-ship, and having made all possible preparations for his expedition, Flag-Officer Farragut received his orders on the 20th of January, 1862, and on the 3d of February sailed from Hampton Roads. Arriving at Ship Island on the 20th of February, he organized the West Gulf Blockading Squadron, and in spite of difficulties of all sorts,—the delay in forwarding coal, naval stores, hospital stores, ammunition, etc., the labor of getting vessels drawing twenty-two feet over the bars at Pass L'Outre and Southwest Pass, where the depth was but twelve and fifteen feet, the ignorance and stupidity of some of the officers, and every other obstacle he had to encounter,—made steady progress. The difficulties were not all surmounted until the 18th of April, when the bombardment of Fort Jackson, the lowermost of the two forts defending the passage of the Mississippi, was commenced. These forts were seventy-five miles below New Orleans and possessed great strength. A continuous bombardment was maintained for six days, by which the forts were considerably damaged, but they still held out stoutly. A heavy iron chain had been stretched across the river, supported by large logs, to obstruct the passage of vessels, and was placed at a point where the fire of the two forts could be most effectively concentrated. Above this chain lay the rebel fleet of sixteen gunboats and two iron-clad rams. Along the banks of the river were land batteries, mounting several guns each.

Finding that the forts were not likely to yield to the bombardment, Flag-Officer Farragut called a council of war, and after hearing their opinions, which were somewhat discordant, issued his general order of April 20th, in which the spirit of the hero gleams out. This was his language: "The flag-officer having heard all the opinions expressed by the different commanders, is of the opinion *that whatever is to be done will have to be done quickly.* When, in the opinion of the flag-officer, the propitious time has arrived, the signal will be made to weigh, and advance to the conflict. . . . . He will make the signal for close action, *and abide the result—conquer, or be conquered.*"

After further and severe bombardment of the forts, the flag-officer gave notice to the steam-vessels of the squadron, of his determination to break the chain and run past the forts, engage the rebel fleet, and having defeated it, ascend the river to New Orleans, and capture that city. It was a most daring movement. The vessels of the squadron would be exposed to the concentrated fire of the forts until the chain was broken and they were all past it; and then they would encounter a fleet nearly equal to their own in numbers, and two of its vessels iron-clads,—at that time an unknown power in naval warfare. To rush on such dangers as these seemed rash, reckless, almost foolhardy. But the flag-officer had weighed well his chances, and believing that cool courage and prompt action were the principal requisites for success, and that the prize to be won justified the risk, he gave the order to start at 2 A. M., April 24th, and meantime visited each ship, and personally superintended the adoption of the requisite measures for the preservation of life and of the vessels, and gave his instructions to the officers as to the mode of the attack. The different plans adopted for protecting the ships and machinery from injury were ingenious and proved effective.

The sheet-cables were stopped up and down on the sides in the line of the engines, thus extemporizing an iron plating over this most vulnerable portion; and hammocks, coal, bags of ashes, bags of sand, &c., were placed in such a way as to protect the engines from shots coming in forward or abaft. The bulwarks were lined either with hammocks or splinter nettings. Some of the vessels coated their sides with mud, to make them less visible, and some whitewashed their decks, that objects might be more visible by night. The signal was made at five minutes before two, A. M., but, some of the vessels having trouble in weighing anchor, the fleet did not get under way till half-past three, A. M. The chain had previously been broken, and the mortar-vessels moved up and anchored ready to pour in their fire as soon as the forts should open. The steam-fleet moved up in two columns, one led by Flag-Officer Farragut in person, in the Hartford, the other by Captain Theodorus Bailey, as second in command, in the Cayuga. The left column (Farragut's) was composed of the Hartford, Brooklyn, Richmond, Sciota, Iroquois, Kennebec, Pinola, Itasca, and Winona; the right (Bailey's) of the Cayuga, Pensacola, Mississippi, Oneida, Varuna, Katahdin, Kineo, and Wissahickon. The right column was to engage Fort St. Philip; the left, Fort Jackson. The fleet were fairly abreast of the forts before they were discovered, and fire opened upon them; but from that moment the firing was terrible, and the smoke, settling down like a pall upon the river, produced intense darkness, and the ships could only aim at the flash from the forts, the forts at the flash from the ships. A fire-raft, pushed by the ram Manassas against the flag-ship (the Hartford) set it on fire, and at the same instant it ran aground; but by the prompt and disciplined exertions of the men it was extinguished in a few minutes and got afloat, never ceasing for a moment its fire upon the enemy. At times the gunboats passed so near the forts as to be able to throw their broadsides of shrapnel, grape, and canister with most destructive force into their interior; and the forts, in the endeavor to depress their guns sufficiently to strike the vessels, lost their shot, which rolled into the ditches. They were nearly past the forts when the rebel fleet came down upon them, the iron-clad ram Manassas among them. Several of these gunboats were iron-clad about the bow, and had iron beaks or spurs. The Cayuga, Captain Bailey's flagship, was the first to encounter these; and soon after the Varuna, commanded by Captain Boggs, found itself in a nest of rebel steamers, and moved forward delivering its broadsides, port and starboard, with fearful precision, into its antagonists, four of which were speedily disabled and sunk by its fire. The Varuna was finally attacked by the Morgan and another rebel gunboat, both iron-clad at the bow, which crushed in her sides; but, crowding her steam, she drew them on, while still fast, and poured broadsides into both, which drove them ashore crippled and in flames. Running his own steamer on shore as speedily as possible, the gallant Boggs fought her as long as his guns were out of water, and then brought off his men, who were taken on board the Oneida and other gunboats of the fleet. Several of the gunboats were considerably injured, but none of them lost except the Varuna. The Itasca, Winona, and Kennebec were disabled, and obliged to fall back. Thirteen of the seventeen vessels composing Flag-Officer Farragut's squadron were able to pass in safety these forts, and had defeated a rebel fleet, destroying thirteen of their gunboats and rams, and the iron-clad Manassas, and compelling the remainder to shelter themselves under the guns of the forts. The entire loss of the Union squadron was but thirty-six killed, and one hundred and thirty-five wounded.

The gallant flag-officer now ascended the river, encountering slight opposition from the Chalmette batteries, about three miles below New Orleans; but they were silenced in twenty minutes, and at noon of the 25th of April he lay in front of the city, and demanded its surrender. Four days later the forts were surrendered to Captain Porter, and General Butler came up the river to arrange for landing his troops, and taking possession of the conquered city. Meantime, Farragut had ascended the river above the city to Carrolton, where had been erected some strong works to oppose the progress of Flag-Officer Foote, should he descend the river. These, on the approach of the gunboats, were abandoned, and their guns spiked. They were destroyed.

New Orleans being safely in the possession of the Union forces, Flag-Officer Farragut ascended the Mississippi, and, on the 27th of June, ran his vessels safely past the rebel batteries at Vicksburg, and communicated with Flag-Officer Davis, then commanding the Mississippi Squadron, and arranged for a joint attack upon Vicksburg. The attack failed, because the bluffs at Vicksburg were too high to be effectively bombarded by the gunboats, and the capture of the city required the co-operation of a land force. He therefore repassed the batteries in safety on the 15th of July, and, descending the river, made Pensacola the headquarters of his squadron. On the 11th of July, the rank of rear-admiral having been created in accordance with the recommendation of a committee of Congress, Captain Farragut was advanced to that rank, and placed first on the list for his meritorious conduct in the capture of New Orleans. He also received the thanks of both houses of Congress. In the autumn of 1862, he directed the naval attacks on Corpus Christi, Sabine Pass, and Galveston, which resulted in the capture of those points. In his duties, as the commander of a blockading and guarding squadron, there was much of detail; attacks of guerillas along the river shores, to be parried and punished; surprises of the weaker vessels of the squadron, to be chastised and revenged; expeditions against rebel towns on or near the coast, to be aided and sustained; and careful lookout to be kept for blockade-runners, who sought their opportunity to slip into the ports of Mobile, Galveston, and Aransas. These occupied much of his time during the autumn and winter of 1862–3.

Early in March, 1863, General Grant, who was then engaged in his campaign against Vicksburg, desired that Rear-Admiral Farragut should force his way up the Mississippi with some of his most formidable steamships, and assault Vicksburg from below, believing that such an assault would aid materially in its reduction. He proposed also that a co-operating force from Rear-Admiral Porter's squadron should run past the batteries of Vicksburg and aid in this attack, and be prepared also to assail and carry some of the river batteries below, when he should have sent his troops down the west side of the Mississippi, as he had already determined to do.

The hero of New Orleans promptly responded to General Grant's wish. He selected for the work eight of his vessels, the Hartford, his flag-ship, the Richmond, a sister ship in size and armament, the Mississippi, a first class steamship, the Monongahela, rated as second-class, and with a lighter armament, and the gunboats Kineo, Albatross, and Genesee. Besides these, there were six mortar-boats, which were to take part in the bombardment, but not to run past the batteries. The gunboats were strengthened, and prepared to resist the terrible ordeal of fire they would have to encounter in passing the batteries of Port Hudson, two hundred and thirty-two miles below Vicksburg, the most formidable line of fortifications on the river except those of Vicksburg. On the morning of the 14th of March, the squadron anchored near Prophet's Island, and at half past one o'clock, P. M., the mortar-boats commenced bombarding the lower batteries, while a small land-force, sent to the rear of the town to distract the attention of the garrison, on attaining their position, opened fire. The steamships meantime awaited nightfall for their movements; and, at half-past nine P. M., with lights out, and their decks whitewashed, to enable the men to see their shot and shell which were piled upon the decks, they moved quietly up the river, lashed together, two and two, and hugging the eastern bank. Dark as was the night, their movements were watched, and signalled by the rebel scouts, and an immense bonfire was instantly kindled, which threw its lurid flames upon the river, in front of the most powerful of the rebel batteries, and would reveal at once the form and position of any vessel which might attempt to pass. The situation was evidently becoming more desperate every moment; but the stout heart of the admiral did not quail for an instant, and his squadron moved on swiftly towards the illumined point, while as yet no gun had been fired. Suddenly a rebel fieldpiece, concealed in the foliage along the shore, opened fire upon the Hartford, and a broadside was returned. Then opened upon the stately vessel and her consort a storm of fire which seemed sufficient to annihilate both. The rebel batteries, extending a distance of nearly four miles, and rising tier above tier on the lofty bluffs, showered their iron hail upon the doomed vessels and the mortar-boats from below, and the vessels of the squadron sent back their replies in tones of thunder. To add to their difficulties, the smoke here, as at the forts below New Orleans, settled murky and thick upon the river, and bewildered the pilots and gunners. The rebels, from their stationary batteries, could fire with more chance of success, but the gunboats were more than once in imminent danger of firing into each other. As yet, however, no one of the vessels had been disabled; but as they neared the line of light, at a point where the Mississippi river curves and the channel runs close to the eastern bank, thus bringing the vessels almost muzzle to muzzle with the water batteries which lined the river-bank, the contest grew still more furious.

The Hartford and Albatross, which were lashed together, succeeded in passing the batteries without serious injury; the Richmond, with the Genesee attached to her, had passed most of the principal batteries, though with heavy loss of gallant officers, when a shot penetrated her steam-chest and disabled her, and with her consort she dropped down to Prophet's Island. The Monongahela and Kineo came next, but the former grounded, and for twenty-five minutes was exposed to the steady fire of the principal rebel batteries, and was badly cut up; but finally floating, through the exertions of her consort she again attempted the passage, but was disabled and obliged to drop down the river. The Mississippi and Sachem came last, and had reached the point directly opposite the town without any serious injury, when the Mississippi grounded hard and fast on the west bank of the river, where she was exposed to the concentrated fire of the entire rebel batteries. Captain Smith, her commander, while every effort was making to get her off, ordered his gunners to keep up as rapid a fire as possible. In the next thirty-five minutes they fired two hundred and fifty shots. At the end of that time it became evident that she could not be saved; and providing promptly for the preservation of his crew and his wounded men, Captain Smith spiked the guns himself, and laid the combustibles so as to burn the ship. He had just fired the combustibles forward, and left the ship, when two rebel shells striking her amidships set on fire some barrels of turpentine, and in an instant she was enveloped in flame. Lightened by the combustion and the removal of three hundred men, she now floated; and turning round, the guns of her port battery, which had not been discharged, now reached by the fire, poured a final and terrible broadside into the rebel town. Drifting on, a mass of flame, she passed behind Prophet's Island; and her magazine exploding, she sank beneath the waters.

Of the whole fleet, then, only the Hartford and Albatross passed the batteries, but the Mississippi alone was destroyed; the others, though injured, were soon repaired, and subsequently rendered efficient service in the reduction of the rebel stronghold. The Hartford and Albatross blockaded for several weeks the mouth of Red River, from which supplies had been sent to Vicksburg;

and when Admiral Porter, in May, having run a part of his squadron past the Vicksburg batteries, relieved Admiral Farragut from this duty, he returned with his vessels to New Orleans by way of the Atchafalaya, and directed the naval operations against Port Hudson until its surrender.

The admiral had long desired to attack the defences of Mobile, and thus effectually check the blockade-running which it was impossible wholly to prevent while that port was left unmolested. The three rebel forts, Morgan, Powell, and Gaines, strong works at the entrance of Mobile Bay, prevented the near approach of the vessels of the blockading squadron, and protected the blockade-runners in entering the bay. An attack on these forts had been several times projected, but as often delayed from one cause or another. It was not till the summer of 1864, that a combined attack of land and sea forces could be arranged. On the 8th of July, Rear-Admiral Farragut had an interview with Generals Canby and Granger, and urged the necessity of an immediate attack. General Canby promised his assistance, but was soon after compelled to retract his promise. On the 1st of August, General Granger again visited the admiral, and a definite arrangement was made for an attack on the 4th. Owing to unavoidable delay, however, the attack was not made till the morning of the 5th, though the troops were landed on Dauphin Island.

The fleet which was to take part in the attack consisted of fourteen sloops of war and gunboats, and four iron-clad monitors. The admiral arranged them for the attack as follows: the Brooklyn and Octorara were lashed together, the Brooklyn being on the starboard side, nearest Fort Morgan—the Brooklyn being, much against the admiral's wishes, allowed the lead; next, the

Hartford and Metacomet, followed by the Richmond and Port Royal, the Lackawanna and Seminole, the Monongahela and Kennebec, the Ossipee and Itasca, and the Oneida and Galena. The four monitors were arranged in the following order, to the right or starboard of the gunboats: the Tecumseh, Commander T. A. M. Craven, taking the lead, and followed by the Manhattan, Commander Nicholson, the Winnebago, Commander Stevens, and the Chickasaw, Lieutenant-Commander Perkins.

The rebels, in addition to three forts all manned with large garrisons, had a squadron consisting of the iron-clad ram Tennessee, regarded by them as the most formidable armed vessel ever constructed, and three powerful gunboats, the Selma, Morgan, and Gaines.

The fleet steamed steadily up the channel, the Tecumseh firing the first shot at 6.47 A. M. The rebels opened upon them from Fort Morgan at six minutes past seven, and the Brooklyn replied, after which the action became general. The Brooklyn now paused, and for good reason—the Tecumseh, near her, careened suddenly and sank almost instantly, having struck and exploded a torpedo; and her gallant commander and nearly all her crew sank with her.

Directing the commander of the Metacomet to send a boat instantly to rescue her crew, Admiral Farragut determined to take the lead in his own flag-ship, the Hartford, and putting on all steam, led off through a track which had been lined with torpedoes by the rebels; but he says, "Believing that from their having been some time in the water, they were probably innocuous, I determined to take the chance of their explosion."

Turning to the northwestward to clear the middle ground, the fleet were enabled to keep such a broadside fire on the batteries of Fort Morgan as to prevent them from doing much injury. After they had passed the fort, about ten minutes before eight o'clock, the ram Tennessee dashed out at the Hartford; but the admiral took no further notice of her than to return her fire. The rebel gunboats wére ahead and annoyed the fleet by a raking fire, and the admiral detached his consort, the Metacomet, ordering her commander, Lieutenant-Commander Jouett, to go in pursuit of the Selma, and the Octorara was detached to pursue one of the others. Lieutenant-Commander Jouett captured the Selma, but the other two escaped under the protection of the guns of Fort Morgan, though the Gaines was so much injured that she was run ashore and destroyed. The combat which followed between the Tennessee and the Union fleet, and resulted in the surrender of that formidable ironclad vessel, is best described in the admiral's own words:

"Having passed the forts and dispersed the enemy's gunboats, I had ordered most of the vessels to anchor, when I perceived the ram Tennessee standing up for this ship. This was at forty-five minutes past eight. I was not long in comprehending his intentions to be the destruction of the flag-ship. The monitors and such of the wooden vessels as I thought best adapted for the purpose, were immediately ordered to attack the ram, not only with their guns, but bows on at full speed; and then began one of the fiercest naval combats on record.

"The Monongahela, Commander Strong, was the first vessel that struck her, and in doing so, carried away his own iron prow, together with the cutwater, without apparently doing her adversary much injury. The Lackawanna, Captain Marchand, was the next vessel to strike her, which she did at full speed; but though her stem was cut and crushed to the plank-ends for the distance of three feet above the water's edge to five feet below, the only perceptible effect on the ram was to give her a heavy list.

"The Hartford was the third vessel that struck her; but, as the Tennessee quickly shifted her helm, the blow was a glancing one, and, as she rasped along our side, we poured our whole port broadside of nine-inch solid shot within ten feet of her casement.

"The monitors worked slowly, but delivered their fire as opportunity offered. The Chickasaw succeeded in getting under her stern, and a fifteen-inch shot from the Manhattan broke through her iron plating and heavy wooden backing, though the missile itself did not enter the vessel.

"Immediately after the collision with the flag-ship, I directed Captain Drayton to bear down for the ram again. He was doing so at full speed, when, unfortunately, the Lackawanna run into the Hartford just forward of the mizzen-mast, cutting her down to within two feet of the water's edge. We soon got clear again, however, and were fast approaching our adversary, when she struck her colors and run up the white flag.

"She was at this time sore beset; the Chickasaw was pounding away at her stern, the Ossipee was approaching her at full speed, and the Monongahela, Lackawanna, and this ship were bearing down upon her, determined upon her destruction. Her smoke-stack had been shot away, her steering-chains were gone, compelling a resort to her relieving-tackles, and several of her port shutters were jammed. Indeed, from the time the Hartford struck her, until her surrender, she never fired a gun. As the Ossipee, Commander Le Roy, was about to strike her, she hoisted the white flag, and that vessel immediately stopped her engine, though not in time to avoid a glancing blow.

"During this contest with the rebel gunboats and the ram Tennessee, and which terminated by her surrender at 10 o'clock, we lost many more men than from the fire of the batteries of Fort Morgan."

The rebel Admiral Buchanan was severely wounded, and subsequently lost a leg by amputation. Admiral Farragut, as humane in his feelings towards a wounded foe as he was gallant and daring in action, immediately addressed a note to Brigadier-General Page, the commander of Fort Morgan, asking permission to send the rebel admiral and the other wounded rebel officers by ship, under flag of truce, to the Union hospitals at Pensacola, where they could be tenderly cared for. This request was granted, and the Metacomet dispatched with them.

The admiral had stationed himself "in an elevated position in the main rigging, near the top," a place of great peril, but one which enabled him to see much better than if he had been on deck, the progress of the battle; and from thence he witnessed, and testified with great gratification to, the admirable conduct of the men at their guns, throughout the fleet; and, in the connection, gives utterance to a sentiment which shows most conclusively his sympathy and tenderness: "Although," he says, "no doubt their hearts sickened, as mine did, when their shipmates were struck down beside them, yet there was not a moment's hesitation to lay their comrades aside and spring again to their deadly work."

It is said that at the moment of the collision between the Hartford and Lackawanna, when the men called to each other to save the admiral, Farragut, finding the ship would float at least long enough to serve his purpose, and thinking of that only, called out to his fleet-captain, "Go on with speed! Ram her again!"

The results of this victory were the destruction of the rebel fleet; the capture of the armored ship Tennessee, and of two hundred and thirty rebel officers and men; the abandonment on the next day of Fort Powell, with eighteen guns; the surrender on the 8th of Fort Gaines, with fifty-six officers, eight hundred and eighteen men, and twenty-six guns; and on the 23d of August, after a further bombardment of twenty-four hours, of Fort Morgan, with sixty guns and six hundred prisoners. By these captures, the port of Mobile was hermetically sealed against blockade-runners, and a serious blow given to the rebel cause.

Rear-Admiral Farragut remained in command of the West Gulf squadron till November, 1864, when he requested leave of absence, and was called to Washington for consultation in regard to future naval operations. Soon after the opening of Congress, a resolution of thanks was passed, to him, for his brilliant victory at Mobile, and the rank of vice-admiral, corresponding to that of lieutenant-general in the army, was created, and on the 1st of January, 1865, David Glascoe Farragut promoted to it. This appointment makes him the virtual chief commander of the naval forces of the United States.

The West Gulf blockading squadron, during all the time Admiral Farragut was in command of it, had had more fighting and less prizes than any other blockading squadron on the coast; and while Admirals Dupont, Lee, Porter, and Dahlgren had accumulated immense fortunes by their shares of prize-money, Admiral Farragut had received little beyond his regular pay. The merchants of New York, understanding this, and recognizing the great services he had rendered to commerce and to the nation, subscribed the sum of fifty thousand dollars, which was presented to him in U. S. 7.30 Treasury notes, in January, 1865, in testimony of their appreciation of his ability and success as a naval commander.

We do not expect any praise, scarcely indeed common civility, in speaking of our generals or admirals, from that English journal which is so thorough an exponent of the prejudices and hostility of the English aristocracy towards us, the "Army and Navy Gazette;" yet that journal has found itself compelled to speak of Admiral Farragut as "the doughty admiral whose feats of arms place him at the head of his profession, and certainly constitute him the first naval officer of the day, as far as actual reputation won by skill, courage, and hard fighting goes."

In the first week of April, 1865, Vice-Admiral Farragut visited Norfolk for the first time since he left it in 1861, and was welcomed to the city by a committee of the Loyal League of that city, with an address, to which he replied as follows:

"MR. CHAIRMAN, GENTLEMEN OF THE UNION LEAGUE, FELLOW-CITIZENS, AND MY BROTHER OFFICERS OF THE ARMY AND NAVY:—I thank you for the kind remarks which you have been pleased to make, and I wish that I had the language to express myself as I have heard others very near me four years ago, in this place, when we had our best speakers standing forth for the Union, and striving with all their rhetoric to persuade the people to desist from their unholy resolution, and cast their votes for the Union. This meeting recalls to me the most momentous events of my life, when I listened in this place till the small hours of the morning, and returned home with the feeling that Virginia was safe and firm in her place in the Union. Our Union members to the convention were elected by an overwhelming majority, and sent to Richmond, and we believed that every thing was right. Judge, then, my friends, of our astonishment in finding, a few days later, that the State had been voted out by a miserable minority, for the want of firmness and resolution on the part of those whom we trusted to represent us there, and that Virginia had been dragooned out of the Union. What was the reason for this act? The President's call for seventy-five thousand men? Why, our arsenals, navy-yards, money in the mint at New Orleans had been seized, and Sumter bombarded. Was it then remarkable that the Government of the United States should call for troops to sustain itself? Would Jackson have submitted to this? No; for I recollect that I myself had the honor to be sent to South Carolina to support his mandate that the Union must and should be preserved. I was told by a brother officer that the State had seceded, and that I must either resign and turn traitor to the Government which had supported me from my childhood, or I must leave this place. Thank God! I was not long in making my decision. I have spent half of my life in revolutionary countries, and I know the horrors of civil war, and I told the people what I had seen, and what they would experience. They laughed at me, and called me 'granny' and 'croaker;' and I said, 'I cannot live here, and will seek some other place where I can live, and on two hours' notice;' and I suppose the conspirators said I left my country for my country's good, and thank God I did. I went from here with the few valuables I could hastily collect. I was unwilling to believe that this difficulty would not have been settled; but it was all in vain, and, as every man must do in a revolution as he puts his foot down, so it marks his life; so it has pleased God to protect me thus far, and make me somewhat instrumental in dealing heavy blows at the rebellion. I have been nothing more than an instrument in the hands of God, well supported by my officers and men, who have done their duty faithfully. I hope, my friends, that this day, with its events, may prove the culminating point of our revolution; and I hope that before long all will be restored to that peace and reunion which has been sought by the Government and desired by everybody; and then you, gentlemen, who have deserved so well of your country by your steady adherence to its Government, will receive the reward which fidelity, and honesty, and moral courage always deserve."

Notwithstanding the hardships and exposures he has undergone in a life of which more than forty years have been spent afloat, the sixty-four years of the vice-admiral's life set lightly upon him, and his eye is as clear, his voice as hearty, his arm as vigorous, and his judgment as sound as when, a dozen years ago, he trod the quarter-deck of a man-of-war in foreign ports. Our brief sketch is altogether inadequate to represent as we desire the character of our naval hero; but, in the words of a brilliant writer in the "United States Service Magazine" for January, 1865, we may say: "When his biography comes to be written, the public, who now see only high courage and indomitable vigor, rewarded by great and brilliant victories, will recognize the completeness and harmony of a character that has so far appeared to them only in profile. The stainless honor, the straightforward frankness, the vivacity of manner and conversation, the gentleness, the flow of good-humor, the cheerful, ever-buoyant spirit of the true man,—these will be added to the complete education, the thorough seamanship, the careful preparation, the devotion to duty, and lastly, the restless energy, the disdain of obstacles, the impatience of delay or hesitation, the disregard of danger, that stand forth in such prominence in the portrait, deeply engraven on the loyal American heart, of the GREAT ADMIRAL."

APPENDIX.

LIEUTENANT-GENERAL GRANT TO THE ARMIES.

War Department, Adjutant-General's Office,
Washington, D. C., June 2, 1865.

[General Orders, No. 108.]

Soldiers of the Armies of the United States:

By your patriotic devotion to your country in the hour of danger and alarm, your magnificent fighting, bravery, and endurance, you have maintained the supremacy of the Union and the Constitution, overthrown all armed opposition to the enforcement of the laws, and of the proclamations forever abolishing slavery—the cause and pretext of the rebellion—and opened the way to the rightful authorities to restore order and inaugurate peace on a permanent and enduring basis on every foot of American soil. Your marches, sieges, and battles, in distance, duration, resolution, and brilliancy of results, dim the lustre of the world's past military achievements, and will be the patriot's precedent in defence of liberty and right in all time to come. In obedience to your country's call, you left your homes and families and volunteered in its defence. Victory has crowned your valor, and secured the purpose of your patriotic hearts; and with the gratitude of your countrymen and the highest honors a great and free nation can accord, you will soon be permitted to return to your homes and families, conscious of having discharged the highest duty of American citizens. To achieve these glorious triumphs and secure to yourselves, your fellow-countrymen and posterity the blessings of free institutions, tens of thousands of your gallant comrades have fallen and sealed the priceless legacy with their lives. The graves of these a grateful nation bedews with tears, honors their memories, and will ever cherish and support their stricken families.

U. S. GRANT, Lieutenant-General.

GENERAL SHERMAN'S REPORT.

Headquarters Military Division of the Mississippi,
In the Field, City Point, Va., May 9, 1865.

General—My last official report brought the history of events, as connected with the armies in the field subject to my immediate command, down to the 1st of April, when the Army of the Ohio, Major-General J. M. Schofield commanding, lay at Goldsboro', with detachments distributed so as to secure and cover our routes of communication and supply, back to the sea at Wilmington and Morehead City; Major-General A. H. Terry, with the Tenth Corps, being at Faison's Depot; the Army of the Tennessee, Major-General O. O. Howard commanding, was encamped to the right and front of Goldsboro', and the Army of Georgia, Major-General H. W. Slocum commanding, to its left and front; the cavalry, brevet Major-General J. Kilpatrick commanding, at Mount Olive. All were busy in repairing the wear and tear of our then recent and hard march from Savannah, and in replenishing clothing and stores necessary for a further progress.

I had previously, by letter and in person, notified the lieutenant-general commanding the Armies of the United States, that the 10th of April would be the earliest possible moment at which I could hope to have all things in readiness, and we were compelled to use our railroads to the very highest possible limit in order to fulfil that promise, owing to a mistake in the railroad department, in sending locomotives and cars of the five-foot guage, we were limited to the use of the few locomotives and cars of the four-foot eight-and-a-half-inch gauge already in North Carolina, with such of the old stock as was captured by Major-General Terry at Wilmington, and on his way up to Goldsboro'. Yet such judicious use was made of these, and such industry displayed in the railroad management, by Generals Easton and Beckwith, and Colonel Wright and Mr. Van Dyne, that by the 10th of April our men were all re-clad, the wagons re-loaded, and a fair amount of forage accumulated ahead.

In the mean time, Major-General George Stoneman, in command of a division of cavalry operating from East Tennessee, in connection with Major-General George H. Thomas, in pursuance of my orders of January 21, 1865, had reached the railroad about Greensboro', North Carolina, and had made sad havoc with it, and had pushed along it to Salisbury, destroying *en route* bridges, culverts, depots, and all kinds of rebel supplies, and had extended the break in the railroad down to the Catawba Bridge.

This was fatal to the hostile armies of Lee and Johnston, who depended on that road for supplies and as their ultimate line of retreat. Major-General J. H. Wilson, also in command of the cavalry corps organized by himself under Special Field Orders, No. —, of October 24, 1864, at Gaylesville, Alabama, had started from the neighborhood of Decatur and Florence, Alabama, and moved straight into the heart of Alabama, on a route prescribed for General Thomas, after he had defeated General Hood at Nashville, Tennessee; but the roads being too heavy for infantry, General Thomas had devolved that duty on that most energetic young cavalry officer, General Wilson, who, imbued with the proper spirit, has struck one of the best blows of the war at the waning strength of the Confederacy. His route was one never before touched by our troops, and afforded him abundance of supplies as long as he was in motion, namely, by Tuscaloosa, Selma, Montgomery, Columbus, and Macon. Though in communication with him, I have not been able to receive as yet his full and detailed reports, which will in due time be published and appreciated. Lieutenant-General Grant, also in immediate command of the armies about Richmond, had taken the the initiative in that magnificent campaign which, in less than ten days, compelled the evacuation of Richmond, and resulted in the destruction and surrender of the entire rebel Army of Virginia, under command of General Lee.

The news of the battles about Petersburg reached me at Goldsboro' on the 6th of April. Up to that time, my purpose was to move rapidly northward, feign on Raleigh, and striking straight for Burkesville, thereby interposing between Johnston and Lee. But the auspicious events in Virginia had changed the whole military problem, and, in the expressive language of Lieutenant-General Grant, "the Confederate armies of Lee and Johnston" became the "strategic points." General Grant was fully able to take care of the former, and my task was to capture or destroy the latter. Johnston, at that time, April 6th, had his army well in hand about Smithfield, interposing between me and Raleigh. I estimated his infantry and artillery at thirty-five thousand, and his cavalry from six to ten thousand. He was superior to me in cavalry, so that I held General Kilpatrick in reserve at Mount Olive, with orders to recruit his horses, and be ready to make a sudden and rapid march on the 10th of April.

At daybreak of the day appointed, all the heads of columns were in motion straight against the enemy, Major-General H. W. Slocum taking the two direct roads for Smithfield; Major-General O. O. Howard making a circuit by the right, and feigning up the Weldon road to disconcert the enemy's cavalry; Generals Terry and Kilpatrick moving on the west side of the Neuse River, and aiming to reach the rear of the enemy between Smithfield and Raleigh. General Schofield followed General Slocum in support.

All the columns met, within six miles of Goldsboro', more or less cavalry, with the usual rail barricades, which were swept before us as chaff, and by ten A. M. of the 11th, the Fourteenth Corps entered Smithfield, the Twentieth Corps close at hand. Johnston had rapidly retreated across the Neuse River, and, having his railroad to lighten up his trains, could retreat faster than we could pursue. The rains had also set in, making the resort to corduroy absolutely necessary to pass even ambulances. The enemy had burned the bridge at Smithfield, and as soon as possible, Major-General Slocum got up his pontoons and crossed over a division of the Fourteenth Corps. We there heard of the surrender of Lee's army at Appomattox Court-house, Virginia, which was announced to the armies in orders, and created universal joy. Not an officer or soldier of my armies but expressed a pride and satisfaction that it fell to the lot of the armies of the Potomac and James so gloriously to overwhelm and capture the entire army that had held them so long in check, and their success gave new impulse to finish up our task. Without a moment's hesitation we dropped our trains and marched rapidly in pursuit to, and through Raleigh, reaching that place at half-past seven A. M. of the 13th, in a heavy rain. The next day the cavalry pushed on through the rain to Durham's Station, the Fifteenth Corps following as far as Morrisville Station, and the Seventeenth Corps to Jones' Station. On the supposition that Johnston was tied to his railroad as a line of retreat, by Hillsboro', Greensboro', Salisbury, Charlotte, etc., I had turned the other colums across the bend of that road towards Ashboro'. (See Special Field Orders, No. 55.) The cavalry, brevet Major-General J. Kilpatrick commanding, was ordered to keep up a show of pursuit towards the "Company's shops" in Alamance county; Major-General O. O. Howard to turn to the left by Hackney's Cross-Roads,. Pittsboro', St. Lawrence, and Ashboro'; Major-General H. W. Slocum, to cross Cape Fear River at Aven's Ferry, and move rapidly by Carthage, Caledonia, and Cox's Mills; Major-General J. M. Schofield was to hold Raleigh, and the road back, and with his spare force to follow an intermediate route.

By the 15th, though the rains were incessant and the roads almost impracticable, Major-General Slocum had the Fourteenth Corps, brevet Major-General Davis commanding, near Martha's Vineyard, with a pontoon bridge laid across Cape Fear River at Aven's Ferry, with the Twentieth Corps, Major-General Mower commanding, in support; and Major-General Howard had the Fifteenth and Seventeenth corps stretched out on the roads towards Pittsboro', while General Kilpatrick held Durham's Station and Chapel Hill University.

Johnston's army was retreating rapidly on the roads from Hillsboro' to Greensboro', he himself at Greensboro'. Although out of place as to time, I here invite all military critics, who study the problems of war, to take their maps and compare the position of my army, on the 15th and 16th of April, with that of General Halleck, about Burkesville and Petersburg, Virginia, on the 26th of April, when, according to his telegram to Secretary Stanton. he offered to relieve me of the task of "cutting off Johnston's retreat." Major-General Stoneman at the time was at Statesville, and Johnston's only line of retreat was by Salisbury and Charlotte. It may be that General Halleck's troops can outmarch mine, but there is nothing in their past history to show it, or it may be that General Halleck can inspire his troops with more energy of action. I doubt that also, save and except in this single instance, when he knew the enemy was ready to surrender or disperse, as advised by my letter of April 18, addressed to him when chief of staff at Washington City, and delivered at Washington, on the 21st instant, by Major Hitchcock, of my staff.

Thus matters stood at the time I received General Johnston's first letter, and made my answer of April 14th, copies of which were sent with all expedition to Lieutenant-General Grant and the secretary of war, with my letter of April 15th. I agreed to meet General Johnston in person, at a point intermediate between our pickets, on the 17th, at noon, provided the position of the troops remained in *statu quo*. I was both willing and anxious thus to consume a few days, as it would enable Colonel Wright to finish our railroad to Raleigh.

Two bridges had to be built, and twelve miles of new road made. We had no iron except by taking up that on the branch from Goldsboro' to Weldon. Instead of losing by time, I gained in every way, for every hour of delay possible was required to reconstruct the railroad to our rear, and improve the condition of our wagon-roads to the front, so desirable in case the negotiations failed, and we be forced to make the race of near two hundred miles, to head off or catch Johnston's army, then retreating towards Charlotte.

At noon of the day appointed, I met General Johnston for the first time in my life, although we had been interchanging shots constantly since May, 1863.

Our interview was frank and soldier-like, and he gave me to understand that further war on the part of the Confederate troops was folly, that *the cause* was lost, and that every life sacrificed after the surrender of Lee's army was "the highest possible crime." He admitted that the terms conceded to General Lee were magnanimous, and all he could ask, but he did want some general concessions that would enable him to allay the natural fears and anxieties of his followers, and enable him to maintain his control over them, until they could be got back to the neighborhood of their homes, thereby saving the State of North Carolina the devastations inevitably to result from turning his men loose and unprovided on the spot, and our pursuit across the State.

He also wanted to embrace in the same general proposition the fate of all the Confederate armies that remained in existence. I never made any concession as to his own army, or assumed to deal finally and authoritatively in regard to any other, but it did seem to me that there was presented a chance for peace that might be deemed valuable to the Government of the United States, and was at least worth the few days that would be consumed in reference.

To push an army whose commander had so frankly and honestly confessed his inability to cope with me, were cowardly, and unworthy the brave men I led.

Inasmuch as General Johnston did not feel authorized to pledge his power over the armies in Texas, we adjourned to meet the next day at noon. I returned to Raleigh and conferred freely with all my general officers, *every one* of whom urged me to complete terms that might accomplish so complete and desirable an end. All dreaded the weary and laborious march after a fugitive and dissolving army back towards Georgia, almost over the very country where we had toiled so long. There was but one opinion expressed, and if contrary ones were entertained, they were withheld, or indulged in only by that class who shun the fight and the march, but are loudest, bravest, and fiercest when danger is past. I again met General Johnston on the 18th, and we renewed the conversation. He satisfied me then of his *power* to disband the rebel armies in Alabama, Mississippi, Louisiana, and Texas, as well as those in his immediate command, namely, North Carolina, South Carolina, Florida, and Georgia.

The points on which he expressed especial solicitude were, lest their States were to be dismembered and denied representation in Congress, or any separate political existence whatever, and that the absolute disarming his men would leave the South powerless, and exposed to depredations by wicked bands of assassins and robbers.

President Lincoln's message of 1864; his amnesty proclamation; General Grant's terms to General Lee, substantially extending the benefits of that proclamation to all officers above the rank of colonel; the invitation to the Virginia Legislature to reassemble in Richmond, by General Weitzel, with the approval of Mr. Lincoln and General Grant, then on the spot; a firm belief that I had been fighting to re-establish the Constitution of the United States; and last, and not least, the general and universal desire to close a war any longer without organized resistance, were the leading facts that induced me to pen the "memorandum" of April 18th, signed by myself and General Johnston.

It was designed to be, and so expressed on its face, as a mere "basis" for reference to the President of the United States and constitutional commander-in-chief, to enable him, if he chose, at one blow to dissipate the military power of the Confederacy which had threatened the national safety for years. It admitted of modification, alteration, and change. It had no appearance of an ultimatum, and by no false reasoning can it be construed into a usurpation of power on my part. I have my opinions on the questions involved, and will stand by the memorandum; but this forms no part of a military report. Immediately on my return to Raleigh I dispatched one of my staff, Major Hitchcock, to Washington, enjoining him to be most prudent and careful to avoid the spies and informers that would be sure to infest him by the way, and to say nothing to anybody until the President could make known to me his wishes and policy in the matter.

The news of President Lincoln's assassination on the 14th of April (wrongly reported to me by telegraph as having occurred on the 11th) reached me on the 17th, and was announced to my command on the same day in Special Field Orders, No. 56. I was duly impressed with its horrible atrocity and probable effect upon the country, but when the property and interests of millions still living were involved, I saw no good reason to change my course, but thought rather to manifest real respect for his memory by following, after his death, that policy which, if living, I feel certain he would have approved, or at least not rejected with disdain. Up to that hour I had never received one word of instruction, advice, or counsel as to the "plan or policy" of Government, looking to a restoration of peace on the part of the rebel States of the South. Whenever asked for an opinion on the points involved, I had always evaded the subject. My letter to the Mayor of Atlanta has been published to the world, and I was not rebuked by the War Department for it.

My letter to Mr. N—— W——, at Savannah, was shown by me to Mr. Stanton before its publication, and all that my memory retains of his answer is, that he said, like my letters generally, it was sufficiently "emphatic, and could not be misunderstood."

Both these letters asserted my belief that, according to Mr. Lincoln's proclamations and messages, when the people of the South had laid down their arms, and submitted to the lawful power of the United States, *ipso facto* the war was over as to them ; and furthermore, that if any State in rebellion would conform to the Constitution of the United States, "cease war," elect senators and representatives to Congrees, if admitted (of which each House of Congress alone is the judge), that State became *instanter* as much in the Union as New York or Ohio. Nor was I rebuked for this expression, though it was universally known and commented on at the time. And again, Mr. Stanton in person, at Savannah, speaking of the terrific expenses of the war, and difficulty of realizing the money necessary for the daily wants of the Government, impressed me most forcibly with the necessity of bringing the war to a close as soon as possible for *financial reasons.*

On the evening of April 23d, Major Hitchcock reported his return to Morehead City with dispatches, of which fact General Johnston, at Hillsboro', was notified, so as to be ready in the morning for an answer. At 6 o'clock A. M. on the 24th, Major Hitchcock arrived, accompanied by General Grant and members of his staff, who had not telegraphed the fact of his coming over our exposed road for prudential reasons.

I soon learned that the memorandum was disapproved, without reasons assigned, and I was ordered to give the forty-eight hours' notice, and resume hostilities at the close of that time, governing myself by the substance of a dispatch then inclosed, dated March 3d, twelve noon, at Washington, District of Columbia, from Secretary Stanton to General Grant, at City Point, but not accompanied by any part of the voluminous matter so liberally lavished on the public in the New York journals of the 24th of April. That was the *first* and *only* time I ever saw that telegram, or had one word of instruction on the important matter involved in it; and it does seem strange to me that every bar-room loafer in New York can read in the morning journals "official" matter that is withheld from a General whose command extends from Kentucky to North Carolina.

Within an hour a courier was riding from Durham's Station towards Hillsboro' with notice to General Johnston of the suspension of the truce, and renewing my demand for the surrender of the armies under his immediate command (see two letters, April 24th, 6 A. M.), and at 12 M. I had the receipt of his picket officer. I therefore published my Orders, No. 62, to the troops, terminating the truce at 12 M. on the 26th, and ordered all to be in readiness to march at that hour on the routes prescribed in Special Field Order, No. 55, April 14th, from the positions held April 18th.

General Grant had orders from the President, through the Secretary of War, to direct military movements, and I explained to him the exact position of the troops, and he approved of it most emphatically; but he did not relieve me, or express a wish to assume command. All things were in readiness, when, on the evening of the 25th, I received another letter from General Johnston asking another interview to renew negotiations.

General Grant not only approved, but urged me to accept, and I appointed a meeting at our former place at noon of the 26th, the very hour fixed for the renewal of hostilities. General Johnston was delayed by an accident to his train, but at 2 P. M. arrived. We then consulted, concluded and signed the final terms of capitulation.

Those were taken by me back to Raleigh, submitted to General Grant, and met his immediate approval and signature. General Johnston was not even aware of the presence of General Grant at Raleigh at the time.

Thus was surrendered to us the second great army of the so-called Confederacy, and though undue importance has been given to the so-called negotiations which preceded it, and a rebuke and public disfavor cast on me wholly unwarranted by the facts, I rejoice in saying it was accomplished without further ruin and devastation to the country, without the loss of a single life to those gallant men who had followed me from the Mississippi to the Atlantic, and without subjecting brave men to the ungracious task of pursuing a fleeing foe that did not want to fight. As for myself, I know my motives, and challenge the instance during the past four years where an armed and defiant foe stood before me that I did not go in for a fight, and I would blush for shame if I had ever insulted or struck a fallen foe. The instant the terms of surrender were approved by General Grant, I made my Orders, No. 65, assigning to each of my subordinate commanders his share of the work, and, with General Grant's approval, made Special Field Orders, No. 66, putting in motion my old army (no longer required in Carolina) northward for Richmond. General Grant left Raleigh at 9 A. M. of the 27th, and I glory in the fact that during his three days' stay with me, I did not detect in his language or manner one particle of abatement in the confidence, respect, and affection that have existed between us throughout all the varied events of the past war, and though we have honestly differed in opinion in other cases, as well as this, still we respected each other's honest convictions.

I still adhere to my then opinions, that by a few general concessions, "glittering generalities," all of which in the end must and will be conceded to the organized States of the South, that this day there would not be an armed battalion opposed to us within the broad area of the dominions of the United States. Robbers and assassins must in any event result from the disbandment of large armies, but even these should be and could be taken care of by the local civil authorities, without being made a charge on the national treasury.

On the evening of the 28th, having concluded all business requiring my personal attention at Raleigh, and having conferred with every army commander and delegated to him the authority necessary for his future action, I dispatched my headquarters wagons by land along with the Seventeenth Corps, the office in charge of General Webster, from Newbern to Alexandria, Virginia, by sea, and in person, accompanied only by my personal staff, hastened to Savannah to direct matters in the interior of South Carolina and Georgia. I had received across the rebel telegraph wires cipher dispatches from General Wilson at Macon, to the effect that he was in receipt of my Orders, No. 65, and would send General Upton's division to Augusta, and General McCook's division to Tallahassee to receive the surrender of those garrisons, take charge of the public property, and execute the paroles required by the terms of surrender. He reported a sufficiency of forage for his horses in Southwest Georgia, but asked me to send him a supply of clothing, sugar, coffee, &c., by way of Augusta, Georgia, whence he could get it by rail. I therefore went rapidly to Goldsboro' and Wilmington, reaching the latter city at 10 A. M. of the 29th, and the same day embarked for Hilton Head in the blockade-runner Russia, Captain A. M. Smith. I found General Q. A. Gillmore, commanding Department of the South, at Hilton Head on the evening of April 30th, and ordered him to send to Augusta at once what clothing and small stores he could spare for General Wilson, and to open up a line of certain communication and supply with him at Macon. Within an hour the captured steamboats Jeff. Davis and Amazon, both adapted to the shallow and crooked navigation of the Savannah river, were being loaded, the one at Savannah and the other at Hilton Head. The former started up the river on the 1st of May, in charge of a very intelligent officer (whose name I cannot recall) and forty-eight men, all the boat could carry, with orders to occupy temporarily the United States Arsenal at Augusta, and open up communication with General Wilson at Macon, in the event that General McCook's division of cavalry was not already there. The Amazon followed next day, and General Gillmore had made the necessary orders for a brigade of infantry, to be commanded by General Molyneux, to follow by a land march to Augusta as its permanent garrison. Another brigade of infantry was ordered to occupy Orangeburg, South Carolina, the point furthest in the interior that can at present be reached by rail from the seacoast (Charleston).

On the 1st of May I went on to Savannah, where General Gillmore also joined me, and the arrangements ordered for the occupation of Augusta were consummated.

At Savannah, I found the city in the most admirable police, under direction of brevet Major-General Grover, and the citizens manifested the most unqualified joy to hear that, so far as they were concerned, the war was over. All classes, Union men as well as former rebels, did not conceal, however, the apprehensions naturally arising from a total ignorance of the political conditions to be attached to their future state. Any thing at all would be preferable to this dread uncertainty.

On the evening of the 2d of May I returned to Hilton Head, and there, for the first time, received the New York papers of April 28th, containing Secretary Stanton's dispatch of 9 A. M. of the 27th of April to General Dix, including General Halleck's, from Richmond, of 9 P. M. of the night before, which seems to have been rushed with extreme haste before an excited public, namely. morning of the 28th. You will observe from the dates that these dispatches were running back and forth from Richmond and Washington to New York, and there published. while General Grant and I were together in Raleigh, North Carolina, adjusting, to the best of our ability, the terms of surrender of the only remaining formidable rebel army in existence at the time east of the Mississippi river Not one word of intimation had been sent to me of the displeasure of the Government with my official conduct, but only the naked disapproval of a skeleton memorandum sent properly for the action of the President of the United States.

The most objectionable features of my memorandum had already (April 24th) been published to the world in violation of official usage, and the contents of my accompanying letters to General Halleck. General Grant, and Mr. Stanton, of even date, though at hand. were suppressed.

In all these letters I had stated clearly and distinctly that Johnston's army would *not* fight, but if pushed would "disband" and "scatter" into small and dangerous guerrilla parties, as injurious to the interests of the United States as to the rebels themselves; that all parties admitted that the rebel cause of the South was abandoned; that the negro was free. and that the temper of all was most favorable to a lasting peace. I say all these opinions of mine were withheld from the public with a seeming purpose; and I do contend that my official experience and former services. as well as my past life and familiarity with the people and geography of the South, entitled my opinions to at least a decent respect.

Although this dispatch (Mr. Stanton's, of April 27th) was printed "official," it had come to me only in the questionable newspaper paragraph headed "Sherman's truce disregarded."

I had already done what General Wilson wanted me to do, namely, had sent him supplies of clothing and food, with clear and distinct orders and instructions how to carry out in Western Georgia the terms for the surrender of arms and paroling of prisoners made by General Johnston's capitulation of April 26th, and had properly and most opportunely ordered General Gillmore to occupy Orangeburg and Augusta, strategic points of great value at all times, in peace or war; but as the Secretary had taken upon himself to order my subordinate generals to disobey my "orders," I explained to General Gillmore that I would no longer confuse him or General Wilson with "orders" that might conflict with those of the Secretary, which, as reported, were sent, not through me, but in open disregard of me and of my lawful authority.

It now becomes my duty to paint, in justly severe character, the still more offensive and dangerous matter of General Halleck's dispatch of April 26th, to the Secretary of War, embodied in his to General Dix, of April 27th.

General Halleck had been Chief of Staff of the Army at Washington, in which capacity he must have received my official letter of April 18th, wherein I wrote clearly that if Johnston's army about Greensboro' were "pushed" it would "disperse," an event I wished to prevent. About that time he seems to have been sent from Washington to Richmond to command the new Military Division of the James, in assuming charge of which, on the 22d, he defines the limits of his authority to be the "Department of Virginia, the Army of the Potomac, and such part of North Carolina as *may not be occupied by the command of Major-General Sherman.*" (See his General Orders, No. 1.) Four days later, April 26th, he reports to the Secretary that he has ordered Generals Meade, Sheridan, and Wright to invade that part of North Carolina which *was* occupied by my command, and pay "no regard to any truce or orders of mine." They were ordered to "*push* forward, regardless of any orders save those of Lieutenant-General Grant, and cut off Johnston's retreat." He knew at the time he penned that dispatch and made those orders, that Johnston was not retreating, but was halted under a forty-eight hours' truce with me, and was laboring to surrender his command and prevent its dispersion into guerrilla bands, and that I had on the spot a magnificent army at my command, amply sufficient for all purposes required by the occasion.

The plan for cutting off a retreat from the direction of Burkesville and Danville is hardly worthy one of his military education and genius. When he contemplated an act so questionable as the violation of a "truce" made by competent authority within his sphere of command, he should have gone himself and not have sent subordinates, for he knew I was bound in honor to *defend* and *maintain* my *own* truce and pledge of faith, even at the cost of many lives.

When an officer pledges the faith of his Government, he is bound to defend it, and he is no soldier who would violate it knowingly.

As to Davis and his stolen treasure, did General Halleck, as Chief of Staff, or commanding officer of the neighboring military division, notify me of the facts contained in his dispatch to the Secretary? No, he did not. If the Secretary of War wanted Davis caught, why not order it, instead of, by publishing in the newspapers, putting him on his guard to hide away and escape? No orders or instructions to catch Davis or his stolen treasure ever came to me; but, on the contrary, I was led to believe that the Secretary of War rather preferred he should effect an escape from the country, if made "unknown" to him. But even on this point I inclose a copy of my letter to Admiral Dahlgren, at Charleston, sent him by a fleet steamer from Wilmington on the 25th of April, two days before the bankers of Richmond had imparted to General Halleck the important secret as to Davis's movements, designed doubtless to stimulate his troops to march their legs off to catch *their* treasure for *their* own use.

I know now that Admiral Dahlgren did receive my letter on the 26th, and had acted on it *before* General Halleck had even thought of the matter; but I don't believe a word of the treasure story, it is absurd on its face, and General Halleck or anybody has my full permission to chase Jeff. Davis and cabinet, with their stolen treasure, through any part of the country occupied by my command.

The last and most obnoxious feature of General Halleck's dispatch is wherein he goes out of his way and advises that my subordinates, Generals Thomas, Stoneman, and Wilson, should be instructed not to obey "Sherman's" commands.

This is too much, and I turn from the subject with feelings too strong for words, and merely record my belief that so much mischief was never before embraced in so small a space as in the newspaper paragraph headed "Sherman's truce disregarded," authenticated as "official" by Mr. Secretary Stanton, and published in the New York papers of April 28th.

During the night of May 2d, at Hilton Head, having concluded my business in the Department of the South, I began my return to meet my troops then marching towards Richmond from Raleigh. On the morning of the 3d we ran into Charleston Harbor, where I had the pleasure to meet Admiral Dahlgren, who had, in all my previous operations from Savannah northward, aided me with a courtesy and manliness that commanded my entire respect and deep affection; also General Hatch, who, from our first interview at his Tullafinnay camp had caught the spirit of the move from Pocotaligo northward, and had largely contributed to our joint success in taking Charleston and the Carolina coast. Any one who is not *satisfied* with war should go and see Charleston, and he will pray louder and deeper than ever that the country may in the long future be spared any more war. Charleston and secession being synonymous terms, the city should be left as a sample, so that centuries may pass away before that false doctrine is again preached in our Union.

We left Charleston on the evening of the 3d of May, and hastened with all possible speed back to Morehead City, which we reached at night of the 4th. I immediately communicated by telegraph with General Schofield at Raleigh, and learned from him the pleasing fact that the lieutenant-general commanding the armies of the United States had reached the Chesapeake in time to countermand General Halleck's orders, and prevent his violating my truce, invading the area of my command, and driving Johnston's surrendering army into fragments. General Johnston had fulfilled his agreement to the very best of his ability; and the officers charged with issuing the paroles at Greensboro' reported about thirty thousand (30,000) already made, and that the greater part of the North Carolina troops had gone home without waiting for their papers, but that all of them would doubtless come in to some one of the military posts, the commanders of which are authorized to grant them. About eight hundred (800) of the rebel cavalry had gone south, refusing to abide the terms of the surrender, and it was supposed they would make for Mexico. I would sincerely advise that they be encouraged to go and stay; they would be a nuisance to any civilized government, whether loose or in prison.

With the exception of some plundering on the part of Lee's and Johnston's disbanded men, all else in North Carolina was "quiet." When to the number of men surrendered at Greensboro' are added those at Tallahassee, Augusta; and Macon, with the scattered squads who will come in at other military posts, I have no doubt fifty thousand (50,000) armed men will be disarmed and restored to civil pursuits by the capitulation made near Durham's Station, North Carolina, on the 26th of April, and that, too, without the loss of a single life to us.

On the 5th of May I received and here subjoin a further dispatch from General Schofield, which contains inquiries I have been unable to satisfy, similar to those made by nearly every officer in my command whose duty brings him in contact with citizens. I leave you to do what you think expedient to provide the military remedy.

By Telegraph from Raleigh, N. C., May 5, 1865, to Major-General W. T. Sherman, Morehead City.

"When General Grant was here, as you doubtless recollect, he said the lines had been extended to embrace this and other States south. The order, it seems, has been modified so as to include only Virginia and Tennessee. I think it would be an act of wisdom to open this State to trade at once. I hope the Government will make known its policy as the organ of State governments without delay. Affairs must be necessarily in a very unsettled state until that is done; the people are now in a mood to accept almost any thing which promises a definite settlement.

"What is to be done with the freedmen, is the question of all, and is the all-important question. It requires prompt and wise action to prevent the negro from becoming a huge elephant on our hands. If I am to govern this State, it is important for me to know it at once. If another is to be sent here it cannot be done too soon, for he will probably undo the most that I shall have done. I shall be glad to hear from you freely when you have time to write.

"I will send your message to Wilson at once.

"J. M. SCHOFIELD,
"Major-General."

I give this dispatch entire, to demonstrate how intermingled have become civil matters with the military, and how almost impossible it has become for an officer in authority to act a purely military part.

There are no longer armed enemies in North Carolina, and a

soldier can deal with no other sort. The marshals and sheriffs with their *posses* (of which the military may become a part) are the only proper officers to deal with civil criminals and marauders. But I will not be drawn out in a discussion of this subject, but instance the case to show how difficult is the task become to military officers, when men of the rank, education, experience, nerve, and good sense of General Schofield feel embarrassed by them.

General Schofield, at Raleigh, has a well-appointed and well-disciplined command, is in telegraphic communication with the controlling parts of his department, and remote ones in the direction of Georgia, as well as with Washington, and has military possession of all strategic points.

In like manner General Gillmore is well situated in all respects, except as to rapid communication with the seat of the General Government. I leave him also with every man he ever asked for, and in full and quiet possession of every strategic point in his department; and General Wilson has in the very heart of Georgia the strongest, best-appointed, and best-equipped cavalry corps that ever fell under my command, and he has now, by my recent action, opened to him a source of route and supply by way of Savannah River that simplifies his military problem, so that I think I may with a clear conscience leave them, and turn my attention once more to my special command, the army with which I have been associated through some of the most eventful scenes of this or any war.

I hope and believe none of these commanders will ever have reason to reproach me for any "orders" they may have received from me, and the President of the United States may be assured that all of them are in position, ready and willing to execute to the letter and in spirit any orders he may give. I shall henceforth cease to give them any orders at all, for the occasion that made them subordinate to me is past, and I shall confine my attention to the army composed of the Fifteenth and Seventeenth, the Fourteenth and Twentieth corps, unless the commanding general of the Armies of the United States orders otherwise.

At four P. M. of May 9th, I reached Manchester on the James River, opposite Richmond, and found that all the four corps had arrived from Raleigh, and were engaged in replenishing their wagons for the resumption of the march towards Alexandria.

I have the honor to be your obedient servant,

W. T. SHERMAN,
Major-General commanding.

GENERAL JOHN A. RAWLINGS, Chief of Staff, Washington, D. C.

CPSIA information can be obtained
at www.ICGtesting.com
Printed in the USA
LVHW040531190122
708837LV00003B/193

9 783752 554441